COWARD

A NOVEL

BY COREY CROFT

FLY PELICAN PRESS

Published by: Fly Pelican Press

Vancouver BC, Canada V6E 1N9

www.flypelicanpress.com

Registration number: 1157856

ISBN E-BOOK: 978-1-9990730-0-8

ISBN PAPERBACK: 978-1-9990730-1-5

First edition

Cover illustrations: Spencer Croft

Photograph: Winston Fong

Cover design: Eric Robinson

Formatting by Indie Publishing Group

Edits: Susan Strecker

DISCLAIMER: Coward is a work of fiction. Names, characters, places and incidents are either the product of the author's imagination and are used for entertainment purposes. Any resemblance to actual persons besides Bob and Kyle is purely coincidental and should be taken as such.

Dedicated to Susan Croft.

I call her Mom. You'd call her Mrs. Croft, then she'd tell you to call her Sue.

You've always known what I am and loved me and supported me anyways, that is the opposite of cowardice.

I love you mom.

When I am king, you will be first against the wall.

-Paranoid Android

THE MAN SAT at the bar with an incurious, almost expecting expression. There was no haste in the way he swirled his whiskey; there was no urgency to finish his drink. He had walked into the heaving bar and parted the crowd to take his seat. He was left unbothered by the rowdy attendees. He casually spoke to the bartender, who answered apologetically, for he was in a rush to satisfy his patrons.

"Two of you and one of me? I like those odds!" A boisterous man in his thirties approached a pair of younger women. They fawned over his introduction. He turned to order a drink. They whispered to each other that he was very attractive.

The man smirked. "Any moment now," he said to the bartender.

"Can I grab you another glass?" the bartender responded. The man nodded.

He looked older than the other attendees at the bar this evening. He was far older than the crowd on any given evening. But had a habit of blending in. He could be invisible in plain sight if he wanted or stand-out in a crowd of millions. A knack? A gift? A tactic for survival?

"My friend Sam is supposed to meet me here," the attractive man said to the women. His lips stretched until his teeth were visible. "My name is Andre Lambert."

Through the alacrity of the hooting patrons, the man turned his head and feathered his eyes towards the opening door. "There he is," he whispered through a playful grin.

A small pale-brown man was squeezed from the anteroom like a soybean. He was nervous and uncomfortable. "E-excuse me, there," he said as he made courteous attempts to snake across the floor. "Whoops I knocked over your jacket, let me grab that," he said to an unobservant patron as he hung the coat back over a chair. He ineffectually patted the shoulders and arms of unknowing people. "Oh, pardon me young lady … pardon me … pardon me … " His sheepish movements did little to stir the unaware attendees. "Sorry about that, I got your purse with my tummy." His heft, even when he sucked it in, inhibited him from cleanly seeping through narrow channels of human islands. He was splashed with alcohol, elbowed and fought irritation which threatened his already-anxious face. "No, no, it's okay, don't worry about it, it'll wash right out."

"He's coming." The old man patted the bartender's prone hand. He turned and watched the pudgy man he had been waiting for struggle to negotiate the festive mob. "Look at him," he spoke to the busy bartender. "The stress, the frustration … the knowledge of his own weaknesses and the strength to do nothing." He watched the younger man stutter and feebly make his way to the bar. "Sam has no idea that I will change his pathetic life."

"Your eyes are breathtaking," one of the younger girls said to the attractive man.

The old man watched Sam sidle up to his left, entirely unaware of his presence beside him. Such was the old man's gift.

"Hey Sam," the bartender said to the newly arrived, pale-brown man.

"I guess my grandmother … " Andre Lambert said to the softly murmuring girls.

The old man with the whiskey tilted his trunk and watched. He watched Sam watch Andre Lambert with subtle envy and mild annoyance.

"Poli-sci … " The girls announced their major to Andre Lambert.

"Oh Sam," the old man let the whiskey dampen his top lip, "you should be excited. I'm excited. I'm ecstatic. How many people get their lives changed in one night, in one fell swoop." Nobody seemed to hear him.

"Sammy!" Andre Lambert exclaimed, seeing his friend.

The old man tilted his head back and finished his whiskey. "Kenneth, would you be a dear and pour me another glass? I am going to excuse myself and use the head and have a cigarette."

He stood outside and smoked. He was eager but restrained. "Life is not a race," he said to a circle of young men smoking nearby. "It is an obstacle course and it is not designed for everyone equally. It is the same contest no matter your strength or speed." The men were puzzled. "Is it not the responsibility for the most capable to feed a line of rope to help another person over the wall? To help the losers? The cowards? The weak and the stupid?" He flicked his cigarette to the ground and squashed it underfoot.

He returned to his seat without challenge.

"Easy there, old man," one of the girls said to a flustered Sam.

"It's time." The man sipped his whiskey and let out a sigh of relief. "Here we go…. Hello, Sam."

PART 1

"BRING ME ANOTHER stack," the man ordered. He tossed the current folder onto a pile of rejected applications that surrounded his chair. "And another bottle of scotch, please."

Sam mashed his palms into his face, dragging them from his forehead to his chin, trying to knead out the puffiness. A guttural half-grunt, half-groan escaped his lips like the air brakes of a trailer-truck.

It was the grumbling of an impotent man who had relented to the reality of his own flaccidity. A resigned captain flipping the switches of a dead cockpit, only for show.

Sam thought about cursing. He thought about the words he wished to use and declined uttering them. "What's the point?" A profound sigh hunched his back. A pouch of dough slumped over his belt. He pinched his fingers around it and sighed again.

"Thank you." The man nodded to his assistant. He tonged a large ice cube into his glass and poured himself a snifter. He summarily glanced at a few folders, throwing each one to the ground with contempt. The assistant bent down to collect the discarded folders. "Leave them for now. They're losers, but not the right loser."

Sam hastily sawed at his teeth, crosscutting through his flared lips with a worn-down toothbrush, arching at the neck with unnatural pliability like a tribesman seeing a giant metal bird flying overhead for the first time. He revisited the argument he'd had with his girlfriend moments ago. She possessed the unique ability of making sure to always leave first, taking the last word with her.

It was the same old song played through brand new speakers.

"Wait a minute." The man's eyes widened as he peeled back the cover of a folder.

Sam's face lost its rigidity and drooped. He spit in the sink and recalled his girlfriend's last words.

"*We* don't ever do anything! *You* don't ever do anything! *I* have hobbies, I have interests, and I'm growing!" Her tinny voice reverberated in his head. It caused him to wince as if she were screaming directly in his ear.

He wrinkled his eyes at the way his mind embellished how she sullenly gobbed the word *you* and melodically sang the word *I*. "I have interests, too," he reasoned with a trap full of bristles and mint foam. But even he didn't believe his words.

"Look at him!" The man slapped the folder on the table and drove his finger against the contents.

The mirror was unkind this morning. He wiped the residue from the corners of his mouth, lightly tugging at his cheek. "Am I getting wrinkles? Is all this fighting with Chloe giving me wrinkles?"

Sam sneered. The lines he had been inspecting seemed to wait for his sour expression, naturally folding into each other like a take-out menu.

"No." Sam shook his head, he could feel the skin on his face jiggle like flan. "Today I will be the good old Sammy I used to be. The good old boy that smiled to everybody he passed and went out of his way to open doors for whoever. Stop being so negative first thing in the morning. Keep our chins up, pal, the day can only get better."

"Him?" The assistant winced with her arms full of folders. "He's so… insignificant. You have diplomats, movie stars, royalty, astronauts, tyrants… Him?"

The morning breeze drifted the ocean's perfume through the maze of low-rise, affordable apartments where Sam resided. The coastal, northwest air was like a perfectly ripe apple, crisp and refreshing without sting or bite. The wintery scene had changed behind a theatre curtain. The backdrop, a pastel-coloured impasto visible behind the various rectangular buildings and timidly budding maple trees on Sam's street was like a Van Gogh upswing.

He was in no mood to appreciate the shed skin of a long winter and the morning's sudden metamorphosis. Nor was he admiring the return of the frolicsome chirruping of swallows, the sheathing of previously omnipresent umbrellas or affable, nourishing sunlight that ate the sidewalk puddles that allowed people to trade their winter boots for sunglasses.

Why am I so grumpy? Sam thought. *It's a gorgeous morning and I can't see it. I want to see the beauty so bad.* Sam thought it may have been a problem with his eyes, perhaps a new pair to help him see the world like he used to.

"Yes, my dear." The man took a big gulp of his whiskey. "His insignificance is one of his strongest suits. I love him."

Even in the tranquility of his street, calm and unclogged by foot-traffic, Sam walked like he was dragging an axe. The sun was pounding down on the main boulevard. "My sunglasses … " He squinted. He stopped and turned towards his apartment. But, he knew if he went back the busses would be full. "Shit." He kicked the cement with the toe of his tattered dress shoe. Then he inhaled. "Nope. Not gonna do that today." He straightened his posture. "It's not the end of the world," he reflected. "It's a new day."

"But the others," the assistant pushed the glasses up her nose, "they seem more interesting. They have greater areas to exploit. More impact, more devastating."

Sam bent the corner onto the main promenade and squeezed among the rope of pedestrians. A tall and slender woman passed him, a matte-peach coloured vegan leather purse slung over her shoulder swung into his arm while she finessed sharply ahead. She spun around, shot him a glare and a hiss, carrying a matching pair of heels in her right hand with sponge-soled trainers on her feet. Sam treated her to a puzzled look. *I'm sorry,* he thought but did not say, *technically, your bag attacked me.*

"No, he is not special, but that's the beauty!" The man laughed. "He is so painfully unglamorous and therefore such a perfect candidate. He has no self-esteem, no prospects, no courage and no hope. He is entertaining because of his dearth of remarkability."

A man with one side of his head shaved to the skull and a lush comb-over moussed from his forehead back, jauntily marched up beside Sam, walking at an even stride. "Yeah, so, fucking … " The man spoke in a voice that was all neck and throat, he repeated his words as a refrain as opposed to allowing his thoughts to pool. "So fucking, that was sick … So fucking … We going to do it again?"

Sam glared sideways at the man. The vapours of his cologne surrounded Sam with spears. He felt hostage to the stranger's potent aroma. The man continued to refuse silence, noticeably speaking over and alongside the tones on the receiver. Sam exhaled critically, hoping the man would recognize his disapproval. The tapping noise from his block-heeled loafers further prodded at Sam. Another glare, a deeper squint: "So fucking … Yeah, anyways, so fucking … "

Just shut up and think about what you want to say, you goddamned idiot! Sam wanted to scream, but managed only to get the words out in thought. He huffed curtly from his nostrils and tucked his head, marching ahead of the man. "It's okay," Sam breathed several lung-swelling gusts, "not everyone respects the noise pollution from their conversations, it's okay, it's okay, he's probably a really nice guy. Maybe."

"So … Fucking … " Sam shook his head and frowned.

"But, sir," the assistant scoffed, "he is so different from your usual projects. It does not make sense."

Sam's foot speed increased to mimic a thrown knife, chunkily stamping on his heel and scraping the toe of his worn black leather shoe against the concrete, missing the ball of his foot altogether. He muttered petulant trifles, already hyperconscious of the visible brownish fibres peeking through the insole, which exposed the lackadaisical craftsmanship and low-grade, plastic-like veneer of his work Oxfords. Two or three times a week they required dollops of unctuous black shoe polish, smeared on and left to cake atop the embarrassingly frayed toe cap, as well the odd glue job to keep the welt from flapping. He did, it seemed, have at least one hobby.

He came up behind a chorus of men and women, bobbing listlessly, floating oblivious like swans sunning in a pond. He craned his neck and shimmied to spot a way through.

A perfect opening that Sam had seen proved to be a decoy; a slit between two office types was a ruse. Unseen between them was small, slow moving, elderly woman with a floppy hat and a bell-ringer hunch pulling a metallic cart full of phallic perishables like daikon and silk squash.

Sam halted and shot upright like a breaker crashing against the face of a cliff. His front foot stomped just short of an obscenely proud carrot, dangling through one of the square holes at the bottom of the basket. His rear foot, poised to move swiftly and forcefully between the stooges on either side of him had little chance to reconcile the suddenness of the stop. His toe skidded behind him, leaving a sooty, charcoal skid mark. The damage his shoe had sustained felt like the real, physical pain of having one of his toenails torn out.

People continued to float in an unintentionally fortified unit as Sam watched the vegetable waggle against the pavement. He noticed his shoelace was unfastened again.

He snapped the string with a frustrated tug from a bended knee. *It's okay. It's just a shoelace.*

"Hey pal, move over if you're gonna be taking up space," a male voice croaked as he coasted past with a familiar redolence. "So fucking …" he continued on his mobile.

Sam let out a prolonged exhale.

"Well, now you are making it sound like a challenge. And, you know that I can never say no to a challenge, my dear. Is that not what the essence of a project should be?"

Sam was not eager to get to work, but anxious to *arrive* at work; to complete the journey to the place where he toiled on behalf of others who harvested the fields and reaped the rewards that he sowed. If you have to ask whether or not you are part of a fiefdom or vassalage, you are probably a serf. Figuratively, of course. Sam was not a farmer. The harvest meant shit strung in a tea bag to old Sammy.

Sam was eager to get to work because he had a routine. Like a knight-errant who lived and died by the poetry of his sword, he was bound by his routine. It was how he preserved what scraps of sanity he had left.

Unable to smoke cigarettes in his apartment, Sam now waited until his second cup of coffee to inhale the first mist of the morning.

His plan was simple.

He would arrive at work thirty minutes before start. To arrive at his destination at the desired time, Sam needed to catch an earlier bus to avoid the peak hour throng and outpace the very same crowd in line at the coffee shop. He fancied the barista, and with that extra time, could squeeze an extra few words out of their daily, though steadily ripening dialogue. If he was a few minutes truant, the rush would cause the girl to become flustered, resorting to a tepid and superficial exchange of greetings; or worse, something about the weather. From there, invigorated by the simple, yet gratifying interaction and the feeling that he still had some appeal to women, Sam would step out of the coffee shop, walk three meters to an awning-covered area and remove a Pall Mall blue from the packet in his breast pocket. He could take his time, replay the conversation in his head and fantasize for a short moment.

"Do you require anything, sir?" The assistant had a pad and pen readied. "Are there any notes that I should take?"

It was his last kiss of freedom. The last moments before he had to don a mask of beige, stranded on a boat, surrounded by familiar strangers.

First, unfortunately, he had to board the damned bus.

"Oh no." The man waved his hand gleefully. "This will be easy. This will be fun. This man, Samuel Florin, he is like free dessert."

Sam hated the bus. Sam hated the lines, the crowds, and feeling like a grain in a human pepper mill. Most of all, he hated the cheating: the line cutting, shoving and selfishness of it all.

Shit, he thought. The line was a tangled extension cord taken out of the crawl space in early December. Jagged and unorganized, bunched together in some parts with gaps and curlicues like a Hemingway letter.

The official regulation, as stated in the public transit corporation's official leaflets, was that no one is to enter the bus from the rear door, it was for exit only. Similarly, no one, aside from the elderly and handicapped, should use the front door for escape. This would allow, in its purest theoretical application, for a smooth cycling of riders to get on and disembark.

Several teeming busses ripped past the stop without slowing, with faces pressed against the windows like jarred herring. When they did stop, the back door was swarmed by a horde that pushed and clawed its way in. The bus driver could be heard robotically admonishing the rogues: "Please do not use the rear door for entering...." Giving up on his own toothless entreaty with the same lack of intensity that it began.

Each time a bus wheezed to a stop, the greediest of the lot collapsed and assaulted the entrance. The people who stood anomalously around the fathoms of columned passengers seized the opportunity to shove themselves towards the coughing doors. Even if they were unable to enter, they would successfully interpose themselves favourably near or at the head of the line.

Sam used his greatest schemes to close the gaps, passively shepherding the people ahead, angling his shoulders and squaring his base to prohibit the encroachment of budgers and stem the opportunity for potential line-cutters.

There were two things that he could not understand.

The first issue was those who stood outside the line and then weaved their way towards the door, wadding at the opening like wet tissue, then slithering back into an advantageous spot in the line. *How can they just stand there so calmly? I would feel like an asshole! I tried it once, it made me sick,* he thought. How could they stand with placid indifference like the portraits of bored-looking, sleepy-eyed bourgeoisie? The lack of eye contact raked against Sam's nerves, how else could they be punished by the nasty side-eye of justice that he was throwing? *Calm down big guy, why are you even getting so worked up? It's not personal. Be patient. Maybe they're in a hurry. So are you, but... be better.*

The second dilemma was the people who allowed this misconduct to happen freely under their supervision, like Nero fiddling while Rome burns. *How can people just sit back and let these atrocities happen?*

"Please." The man smirked. *"This young man will do all the work himself. Look at him. He is so weak and pathetic. It makes you question whether all lives truly matter. Or, if you can make an inconsequential life have consequence."*

Sam eventually scraped into a bus, flaring his elbows to prevent the collapsing line from overtaking his position, dropping the exact change into the coin slot. *What a lovely sound.* Sam wanted, just one time, to be asked to press the bar and drop a day's worth of coins into the container below, it seemed better than an orgasm.

The bus was a sultry and acute microcosm of society to Sam. He tried to make himself as small as possible, removing his messenger bag, folding his shoulders, and tucking himself into a spot that would not limit the corporeal freedom of anyone else. He ignored the mobile dancing in his pocket, moderated the sound and speed of his breathing, avoided making prolonged eye contact, and become as inconspicuous as possible.

Sam would have done so well in Tokyo.

The bus driver powerlessly beckoned people to move to the rear. Few did. Sam grumbled at the congregating mass at the front, unable to pass between backpacks and crisscrossing legs, knitted at the knees.

"Please step behind the yellow line," the bus driver lethargically demanded without looking at Sam.

"Okay, okay, sorry, sorry …" Sam apologized. "Ex-excuse me, pardon me," he peeped unassertively at the crowd blocking his passage. Music spewed from everyone's headphones. Sam tried to twist himself through, but found no success.

"Sir, please step back." The bus driver tweaked his original tone with drops of peremptoriness. "It is an offence to block the conductor's view of the side mirrors. Please step behind the yellow line."

"Okay, okay … " Sam said with hasty contrition, sweating at his nape.

Some people abandoned their seats as the cord was pulled and the bus neared its stop; they moved towards the front, further testing Sam's ability to straddle the yellow line. He was left without anything to grab, praying that his squat equilibrium could handle the change in momentum.

The bus vaulted to a stop, sending him crashing into the front window.

The exiting riders carried Sam like a rapid.

"Sir, please step off to allow the others the chance to exit the bus." The bus driver rolled his eyes beneath semi-dark transitional lenses.

Sam took a step to the ground and clung to the door like a branch hanging over a waterfall, to mark his spot as first back on.

The bus driver raised his voice. "Please make room!" He lowered the ramp for a mother with a carriage and a decrepit-looking man in a motorized cart. The mother flicked her cigarette and entered, blowing her smoke in the bus itself. The old man in the imperial red scooter beeped at Sam as he wheeled on. Neither paid for their journey.

"Have to wait for the next bus, sir. Should be right behind us," the bus driver dispassionately informed Sam. "Please do not enter from the rear door. Please move to the rear...." The doors swung shut.

Sam's protesting expression turned to a sigh. The doors swung closed as he lowered himself from the bottom step. He realized that he did not grab a transfer.

"Back of the line ye fuckin' bum," shouted someone in the procession.

His face lit up with a deep inhale. A second later "Okay" slithered inaudibly from his lips. He walked to the back of the line with his head buried in his chest.

"I just don't understand why him, sir."

Sam entered another overcrowded bus and wormed his way to the middle, grabbing the overhead rail. The inescapable sunrays made him squint and irritated his sinuses. He sniffled carefully. It was not enough. I*'m sorry!* he thought as he forced a wet snort to prevent leakage.

"Ugh, gross," a young lady piped. She glowered hatefully at him. "Oh, nothing," she said into her phone. "Some guy on the bus who's obviously never heard of Kleenex." She paused. "I know, right?" Another pause. "I'm so hungover right now, bloody fucking hell. I think I might have forgot to use a condom with that guy last night.... Well, I was wasted, you know what tequila shots do to me... Shut up! I do not ... Well you do, too, little slut. Ha-ha."

Sam breathed cautiously and glared at the girl. Her voice was clarion, a glowing red icepick through the sounds of newspapers ruffling and road passing beneath them.

"Do these people not have any self-awareness?" He shook his head, thinking.

He periodically caromed side glances at the girl—a slight protest to her rebuking him and carrying on in such a disruptive manner. Despite the transparency of her conversation, her face was seldom visible, buried in knees that were pulled up to her chest across two seats. She seemed unaware of the increasing askance looks from other passengers.

The world needs a hero.

Sam beheld the faces of his comrades and their curt, sharply released breaths. He was working up the courage; selecting the proper mien of austerity, calmness, authority, firmness, and emotionlessness. He felt the solidarity of the movement mounting and aligning wordlessly behind his own. *I have to be composed but direct, lawful but not oppressive,* he was thinking, *things could take a very drastic turn if I seem aggressive, a man shaming a woman. Despicable.* His head was swimming, he felt his hand clam against the bar, becoming slippery. He was working out a tone that he could use to say 'excuse me'. It could not be too passive; it could not be too cruel. He could sound laid back, but she may not pay him any mind. He could try a sincere look with a pseudo-pleading tone, but that may strike everyone around him as effete, and his message would be lost in his lack of masculine edge. He was defeating his own crusade before he had taken up arms. He rallied against his own lack of fortitude. *No, I'm not alone ... we're all in this, together.* He nodded to himself. *I'm like that guy in Tiananmen Square. One hand with a briefcase, the other telling a tank to go back where it came from.* He forged steel in his eyes and locked his sights on the nuisance *Like Moses to the Pharaoh: Let my people go.*

"Ugh, what a creeper! This perv keeps looking at me," she screaked. "Fuck you, pervert!" Her voice rose to a shriek at Sam. His face was stupefied and incredulous.

"No kidding, listening to our conversation and creeping on me, so rude." She carried on as before. "I should have peed earlier, I don't want to get another fucking UTI. I can feel it starting already. You got cranberry juice?"

The passengers collectively glanced dismissively at Sam, shrugged, and turned their attention neatly back to their phones, books and newspapers.

He had been swiftly vanquished.

Sam dusted eyes with a man in a three-piece suit overlain with a beige raincoat who had been staring a burning hole at the young lady from behind. Sam sought to offer a sympathetic cringe with the man, to save face, and find some camaraderie in the episode. Just as Sam made contact with the stranger, the man in the beige raincoat quickly pulled his eyes away and fanned the long, vertical broadsheets in his tight, pink fists.

It's still okay, still very okay, he thought with a hearty shake of his head, *the bus is always stressful, but I made it.*

"You see?" the man asked. "Yes," the assistant responded with a slow nod. "He is a disaster, an ineffectual waste of a man. What will you do?"

At the office building, Sam glanced through the coffee shop window to espy a lineup that lengthened every second. He *could* go upstairs and pour himself a cup of brown-water from the urn in the office and hustle back outside to have a cigarette. That became unnegotiable when he spotted her; collecting bills with her right hand and dolling out coins with her left. He inhaled through his teeth, and shivered beneath the breezy shade of the awning.

Sam swung the door open and stepped aside, allowing two men and a woman to exit: Suits, passing through the opening without a crumb of eye contact. Sam curled his lips, ready to say 'you're welcome', but received no thanks for his effort. Another stream of formally dressed business-types exited in a duck-row fashion, each holding paper cups; none of the individuals offered gratitude for Sam's service. The penultimate man to exit reached his arm across Sam's torso to push the gaping door open a hair farther, turning to his female associate, winking, and said, "There you go, Ella." The woman thanked the man she called Peter. Sam whispered, "You're welcome," under his breath.

Luckily, the morning crowd at the caffeine stand moved efficiently. The customers did not gambol about the entirety of the menu; they had their choices loaded in the chamber, ready to disgorge at their earliest convenience.

The barista was named Kay, at least on her name tag, Kayoko in full. The coffee shop generally employed students, and a large proportion were those with English as a second language. In their first encounter, Sam embarrassed himself, something he still remembers as he approaches her nearly every day, when he spoke very slowly and patronizingly, assuming that Kay was one of the foreign exchange students that was hired by the shop. He very slowly and roundly asked for a coffee, overly-pronouncing each syllable like he was speaking to an infant. The barista, evidently Japanese in descent only, responded, "Yeah dude, one cuppa joe, black, two-fingers of room?" in a smoky, almost boyish way. Sam left a five-dollar bill for his two-dollar coffee and slunk away in prostrating retreat.

Since then, he felt he had worked his way back, having friendly conversations and learning more about her. He was intimidated by her, though she stood perhaps chest height in comparison. Her hair and make-up constantly changed in style and colour, as did her jewelry with the exception of a septum ring. Staring into her jasper-black eyes was the high point in Sam's day. *As soon as I break it off with Chloe, I'm going to ask Kay for dinner,* he often thought.

Kay was working with someone who Sam had never seen behind the counter. The nametag read 'Krys' with two symbols drawn beside the name; two circles, one with an arrow and one with a cross. The two baristas were alternating positions, one person pouring the drip coffees and working the till, the other operating the levers on the espresso machine.

Sam slotted in behind a tall man with a heather-grey checkered-suit and big head. He could see the temple tips of sunglasses sitting on the man's ears above a wireless earpiece with a blue blinking light.

"Two, uh, what's a macchiato?" the man asked with vowel sounds that hung open as windows in the summer.

"It's like an espresso with a bit of foam on top," Kay responded.

"Nah, nah … too many cals." The man patted, then rubbed his stomach. "What about, uh … flat white?"

"It's like a latte, with less milk," she responded.

This went on for another several beverages. Sam could hear the sounds of exasperation ring-out behind him. He could see the now folded-armed Krys, without orders, scoff and trot sassily to the second register.

"Next!" Sam was brusquely summoned.

"Hey man, can I get …" he opened robotically, his attention channeled on Kay explaining every drink to man wearing his sunglasses indoors.

"Man?!" Krys bleated. "Do I look like a man to you?"

Sam stammered. His attention had been fixed on Kay, waiting for her to glance in his direction.

Krys, as the nametag indicated, was impishly built with a short undercut hairstyle, a light purple rinsed into their mop. Krys wore a loose-fitting black shirt that extended down to their knees, with lithe and delicate-looking fingers slightly protruding from long sleeves. Earrings on both ears and a necklace made of thin silver that looped around a cylindrical amethyst gemstone, smoothed and shaped to a point.

Sam's eyelids pulled into his frons. "I didn't mean *man* as in man, I meant *man* as in dude … or human?" The inflection at the end of his plea and the penitently crossed fingers on hands pulled towards his sternum demonstrated, with hope, of his apology for any miscommunication.

"The world is becoming non-binary, *man*," Krys mocked. "Assuming my gender is a micro-aggression, that's literally so bronze age. It's problematic that you are pushing heteronormative values and alienating vocabulary in the safety of my work space. Intersectionalist!"

'I'm really, really, really sorry. I don't even know what an intersectionalist is. I don't mean to be one. Is it bad? Oh god. I'm so sorry. I just wanted a cuppa joe. I didn't mean any harm."

Beside him, the heather-suited man had casually removed his sunglasses and leaned over the till, smarming Kay.

"I bet you're Japanese; are you half something? White maybe? Swedish? Very exotic. I've spent time in Asia. Mostly Thailand. Japan is nice, so many bars and girls. Nikka, whiskey bars, am I right?" The man reached into his pocket. "Here's my business card. I'm in town for a week, but I know Japanese girls are very ... accommodating."

Sam continued to apologize, hearing something about mansplaining from Krys, keeping an ear on the conversation to his right.

"Well, I work *here* and I go to *school*. I'm pretty busy and don't really have any use for a corporate accountant, you know, because I don't run a business, or have any money," Kay answered.

"That is a lovely accent you have," the man responded. "I'll let you think about it; my cell number is right there." He concluded by clicking his teeth and shooting her with a finger pistol.

Sam finally got his coffee, sliding the barista a twenty atop the faux-granite countertop and whispered, "Keep the change."

"You can't buy acceptance in today's society, oppressor." Krys sucked their teeth and broadcasted.

Sam raised his eyes from the supine banknote to the barista's hexagonal scowl. He immediately disengaged, cleared his throat and pressed his lips together firmly, nodding dejectedly as he stooped away from the counter.

He stopped to add a splash of cream at the condiment station located beside the drink pick-up bar. "Hey." Kay reached across and tugged Sam's arm, stretching over the counter. "Sorry about ... that. She ... he ... They is new and still kind of feeling it out, I guess. I've heard the words 'toxic', 'consumer' and 'privileged' so many times this morning I think my head is going to explode. I don't see it panning out with … them."

Sam smiled. "It's okay … I should probably stop calling everybody man, man. Damn it."

"Although," Kay giggled and glanced towards the Mason jar tip cup beside the till, "I think … they … are intimidating people into paying us through the nose, too bad it's probably out of guilt."

"Yeah." Sam rubbed his arm and felt a dampness throughout the cotton blend dress shirt. "I didn't know what else to do. That was terrifying."

Kay and Sam exchanged a tacit recognition of the farce with flippant hand gestures.

"You're so late today, no time to chat." Kay's candy apple painted lips pouted. Sam wanted to compliment her on today's makeup: a faint crimson blush under her eyes that gradually faded as it climbed her cheekbones. It made her irises look darker and her skin look lighter, washed out, but in a good way. Her lipstick was thick, syrup-like, and reflected the potted lighting above her head; every time she spoke, they had to unstick from the centre to the corners of her mouth, almost audibly.

"Yeah … just a rough morning," Sam responded.

"I hear that, I gave myself this hangover eye shadow-thing because I woke up feeling like shit from staying up all night studying. I look like a mess. I'm sweaty.… I didn't even go out last night."

"I think you look … " Sam blinked with frankness.

"Su-pa kawaii," the man who had given her his business card added, poking between them grab a sleeve for his beverage. "Don't forget to use my digits." Another finger-gun salute.

"Oh, you honour me," Kay exaggerated the accent and bow of a Geisha. "Fucking idiot … what accent?" She rose with her middle finger extended while the man swaggered towards the exit. "Those guys are the worst; the ones with Asian fetishes. You'd think that if you have an interest in people of another race, you would do a little background research to not sound like a fuck-boy piece of shit whenever you talk to them. Ugh … Greasy-ass douchebags, I knew this makeup would bring all the creatures out from under the stairs. Men *love* the look of a drunk girl. Why is that? Is it because they seem easy? Like their defences are already down? Ridic. It's no make-up from now on. Ponytail and just moisturizer. That guy didn't even take off his sunnies … indoors! I mean, who does that? Almost as bad as resting them on the back of the head. People are the worst. Sorry … you're one of the good ones, Sammy."

Sam choked on his own breath, kicking up a thin cough. *I'm* one of the *good ones*! He puckered his face, trying to not smile as he looked at Kay. *She gets it. She can see the nice, good guy that hasn't been worn down. She is the best part of my day.* Sam burned to tell her that. He worried that it may ruin her day. He said nothing.

"I'm sorry to rant.… All I do is listen to people bitch and moan here and at school. That felt good, thanks." She patted his hand, placed on the counter to steady himself while coughing. "I'll let you have your smoke before work though, have a better day than me, Sammy! Can I call you Sammy?" Kay asked with a compressed smile as she returned to the frothing and steaming of milk and milk substitutes.

Yes! he thought in an air-horn sound, *call me whatever makes you happy!* He nodded and fought over-smiling as he spun around to make his exit. The sound of coffee pucks smashed from the porta-filter rose above the chatter of patrons.

"Are you sure you don't want to try a fair-trade blend? It's more expensive, but it's not the money that's the issue. The farmers in Java, Colombia and Ethiopia are the remaining slaves of the globalized world. Yes, it still exists, and you're supporting it. Haven't you taken enough … "

Sam could hear Krys' voice bemoan a customer as he felt the breeze of the open door expose on all the areas sweat had been escaping on his body. Everywhere.

"Interesting," the man said, swirling his glass of scotch.

There were four working elevators in the lobby of the tower where Sam worked. Another two had been out of commission since February, and not a day passed when at least one person could be heard cursing with indignation about the inconvenience. It was overhearing such whining that made Sam aware of his own petulance and inessential commentaries about the most trifle of things.

At the rear of a waiting mob Sam turned his wrist to check the hour. He pressed two fingers into his stylish pot; his head dropped and shoulders rolled inwards while he waited for his abdominals to stymie his probing fingers: the same ones he used to scoop peanut butter out of the jar the previous night. Only with a robust outbreath could Sam feel the curvature of what he hoped was stomach muscle. Engulfed by idle murmurs of grumbling, stale coughing, dry sniffling and affected throat clearing, he contemplated the stairs.

He glanced over to the metal door leading to the staircase where a man fully garbed in cyclist's apparel, spandexed and chamoised, moved his long Dutchman's legs up the stairs two steps at a time. Still wearing his sunglasses and helmet, he sipped from a clear tube that poked from his backpack. With a bicycle wheel in hand he was up the first flight before the heavy door swung closed.

Sam pushed open the fire exit, the cyclist's shoes were cheeping with fury overhead. After the first small series of stairs, Sam's trousers became overextended sausage casings around his tumefying stems. By the second series, hot liquid was squirreling out of his sundry folds and pits. By the third, he was heaving and reliant on the railing, and midway to the fourth he could hear the claps of each foot echo through the stairwell, decreasing in speed and increasing in weight. There was a short feeling of renewal after the fifth, when he approached an elderly woman taking slower, calculated strides.

"Each day better," she said in a Portuguese accent to Sam with a slight pant and full smile. Sam released the rail and eradicated the remaining steps.

On the next flight he came upon a rotund, middle-aged woman: stalled-out, seated on the riser with her heels removed and vexation ribboning her forehead.

"Can I give you a hand, miss?" Sam offered his hand.

"No!" the woman barked before sobbing languishingly. "I need to do this!" Sam was unsure if she was speaking to him or to herself, her head buried and her thumbs plunged into the palm of her foot.

Sam tasted brackish water mixed with hair product as it seeped into his mouth. A clingy skirted and flowy-bloused woman in running shoes powered by him soundlessly, her ponytail swaying back-and-forth as she darted effortlessly up the stairs. Sam's leaden breaths pulled in her handsome aroma. He tilted his neck and stole a slivered peek of her athletic back-end, he nicked the edge of a step and nearly doubled-over and down the staircase. His wet paw slipped down the railing; only by luck did the sweat dry and his fingers catch the stainless handrail to save his vertebrae.

His lungs contracted like an octopus in flight. He felt needles in his unlubricated throat. He closed his eyes and waited for the cigar-burns in his vision to clear up. The older lady greeted the middle-aged woman from below.

"Hello, Paula!" The older woman's voice smiled.

"Hi, Doris," Paula said through cached crying.

"I tell you, sweetheart, each day better." Doris beamed.

"Ugh, my doctor says … " Paula cued up the searchlight for sympathy.

"Nope! I can do this!" Sam shook his head, seeing milky droplets wiggle free from the tip of his nose. He grunted up the remaining stairs, the women's voices faded.

"How will you do it, sir?" the assistant asked. "Like I said," he began, "this will reveal itself after I get the ball rolling. A little nudge is all he'll need and he could do some damage. Besides, who would expect a lump of clay like this to wield any special power?"

As he achieved the floor of his office, not even the top floor of the building, his clothes felt tight and damp. The soft blue of his shirt was blotched with dark, soggy islands of perspiration.

Sam focused on leveling out his breathing as he stamped down the corridor to his company's office. His clothes chafed and rode up at every extremity. "This is like puberty all over again." His pace quickened involuntarily when he saw the water-fountain, instantly hyper-aware of his unbuttered throat. His mouth felt like one glued-together ball of sawdust and floor sweepings.

"Sammy, hey." His boss Harry Chen's robust, Styrofoam-voice modulated as he emerged from the office unscrewing the lid of a large water bottle with a bright orange 'Non-BPA' sticker smacked on the centre. "Are you all right?" Harry asked banally. "Did it start raining? Son of a … I had a bike ride planned with my partner after work…. Oh jeez, just my luck. Of all the … I didn't even see any clouds!"

"No, Mr. Chen," Sam mumbled, purging any saliva he could to lubricate his mouth, "I … uh … decided to take the stairs."

"Ah," Chen said, his eyes roving up and down the moistened pile of flesh before of him. "Well." He tapped his water bottle against his summer-grey pant leg, "Good time of year to work off the turkey tummy, am I right?"

"W-What?" Sam's mouth clung to itself like pancakes on an ungreased skillet, "I … I mean … pardon me?"

"The fall flab. The winter weight. That spare tire you've been lugging around," Chen joked, testing the spurt of water with his fingers before placing his bottle beneath the languid fountain.

"Uh, I guess yeah …" Sam cleared his deadwood larynx. "Got to start with the little things."

"Naturally," the boss patronized, "for some of us, it's an all year-round thing, but huffing up a few flights of stairs, you know, can really put it into perspective."

Sam blinked and nodded, trying to look interested. He could feel his gaze being pulled away from his overly-jovial superior towards the limping stream of much desired refreshment. He could hear the water trickle become less hollow, increasing in pitch. That sound alone charmed whatever residues his body was using for brain function to descend from the roof of his mouth and wet his teeth.

"Wait a minute," Chen said lifting the hand that held the bottle, pointing his finger at Sam with the gift of astuteness. "Your partner, she's a real fit one, isn't she?"

Sam followed the replete bottle with fully attentive eyes.

"Y-Yeah." Sam bounced his head with fatigue. "She got her personal training certificate, Pilates instructor designation, and a dietetics course online, and she's studying to be a yoga teacher and … "

"Well, there's your ticket!" Chen slapped his thigh, moving his hand to pat Sam, pulling back from the dampness, spilling some water between the two. Sam's heart squeezed as he watched the water splash the ground. "Woops." Chen released his trademark laugh, a hearty baritone that had all the sincerity of the king's most ambitious courtier.

Chen emptied the bottle. "Always empty the first bottle," he said, winking. "Never know what the pipes collected overnight."

Sam felt a stool get kicked-out from under his spirit. All the moisture left his mouth: unmixed grout meal was the taste he was left with.

"Are you okay there, Sammy?" Chen asked, his finger still drawing the lethargic wellspring from the fountain.

"Y-Yeah," Sam flushed, "just a lot of … "

"Heat?" Chen finally pulled the bottle away and took a few gulps. The water rattled down his throat with the same upbeat tempo as when he spoke. "Yeah, like winter wasn't days ago! Must be the ocean. I'm not complaining, I dusted off the old twenty-one speed over the weekend, felt great to have the wind in my hair." Chen smoothed his hand over his thickset pompadour, groomed perfectly. "Doing the seawall after work, just a little 25K."

Sam's eyes disappeared, as he dropped his head without utterance. There was nothing wrong with his young boss, slightly younger than Sam in years and decades younger in disposition. He was a decent man, an ivy-league carpetbagger, able to swoon clients and upper-management types with his pretentious guffaws and distinguished contralto. A squirrel with a razor under its tongue.

"Just woke up with a headache." Sam blinked matter-of-factly, unable to even imagine matching the unceasing enthusiasm of his boss.

"Well." Chen momentarily mirrored Sam's inertia. "Nothing I can do about that old chestnut." He fastened the lid of his water bottle. "Make sure you stay hydrated, though." He pepped back to his regular complaisance. "Looks like you might have lost a few ounces hustling up the staircase." He turned to enter the office, stopping a few strides away. "Oh, Sammy?"

"Yes, sir?" Sam halted his well-fasted raptor-upon-carrion movement towards the fountain.

"Meeting in five." He lifted his elbow and pulled back the comfortably tailored sleeve beyond his wrist to check his alligator-strapped, stainless Breitling. "Hurry in and grab a seat in the conference room, we've been jabbering for a while. I have a big announcement to make." He concluded with a knowing smile. Sam screwed his eyes upwards before swooping in for a few voracious and unaesthetic mouthfuls of water.

"Big announcement?" His eyes widened as he drank. "He must be getting a promotion. What else could it be?" Sam chewed at the water; his mouth, then throat, and then brain, all felt purified.

"If he goes, does that mean …" Sam felt a thrum of vitality pluck at his spine.

"It's settled. I will meet Sam tonight. Tonight will be the last day he ever has to be such a coward."

Sam's breathing had not yet settled as he entered the office. "Sure, Chen only cares about himself," he mused without angst. "But there was something in his look, something knowing, or telling." He dropped his bag on his flimsy rolling-chair. "Maybe he knows I've been too scared to ask for a promotion," he optimistically reasoned.

The office held twenty employees. They were seated in little clusters, similar to an elementary school, assigned by department and subsequent categories. The office always felt cramped and the shallow ceilings did little to expand the room or creative areas of the mind. The median age was hard to pin down. The monochromatic oatmeal-coloured walls and carpets made nearly everyone seem middle-aged; it had all the charm of a hospice. Age, sex and race ran together in a homogenous pastiche where fake smiles and forced conversations stretched the paint to the margins of the frame.

Sam's face melted in to a frown and he felt the energy drain from him as he walked in to the office. Was it the source of his grumpiness? Was it working in general? Was everybody miserable at work?

It was fine, just boring. Sam was hired because he applied. There was no passion. At that time, Chloe was still in college, he had just completed his degree, and financial support was the only impetus. Luckily, he had ingratiated himself with the staff; he arrived a fit, spry young buck who spoke with respect and posed no threat. If there was one critique, it was that he was *too* nice.

Was he stale? When did he stop trying? Did he ever really start trying? Was it a fable of entire existence: Lying back and letting life take shape around him, frustrated when he was left behind. *I just want to be a nice and good man, neither a leader nor a follower, just a simple and easy-going guy.* Life moved too fast for Sam's slow, uncalculated strides.

Small talk had become a cloud of mosquitos that he could not swat away. There was a time when Sam, mixing the powdered cream into his cuppa of stale decanter joe, would listen about children, sports, picnics, home gardening, rented paddle-boat adventures, fast food documentaries, and other mundane activities his coworkers felt the need to share with him, with or without his request. And he responded in kind, kindly.

In six years he had heard the gamut of leisure-day activities, all becoming an indictment on the lack of amusement in his life. He had a feeling that people could sense his loss of patience for banter; either from a lack of genuine reciprocity or the look on his face, which he had been informed seemed tired or depressed. "Maybe I've become the stale, boring representation of how everyone seems to me," he reflected. "I'm still polite, though." Polite enough to cringe with august silence at the systematic, fluffy recitals every Monday morning.

There was only one person who did not seem to acknowledge Sam's mounting distaste for small-talk, his cluster mate, Michelle. She was young and bright with the new-car smell of a recent university graduate. She was ninety pounds of grating amicability. *Her folks gave her too much confidence*, Sam thought.

"Hey Sammy," Michelle said, returning to her desk to grab something.

"Hi, how are you?" he greeted in a khaki tone.

"Oh! I'm great. What a beautiful day! Do you think we can work outside today?" She laughed with the artful pride of someone who invented a joke.

Sam's face flushed with antipathy. He converted a grumble into a thoughtful exhale, cut off before he could respond.

"I'm kidding, I'm kidding." She giggled, too hard. "But seriously how was your weekend?" she asked, continuing before he could reply. "Mine was great! Me and my fiancée, did you know I was engaged? Well, I am, his name is Edwin, he is a big-time accountant. I know, right? So boring. Well you're wrong! He is, well *we* are, total thrill seekers, like to the max. *We* went for a hike on Saturday, it was rainy, so we had to buy all this gear, *and we* bought matching rain suits, so cute! *We* did the North Falls, but at the top, you'd never guess, it was sunny! Above the clouds! Wanna see a picture?"

"That's great…" Sam's body was pulling him towards the conference room door.

She scanned her mobile. "Oh no, that was on *our* Nikon, silly me."

"We should probably…" He held his watch up with emphasis.

"*Anyways*, then *we* went out for some food and drinks, I know, should be watching my weight for the wedding, but anything with soda is okay. So many limes, ha-ha, I think the bartender hated me. I made him use so many on each drink. But, you have to spoil yourself, right? The hike was tough and *we* figured that *we* earned it. Well, *we*, all my friends were there and we all drank vodka-sodas, so many. He had to cut more limes. Lime everywhere! It was so great, *we* danced and had so much fun. Edwin is such a good dancer. *We* are taking swing lessons to surprise our guests at the wedding. Isn't that neat? But *we* had to go home early because Sunday *we* were going kayaking. Have you ever been? It's such a trip. *We* love it so much. *We* bought matching kayaks when *we* first started dating. Both are red, like my bridesmaids' dresses and the groomsmen's bow ties. So cute, right? Anyways, *we* kayaked all day, *we* were so tired, but *we* still went to yoga at night because, well, *we* wanted to feel rested, you know, ready for the week at hand. You ever notice how sometimes exercise can make you feel more relaxed and rested? *We* always say that, two peas in a pod, *we* are."

Sam could do nothing. He heard but did not listen. He nodded and smiled woodenly while absorbing very little. He felt a twitch in his eye when Michelle overly-sweetened the word *we*; stretching the letter 'e' like pulling taffy. He noticed that she stopped. The serene quiet had grown anxious.

"Well?" she blurted with one thin eyebrow lifted.

"I'm sorry," Sam shook his head, "I missed the last part."

"Why are you so wet?" Her cheeks pulled up.

"Oh … I took the stairs, and … "

Michelle's face lit up. "Are you running stairs? Edwin runs stadium stairs! Oh my god it's such an intense, cool, new school work out. His rowing team used to train like that in University and he still keeps in touch with the coach. Once a week *we* go and run all the stairs. He's so good, such an athlete, probably could've been an Olympian! *We* get such a burn in the quads, hams and glutes! *We* just pour sweat and then treat ourselves with our one luxury: sweet potato fries. *We* love sweet potato fries."

"No, no … just the fire exit. The elevator was packed." His lips creased inward, squinting but not blinking.

"Oh!" Michelle responded in two syllables; the second an octave lower than the first. "Well any exercise is good exercise, that's what my fiancée always says."

"Yeah, I … "

She tilted her head and smiled with greater-than satisfaction. "If he wasn't such a great accountant, Edwin probably could've been a top-notch personal trainer! I can ask him if he has any tips for you. If I remember, of course, we always get caught up in conversations and just run out of time, not things to say. It's like, oh my god, it's bed time, we have to be up in eight hours and we are only half done with our talk. Bookmark it for later.… We really should create a conversational bookmark; wouldn't that be an amazing invention? Maybe not invention, but a pretty genius device? Something to pick up where we left off, probably so many good topics just left there, lying on the floor, sad really. Maybe like an app for the phone? I'll never have time to create that. Pity, pity. Oh well."

If there was any discontent, Sam could not see one ounce. Her demeanour did not sag in the slightest.

"Harry says he has a big announcement.… He said that he was hoping to get a …" she began anew.

Sam's work phone emitted a low warble.

"Sorry Michelle, I should take this," he said with relief camouflaged as regret. "Samuel Florin."

"Okay," she attempted to whisper but rasped in a still-loud voice. "Don't keep us all waiting."

He squeezed a fraud's smile and waved.

"What's up, Andy?" Sam dropped the act and turned his focus to the line.

"How'd you know it was me?" Andy responded slyly.

"You're the only one who would call me on Monday morning, first thing, when I just get to my desk," Sam answered.

"Fair play, old Sammy boy," Andy continued. "How goes?"

"Ah, you just saved me from that annoying little twat I sit across from. She just won't shut up." Sam turned on his monitor and shuffled some papers on his desk.

"The Asian one?" Andy said in a playful tone, "She's pretty cute. So petite, so …"

"Oblivious. Clueless. Annoying. Self-centred. A try-hard. And engaged, sorry pal," Sam rattled off.

"Engaged? So young, what a waste. What's with kids these days?"

"I don't know, man. Maybe they just want security. A family. Or they get a taste and … "

"And move in with their sweetheart and spend, what, almost a decade hating their life."

Sam was silent. "I don't *hate* my life."

"I'm just joking you." Andy pulled back. "Did you do anything on the weekend?"

"Plans kind of fell through …" Sam realized that he was the only one left in the bullpen, everyone else was in the conference room. "Ah shit," Sam broke off, "I have to go to this meeting."

"Monday at Mahoney's? The usual?" Andy asked.

"Yes sir," Sam responded.

"Love you."

"Love you too." Sam docked the receiver.

"Nice of you to join us, Sam," Chen ribbed .

"Yes, sir." Sam bowed and took the only seat remaining, front and cen-tre beside Michelle.

"Thanks for all being more or less on time." Chen initiated the sermon for their habitual Monday powwow. Little information of value or use was generally disseminated at this time, a formality of checking in and hearing about the odd milestone. But today was different.

Sam began sweating again, slightly, but enough to feel the individual drips force out in rivulets down his back. He was interested in today's meeting, tardiness notwithstanding. "If Chen's out, then a shake-up is in order, and I could find myself promoted." The invariability in the com-pany meant that opportunities came at a sloth's mile. "I mean I haven't *asked* for a promotion. But I have hinted at it. Haven't I? I meant to. I just worry … what if they say no?" He had not even been aware of a posting and all heads accounted for meant that there was no immediate vacancy to fill.

"And, I trust everybody enjoyed the weekend, anyone get up to anything fun?" Chen said with his leg on a stool, water bottle in his hand, buoyant. Michelle's hand shot-up like a junkie.

The air-conditioner hummed in the background. Whatever particles it kicked in to the air always made Sam sleepy and nauseous.

He allowed himself to drift away, only brought back to reality by the noise he made each time his back moved from the padded backrest of the metal folding chair; a tearing sound filled the cramped room.

"And then this morning *we* made smoothies with the blueberries *we* picked in the valley a week ago and some cashew milk *we* strained through a cheese cloth!" Michelle had just concluded in a 'how long have I been out for' moment for Sam.

"Yum! That sounds terrific," Chen approved in a news anchor's voice.

"Can we have work outside today," a faceless co-worker said out of turn to a mixture of chippy snickers and uproarious laughter.

"Ahh," Chen traced his finger beneath his eye, "thank you for that." He slapped his knee for good measure.

Instantly, the manager adjusted his posture. "Some serious news. In two weeks, I will no longer be with you, my good people."

A stir of tepid surprise oozed from the crowd.

"I know, I know," Chen waved his palms, "I have been here for six years, actually, Sam and I were hired on the same day...."

Why does he have to remind everyone that we started the same day. Sam felt the blossoming of impatience and fatigue from the recycled air settle upon him. It demanded that his eyes close and place a weight on his head that caused it to dip over the ballast, like every other Monday.

The office, six years ago, was not dramatically different from the one today. Sameness is the hallmark for office types and jobs like these, ideal for the complacent and unambitious. Sam and Chen, then referred to as Harry, were seated at a dyad as Sam and Michelle were presently. Sam had earned his diploma from a local college and needed a full-time position. Harry was about to graduate from a private university and was given an internship at the office, a satellite of a larger company owned by his father, *Chentex*. Sam immediately disliked Harry based on his haughty, patronizing and synthetic attitude, which, to his credit, he was able to harness and sleek to a fine skill.

"In my time here, I not only became the youngest manager in company history," Harry Chen said with closed eyes and joined hands, "but also the first minority to accomplish the same task." His boasting continued: "I reduced costs, increased productivity, eliminated the dead brush while *creating* jobs. I was on the board before graduation!"

Sam would have been jealous if he had thought that his level of compete, intellect or effort was anywhere near that of Harry Chen's: it was not.

Very much, not. The old-timers, the negligent and slackers, *they* were jealous; Resenting this wunderkind who was riding on a steed of nepotism, pointing his shrewd claymore at things that were not broken and had always been that way. "He just has book smarts," some would grumble. "It's because his daddy calls the shots," others would chaff.

Sam was aware of the familial favouritism, but plants in the sunspot have little choice but to grow, and those with ambitious stems will grow the fastest, shading the others.

"Some of you know my father, well, let me tell you he had little hand in my success. I was my own man, perspicacious and hungry! Look at us! We are now a thriving, innovative wing of Chentex. We are diverse and young. As we say in the organization, *Diversity trumps adversity!*" Harry extended his upturned palms, priest-like.

Sam remembered a staff meeting Chen called after he'd only been managing the office for a few weeks. The email notification came through with the subject line, *Innovation is the Key to Success!* Sam groaned as he shut down his computer and picked up a notebook and pen, mostly for show. By the time he shuffled in the conference room, the only remaining seat was a small, plastic chair with a cracked frame. When he was told to take a seat he responded, "No, thank you, I'd rather stand."

"So!" Chen started, clapping his hands together in his usual, over zealous and completely insincere way. "I'll just get right to it. The brass brought me on board to make sure we turn a profit and be the best we can be." Sam rolled his eyes. What did that even mean? "This week we'll start the process of moving to a higher-visibility, more cost-efficient space." A smattering of applause rippled through the room and Sam wondered why he'd never thought of such a simple idea. Harry Chen bowed with false modesty. "Thank you, but no need for kudos. I'm just doing what anyone would in my position. Which, by the way," he winked, "is top dog." Sam felt nauseous.

Man, Sam thought, *there's something I hate about this guy.* A feeling of internal defeat softened him. *I don't hate him; I respect him.... I just don't like him. I stayed at the same position and he just kept climbing. He got smarter and I feel dumber, just coasting along. I got cozy... lazy would be a better word. Even new recruits have been hired for jobs I could've done. I could take night courses, ask for extra work, something.*

"I was sad to have to let so many people go when I first came on." Chen patted his hair. "It is the toughest part of the job. But without laying off so many underachievers, I wouldn't be surrounded with the winners that I am today!" A brew of resentment and self-adulation simmered in the room.

At least I kept my job.... When many had been sliced away like lumps of useless gristle, Sam had remained. He was not training to be the fastest, the strongest or most cunning. He galloped astride the middle of the herd and kept his head down. *It's going to be the 'same old' from now until I die.*

"It was a time for new ideas. There was no favouritism. If not me, then any self-starter with a focus on streamlining and budget could've been the chosen one. The same old wasn't working. The ox-headed ways of doing business in the past were just that, passed." Chen had locked an earnest eye on Sam.

The 'same old' mantra may not kill a man, but corrodes the elastics between the bones, making movement more difficult and agility, a memory. Sam's 'same old' response was his most dependable tool in the chest when asked how he was or what he did. It is likely that the 'same old' rejoinder, a stone to build a conversation, was now like an Inuit building an igloo from the inside, encasing himself, forgetting to leave an opening for an exit.

"And so a replacement is in order. The board has so graciously given me the opportunity to take the next step, or rather, build a bridge to continuing the path of my career." He linked his fingers together. "I feel that anyone and everyone here has the skillset, proactive attitudes and intangibles to run the office. I really do. On the plus side, aside from the one person chosen to fill my shoes, no one else will have to change departments, desks or anything whatsoever. No change!"

There was some whispering, but the room had grown courteously deferent to the manager's long pauses. Sam was alert. He glanced around the room nervously; he tried to be inconspicuous. His shoulder had pulled farther than he had anticipated and his shirt peeling from the backrest made the sound well-crisped toast being smeared with jam. He could not see his own face, but it felt like the expression of a gambler, his life depending on a ticket-in-hand, watching a ball sail towards the basket as the horn sounded.

"I hate to drag these things out," Chen took an alpha-sized sip and smacked his lips with disporting satisfaction, "Michelle Nguyen!"

Perfunctory clapping followed as the young woman rose quickly to shake the outgoing boss's hand. Sam's shoulders capitulated downwards in accordance with his dropping head.

After the jocular, big smiling handshake and hug between Chen and Nguyen, Michelle was given the floor for a few words.

"Oh my god, guys ..." Her hands speedily pump-faked. "This is so exciting. It's a surprise, well, not really a surprise, but more of a shock ... well no, that's not the right word either. I don't want to say that I was expecting this, but I would be lying if I said that I wasn't...."

Her energetic timbre washed over Sam like tinkling chimes of ice cubes dropped down the neck of a metre-long Collin's glass. He filled his lungs with a heavy, deplumed breath and felt his shirt shrink around his trunk, flirting dangerously with the stitch-work.

" ... and" she was still talking "*we* just picked out the flowers and honeymoon, so this is going to be a big plus for my fiancée and me." She clasped her hands. "Harry has done a great job and I have no doubt that I can pick up where he is leaving us, which is in good hands, I swear, ha-ha. I want to continue to do the same things that Harry had started, increase productivity and decrease overhead costs. We are both graduates of the same program at the same school, and so we both have the same philosophies about the corporate ... "

Sam ignored the remainder of Michelle's valedictory. It had the smell of nepotism, favouritism, once again. He would only be able to bathe himself with that thought until the afternoon, maybe until the next morning; he already had the inkling that deep down he knew she was a sound incumbent, but ignored the fact to splash around in his own angst.

Back at their desks Michelle leaned in and patted the back of Sam's mouse-gripped hand: "Sammy, I'm so happy!"

"Yeah, congratulations, Michelle," Sam said half-heartedly.

"Big secret … I kind of already knew," she whispered quickly.

"What?" Sam responded with genuine surprise. "How?"

"Well, Harry and Edwin are old high-school and then university friends. Come to think of it, they're family friends since childhood. He's actually in the wedding party! I never mentioned that? Crazy. Well. He told Edwin that he was getting a promotion and that he picked me to take over his role. Isn't that crazy? I've been here for what, six months? *Six months*? That's got to be some kind of record. Some people have been here for over ten years. More! You've been here for, like, five or six years! Isn't that crazy?"

"It's insane," Sam authenticated solemnly with genuine candor.

"Don't tell anyone," she giggled, "I don't want people to think that I got the job because my fiancée is life-long, best friends with the manager, might rub people the wrong way."

"You don't say." His eyelids sagged.

"But you're safe."

"I'm 'safe'?" He winced.

"Yes, we will probably do another shake-up, I have noticed a lot of time wasted here, a lot of chitchat, people not being all they can be, you know? Maybe release one or two of the old-timers and either combine departments or bring in some fresh faces. Can't have all these people thinking this is a social club where they can talk about their personal lives all the live-long day!"

Sam nodded. "Well, thank you for the show of faith."

"Just keep up the work or else!" Michelle jokingly warned. She slid her index finger across her throat, before succumbing to a fit of giddiness that shook her tiny body.

Sam took his lunch outside to a little bench in the pavilion. He grabbed a salad from the food stand in the lobby. He was famished and wanted a sandwich, a bag of potato chips, a cola, a sweet for dessert, and maybe another sandwich. "Food is your coping mechanism," Chloe often said, which he rebuked, slept on, and came to agree with. The tightness of his work clothes, the difficulty with the stairs and the fact he was currently sweating beneath the shade of a tree further informed him that he should treat his body better, starting with the puny salad that ridiculed him with its well-intentioned leafiness.

Maybe, he thought, *given the circumstances of the day, I earned a little cookie.* The food stand offered a variety of baked treats and Sam had a penchant for peanut butter cookies with chocolate chips. "I *did* do the stairs, which I can do again after lunch, up and down, twice each. And, the whole being overlooked for the job thing ... " He snapped the spine of a piece of Romaine lettuce with his plastic fork. "I didn't even know there was a job to be overlooked for." He sighed as he crunched the balsamic oiled leaf. "I probably wasn't even close to being considered, given that I didn't even know about it.... What can you do?" Sam shrugged, not bothering to answer his own question.

"Can I sit?" A mellow female voice broke Sam's vacant trance and lettuce chewing.

"Kay!" His aperture opened. "Of course!"

"Twins!" She held up a matching salad and smiled. "You on a diet too?"

"K-Kind of," he started, "w-well, not really, I mean I have to lose some weight, but, maybe as of right now, I mean, it's a good time to start, but, I mean, I guess, I don't ... yes."

She snickered at his stutter. "Aww, too bad, I like the dad-bod look."

"I ..." he flustered, unable to determine if there was sarcasm in her remark. "Why on earth would you be on a diet?"

"I feel skinny fat," She peeled the lid of her salad with a slight sneer. "Soft and skinny, all at once."

"But you look ... " He stopped himself, forced a blink. "You're already really shape in good."

"Ha-ha, what?" She threw him a tilted expression. "Well, I'm young and my genetics are misleading, but that doesn't mean much in the long run. I feel weak. I feel stringy and pudgy. I look better with clothes than naked."

Sam was at a deficit for words. "Well, I'm sure you look perfect, when you're um … "

"Naked?" She laughed. "Well you couldn't be a doctor with a tongue that gets twisted that easily."

"I'm also not a fan of blood," he grinned, "so this is the life that chose me."

"I've had too many late nights of stuffing my face, drinking with my roommates, social events," she said. "I also went on a run of dates where the guys kept insisting on going to expensive restaurants and buying the bar…. I just feel kind of … woof." She lost her track as she tore open the dressing packet with her teeth and squeezed-out the dressing.

"Well, obviously if you're going on all those dates, you're doing just fine." Sam fought sullenness.

"I'm a student," she said frankly. "A free meal is just that … I mean, maybe I could've gotten lucky, but most of the guys I've seen are not even *close* to my type. I mean … You give someone a chance because, you know, love or at least attraction can be in the anywhere. But, I don't like guys my age, or trust them … and the guys I have gone out with … Put it this way: If you are a lawyer, an accountant, a doctor or whatever high profile career-douche, why are you taking out a coffee shop girl if not to just fuck her and not call her again? Do you really want to take *this* home to mom and dad? They're all the same in the end. All liars."

Sam strained. "Well, you said love, o-or attraction, can be anywhere, and you *are* a very good-looking girl." She smiled as he continued. "I mean I think you're pretty cool, so … maybe they are leading with physical attraction and seeing … "

"Bullshit." She stamped. "This city is full of fake, insincere, wannabe Wall Street, wolves in sheep's clothing, predatory, high on their own smell, spoiled rotten, trust fund baby, silver spoon, scumbag human beings."

Sam nodded: "I'm a guy and I can't argue there. I think I dislike about 99 percent of people I encounter on a daily basis."

"Fool me once, shame on you … fool me seven, eight, nine times … well shit, man."

"Hey, it's okay...."

"Oh I'm not upset." She stabbed at the salad. "I make my own choices. I don't have to say yes. I don't have to date suits that order triple-shot espressos and tip with their number written on a fifty-dollar bill. But, I have. I'm sure women are no better. I'm obviously not."

"Rough weekend?" Sam asked sympathetically.

"Ha-ha," Kay laughed, "nah just in a mood ... How about you?"

"Same old, you know."

"Well ... no ... I don't know you. What's the same old? What's Sammy's 'same old' all about? What do you button-ups do? Hang-gliding? Para-sailing? Hiking and then go to a night yoga class to calm back down?"

Sam took a posture-straightening breath. "Nothing." He slumped back down.

"Oh jeez, you nine-to-fivers really *do* lead boring lives. Girlfriend? How many years? Married? Children? Grandchildren?"

"Nah," Sam said, "well yeah, I do have a lady." He exhaled his spirit.

"Oh. Rad. How long?"

"Too long," he spat reflexively, "I mean, a while, I mean eight years ... " He repeated, "*Eight?!*"

"You seem ... surprised? Engaged?"

"No!" he rebuffed. "If anything, only in daily combat."

"Nice guy like you? Don't see you as the fighting type... guess we all got..."

"To be honest," he interrupted sharply, but retained his composure, "I can't remember a time when I started a fight, or a time we didn't fight." He gnawed at his thumbnail. "Us nine-to-five types ... we get in these routines, you see ... "

"The same old?" Kay twisted Sam a look.

"Exactly, and, before you know it, you're fat, paying off student loans, hiding donuts, getting overlooked, back hurting all the time, sleeping on a couch, joint bank account, only name on the lease, yelled at when the toilet seat is up, with a girl who blames you for everything that's wrong in her life, even though you've done everything for her for the better part of a decade!"

There was a silence, not awkward, but a pause for a commercial break.

"Do you," Kay fiddled her fork in the greens, "ever tell *her* that?"

"Well, I … " He glanced to see her staring sincerely in his eyes through faded-red makeup. "No." He dropped his fork in the plastic salad container. "We haven't talked about 'us' so much as 'her' and 'me' as separate entities for a while. No discussion of marriage, children, settling down, vacations, future plans, nothing. Just that I need to lose weight, be more attentive, take ownership of myself, have more ambition, get more hobbies, support her career, make better money, all that fun stuff."

"Sounds more like a dictatorship," Kay continued. "Is the sex at least … "

"What sex?" Sam blurted. "Sorry, it has been a long time. You usually have sex to blow off a fight, but if the fighting never stops …"

"She's probably cheating on you.…"

Dead air.

"Sorry … knee-jerk … " Kay backtracked.

"Nah, it's cool … I haven't. If that was the next question. But I've thought about that possibility with her. And my friend Andy has suggested it." He held out his fingers. "More times than I have bones in my body."

"Two-hundred and six?" Kay asked with more interest than sarcasm.

"Give or take." Sam smiled painfully. "But, I'm sure it'll all work out for the better."

"How long have you been telling yourself that?"

Sam began to calculate aloud, "Eight minus … five years, or so."

"Jesus Christ."

Sam rotated his watch. "Well, Kay … "

"I'm sorry I ruined your day, Sam," she muttered with compunction.

"Not at all … " Sam answered in slow earnest. He turned his body to face her directly. "I'm glad that I finally got to talk to you, you know, not over a counter. Not with some customer biting at my heels or some … person … berating me for calling them the wrong … "

"Oh fuck!" Kay grabbed Sam's arm. "I've left Krys in there way too long! There might be a protest or a picket line or some shit!"

"Oh! Yeah. I had better get back as well." He wished to spend the rest of the afternoon exactly as the previous quarter of an hour had been.

Kay stood up, tossed her half-eaten salad into the garbage can and brushed her backside off. "These things never fill you up." Sam smiled and nodded.

"Hey." She stopped as Sam rose, discarding his own fully eaten box. "I hope things get better, and if you ever want to talk … just write your number on a dollar bill, or a quarter, or a penny." She lifted her hand and waved with her thumb tucked into her palm and grinned. Sam felt the floor disappear beneath him and the pavilion turn into a blind galaxy of pock-holed brilliance.

Sam was riding a little higher. He absent-mindedly marched straight for the elevator instead of curving to the stairwell. *At least I won't be a sweaty mess,* he thought as he picked at his teeth.

Reaching his seat, Michelle's arm was extended and crooked, drawing attention to the timepiece slung around her bony wrist. She was peeking at Sam from under her bangs, moving her eyes between him and her rose gold watch.

"*Watch* broken?" she questioned before continuing. "Better *watch* out with the long lunch breaks, I hear the new manager is a real stickler for lateness, ha-ha."

The laugh, a sprinkling of sugar that made no impact on the vinegar taste, did little to conceal the subtle reprimand with any sort of levity. "I'm only a few minutes late," Sam said with confidence, immediately feeling less confident about having had to justify his actions to his would-be superior.

"Well, time is a construct," she said satirically, "but we feel that a routine observance to the rules is the only way to properly ensure a full and active participation in daily business and operations, Samuel." She spoke as if rehearsed, her eyes became sharp and focused. "How did that sound? Manager-like?"

"Well … " Sam desisted, thinking that she herself was often absent long after the metaphorical lunch bell. "You didn't leave the office for a lunch with Edwin?"

A concert of ha-has boomed from the opening door of Chen's office. Out emerged two handsome, well-built men, referring to each other as 'Channy' and 'Chenny'. Both Harry and Edwin bore striking similarities, Sam thought, probably from growing up together. They were both ath-letic men with square jaws and high, durable cheekbones wearing suave business-chic suits; each had the same neo-ducktail hairstyle pomaded without flaw; and each spoke and laughed with the rich bravado of a private golf club member.

The similarities in their intonation was uncanny. They each articulated superbly with a peach-fleeced flocculence as if their lungs were in their maws.

"Chenny," Edwin said while shaking hands, placing his left hand on the manager's right shoulder. "That was great, really, and we'll be even closer when you move offices."

"Don't I know it, Channy." Chen patted the fiancée's shoulder three times. "Still up for hitting the links next weekend?"

"Bro," Edwin Chan moved his arms apart, "I wouldn't miss our eighteen for anything!"

"Ha-ha! Good, good!" Harry Chen laughed.

Michelle's eyes lit up fondly while Sam turned his head. "I guess that's *not* a fake laugh?" He questioned his longstanding belief while listening the dueling clang of rich man laughter, the most phonetic of all laughter.

They walked abreast towards Michelle and Sam. Michelle straightened her back while Sam busied himself over some documents lying on his desk.

"Thanks for giving Mimi a chance, Chenny," Edwin said, placing a hand on his fiancée's shoulder. "You think she's got the goods?"

"Ha-ha, Channy!" Chen patted Edwin's shoulder. "There was never a second thought! It wasn't a decision so much as a wait-and-see kind of game."

Sam peered up at Chen, who had, perhaps only in that moment, cast a disparaging, unpitying look that was laced with, what he took as, mild disgust. Either way, Sam caught it. Chen regained his exultant countenance and carried on: "Hardest worker and kindest soul in the office," he said with volume that had noticeably increased, though it did not decrease the clarity of his speech.

All three nodded.

"Well sweetheart, I have got to get back to the number crunching," Chan said as he and Michelle pecked. "*We* are so honoured." Edwin stressed the pronoun the same way as Michelle.

"I'll walk you out." She stood up as all three slowly made their way to the exit, laughing and not looking back at Sam, left alone at his desk wearing a puny russet crown.

"Clear my schedule for the rest of the day." The man laughed. *"I will meet young Sam tonight, and his life will be changed forever."*

Sam thought about Chloe on his way home. They had not communicated throughout the day, which a few years ago seemed unfathomable. Back then, if either had failed to receive a timely response to any number of inconsequential messages in the course of a day, panic crept over. It had a cuteness that now scrambled Sam internally; he wanted to simper at the memory, but in the instant that the milky warmth of nostalgia began to drizzle down, it hardened in his heart and lumped his throat with sorrow.

Sam's hard-put face stared at back him in the dimmed mobile. He opened the screen: Nothing. In the beginning when they quibbled, one of them broke down before noon. Now, it was rare to hear from the other, and scarcely anything good. The war never stopped, the communication never started.

What a simple, stupid thing to take for granted. Waiting, even hoping for some kind of nonverbal, touchless validation. He longed for the times someone reached out to him with plans he would begrudgingly oblige; waiting for a patio table at a café like so many he could see from the bus. He felt an anger and hate at the people sitting in the sun, taking pictures of their food. *No,* he thought, *Stop it! I don't hate them. I just want a seat.*

He was tired of wishing a return for the 'good old days' of Chloe.

Sam had an affinity for digging up the past, the glory days when Chloe could do no wrong. But even those cherished memories were corroding with the present situation; an autopsy with rusty, unsharpened blades. Simple things like making homemade juice with fruit they cheaply acquired from the Chinatown markets, strip-quizzing her with homemade cue-cards for her midterms, or just a simple cuddle on the couch to watch a movie but talking about their ambitions through the entire thing. The strain to really feel those times and not just recall them was like watching a badly damaged film reel, where blurry optics and distorted recording seemed pointless and almost disturbing.

What he really wanted was to enjoy the present and not press his eyes to see at the past, squeezing the juice from an atrophied lime. He wanted something, or someone, that let him be carried by the gentle surf of tender thoughts, and did not harden abruptly, like instant cement.

I don't want what I had with her, or I do… but not with her, he thought. *It's not about better… it's about different. I need change and the good and bad it brings.*

The cord dinged as he pulled it. *I'm praying to a dead god … milking a goddamn bull.* He slunk off the bus.

He flashed his mobile in front of his face again. Nothing.

What did he expect? He tucked the device into his pocket. She only would have texted him to tell him the sink was broken again or call him some awful name. The two had given up on making evening plans, or even divulging one's whereabouts. *She knows where to find me*, he thought defiantly, referring to being either at home or at Mahoney's pub with Andy. *I never know where she is.* How long had he been confusing butterflies with ulcers?

Relief and apprehension hit Sam when he neared his door. He was relieved to be home, but ill-at-ease that a fight that may ensue. If the apartment was empty when he returned, he felt dismay. Not at being unable to resume fighting where they left off, but not knowing where she was. His ego hurt every time she avoided his contact, responded snappishly, telling him nothing of substance. Like living in a warzone, he could settle in with the illusion of solitude, but could be hit with a bomb at any moment.

He opened the door with a limp "Hey" that drifted directly out of the open window. Sam let another feeble warble teeter from his lips, doing little to inflate the room.

"Ahh." He exhaled with relief and moved to the kitchen where he patrolled the pantry for something to eat. He came upon a note that read *Gone Out* written in black sharpie with bitter corners. *She writes like a boy when she's mad,* Sam thought, comparing it to the cute letters full of swoops and hearted tittles that he still kept in the dust-jacket of a hardcover she had given him for their first anniversary. She was then a penniless undergrad and bought a copy of Master and Margarita for a dollar at a school book sale. The price tag was half scrapped off: the cheapest things have the most resilient price tags.

"How did it get like this?" He leaned on the counter and sighed. "We'd probably both blame each other. I think I can accept my fair share of the fault. Just like the bus, just like work, just like everything." Sam felt like he stopped trying to be positive and let every little thing bog him down, allowing it to seem way worse than it was. Instead of looking for the bright side, he dwelled on the dark. He was tired of being pessimistic. *Maybe,* he thought, *I'm making things worse than they are.*

He decided to ring her.

First time nothing. Second time nothing. He rummaged through the fridge, mostly her food; kale, spinach, berries, avocado, seeds and legumes, rice cakes, lean fish, tempeh, tofu, and a little container of Greek yogurt. He ate the yogurt; it was just okay. She picked up on his third attempt.

"Is the sink busted again?" she answered hurriedly.

"No, no, ha-ha," forced laugh, "I just wanted to see … "

"I'm busy Sam, we're biking from the studio to Bikram and my earpiece kept beeping during my playlist."

"Sorry, sorry … Are you going to be home for dinner?"

Chloe groaned. "Ugh, no I don't … No, okay?!"

"Um, well that's fine, that's fine, it's Monday so … "

"So *you know* that I teach in the morning and afternoon, then have class at night, it's a long day, okay? You never listen, I told you this morning that I had a long day and not to stress me out, and now, I'm riding across the bridge and what are you doing? You're stressing me out! How can I find my Zen when you're stressing me out?" There was an inaudible word and Sam made out "Of course not you, silly," followed by gentle laughter.

"Who are you talking to?"

A silence.

"Jesus, you're nosey, aren't you?"

"What?" Sam raised his hand in defence while on the phone. "I just was wondering … "

" … Fucking Chandra, for the love of god."

"Sorry, sorry … " He shook his head. "Do you want to come with Andy and me to Mahoney's tonight? After you're done? Your friend might like Andy."

"And sit in a dank pit with you and listen to him talk shit? Ugh, not!

No, it's a beautiful day and if it's still warm, me and Chandra are going to a patio for wine after class."

"That sounds nice," Sam said with hope, "maybe … "

"Yeah, that's why I'm doing it!"

Sam paused and allowed enough time to be included. "I hope you are enjoying the sunny day."

"I'm trying to, Sam," she said, like he was a dark cloud.

"Okay, well, say hi to … " He heard the smack of three beeps end the call.

That's the difference between the two of us, Sam thought as crumpled up the note. *If I had hung up on her, she would have pulled off to the shoulder, called back to cuss me, my mother, my whole entire life and future.*

Sam put down the phone, hoped that she had inadvertently hit the receiver, and reached into the cupboard for the peanut butter, spoon already in hand.

PART 2

SAM MET HIS best friend Andy at Mahoney's Irish Pub every Monday, and sometimes throughout the week, but always on Monday night; Monday night was locked in. The pub had both a geographic convenience for the two men, and offered a sentimental factor, reminding them of the halcyon days of college where they had been dormmates at the college nearby.

Mahoney's was quiet and had Guinness. The male servers wore all black and the women wore green tartan kilts. It forwent much of conventional extravagance most Irish pubs fall victim to: the gaudy overlapping of ornaments vomited on to shelves, pictures of Larry Bird or the Blarney Castle, framed prints of *Slainte* or other Irish proverbs and idioms in Celtic font. The others were clichéd joints, decorated by a non-Irish, pissed-up on chartreuse coloured Harp, exhilarated by their one and only trip to Temple Bar.

The owner even refused to add green dye to his lager on Saint Patrick's Day, and preserved the demurred tobacco-discoloured hardwood paneling, spalling brick, and panes of stained-glass. The Irish bar was never bright, but never quite dark. The impassive light from the soft bulbs that hung throughout the bar like cavern torches always seemed to give off an early evening, fall transcending to winter feel. The oaken wainscoting responded to the dim light with a warm amber-orange relucence.

Sam's eyes took a moment to adjust to the darkness of the pub as he entered through the fortress-like front door, three little steps down from the street level. Neither light nor sound was able to escape past the iron-barred, heavy wood-slatted door, which led to another door, half-glass with the name of the pub scrawled like a detective's office.

After succeeding the first door, Sam was shocked to find himself squeezed in amongst a crowd into the mudroom, already poor for space when empty due to an old, boxy cigarette machine.

"Hey Sam," a bartender named Sean morosely addressed.

"Sean, what the hell is going on?" Sam blinked to accustom his eyes to the light, the wooden door struggled to nudge him farther into the persons-clogged entryway.

Sean sighed. "I guess, it's finals week, or after finals, or something at the university." He rubbed his forehead. "At any rate, it's a pub crawl, or pub night for the students. I don't know man."

The clamour of hoarse and astringent, male and female, hollers and shrieks made the bartender cringe the left side of his face tortuously, moving his hand to smooth it back out. "This is my Friday and I just wanted a quiet little night, watch the game, maybe pour a few draughts." A cheer erupted in concert, even concerning the few others in the tiny vestibule. Sean soughed ruefully.

"Andy is already in there," he said through his palm. "Of course, we kept your seats, it is Monday, after all."

"Thanks Sean." Sam patted the barkeep-turned-doorman on the arm. "How are the other regs holding up?"

"Either pissed-off, pissed-up or down the street," Sean returned. "Anywhere but where their mail comes."

Few things rival the undermining consequence of having to enter a party scene while stone-cold sober.

Sam sucked in his stomach and tried to make himself public transit small. *Lucky I don't have a beer yet,* he thought as he was bumped and jerked by the festive mob, all wearing the blue with gold trim of their university's sporting-colours. He was stunned by his routine being knocked so far off its regular alignment to be irritated. That would come soon. Tomorrow's promising future are always today's worst drunks. He meekly wound around the boys and girls, all at least a decade his junior, and was succoured by the decision to change from his work attire to a more casual dress. Splashes of house lager and vodka soda sprayed from all angles like a clubhouse after the pennant.

All Sam had wanted was a laid-back jaw session with his pal.

Andy was leaning against the corner of the bar in their usual spot, unseated and chatting up two sorority girls, evidenced by the Greek lettering on their tops. He was still in his Muscovite-grey fitted suit, mauve button-down, no tie. Three buttons undone.

"I work in sales," Andy said to the girls.

"Are you sure you're not a model?" one of the girls asked him.

Andy threw his head back, combing his hand through black hair, streaked with premature grey, weaponized as an elegant sagacity for younger women. "Nope, computer sales, *mon cherie*."

"You don't have a computer salesman's body," the other girl remarked, squeezing his broad, sculpted shoulders to his manta-ray latissimus dorsi muscles.

"I used to swim competitively. Keeps the physique nice and svelte," Andre Lambert responded with confident charm.

"How old are you?" the first girl asked.

"Old enough to be as far from wise as I am from dumb; and still say girls and booze are my two favourite things in the world." It did not matter what he said, his classic handsomeness and depthless charisma allowed him to say almost anything.

"Your eyes are breathtaking," the second girl climbed over her friend to add, "where did you get them from?"

Perhaps the greatest strength Andy had, which he long recognized to employ as a stratagem, were his eyes. His face worked like a treasure map to guide the onlooker directly to his baby blues. The term piercing gets thrown around, but Andy's were knifelike, and he was all too aware how to penetrate women, men, and potential buyers with his.

"I don't know," Andy said with skillful coyishness, scratching the back of his head. "I guess my grandmother, we were very close, so she left me the gemstones she never put in her will."

The two girls cooed in unison.

Sam had slipped his way to the bar and lifted a finger to a flustered barkeep who began the ceremonial pouring of a Guinness. He nodded to the older man on his left, Glen or possibly Frank, he was not sure, though he'd neighboured a barstool with the guy for years, even partaken in heart-to-hearts and sloppy pub carolling around Christmas.

"Fucking kids," muttered Glen or Frank. "At least your mate is having fun." Sam curled his lips in and nodded.

"They are beautiful! And I was close with my granny, too!" said one of the girls.

"I was way closer with mine, and my grandpa, and my great-grandma, too!" the other one-upped her sister.

Sam was standing behind the girls, waiting for Andy to notice him, eavesdropping.

"Yeah, family is important," Andy said, Sam shook his head. He knew Andy was punching for points, and also knew the subject would change very soon. "So what do you girls study?"

"Poli-sci!" The spoke harmonically, turning and smiling to each other.

"Ah! Jinx!" Andy started, "So … Do you two do everything at the same time?" The girls turned to each other coquettishly. Andy had landed his jab and pulled back. "Political science … Sounds so important, yet something I know so little about, I would love to hear more about it. What will you do after graduation?"

"Well, it's basically the study of the inner-workings of political mach-inations on a national and international scale," one girl began, the words not synching with the metering of her idiosyncratic, upward inflections on every second word.

"And we both plan to pursue a life of politics, I myself like civic pol-itics," the second girl interrupted. "And I'm interested in federal institu-tions," the other broke in. "My daddy is on the transportation committee."

"My father," the other broke in with pomp, "works in international diplomacy."

"Woah, that's amazing." Andy's enthusiastic voice outstripped his expression.

"I don't see him too much, never have … " she broke off.

Sam watched as Andy flickered with the cunning smile of a wolf, he knew what came next.

"That is so sad." He placed his hand on her shoulder. "My dad worked a lot, too. You never know what you have until it's too … Sammy!" His somberness was quashed entirely.

The first girl stepped back and stumbled slightly on Sam's foot then shot him an unwelcoming glare.

Sam was passed his beer and caught himself blowing on the foamy head like it was hot coffee. He was watching Andy with a knowing smugness.

"Good day, Andre," he said, tipping his glass towards his friend.

"Sam, I'd like you to meet my friends…. Well, ladies, I didn't catch your names."

"Stephanie." One girl pointed to the other girl whose glare became a fake smile. "And I'm Rebecca."

"Steph and Beck!" Andy smiled and picked up his untouched pint.

"Oh my god, that's what we call each other," Beck adulated. Steph smiled nervously. "What's your name? Or should I just call you Blue-Eyed Beautiful-Man?"

Andy laughed. "Nah, that's what my mom calls me, too many syllables, anyways … My name is *Andre Lambert*." As he often did with women, especially white and especially young women, he pronounced each name with a melodramatically French accent, though unable to replicate the guttural 'r' sound and a caricature artist's inflating of the vowels. It was a neat trick and it worked. Truth told, it was a terribly flat accent.

"Oh wow! Are you French?" Steph asked. Sam rolled his eyes.

"*Enchanté*." Andy winked, then kissed the backs of their hands.

"We have to go to the bathroom," Beck said with far too much excitement and grabbed her friend. "The line is probably forever; will you wait for us?"

"*Mais oui*! We'll be right here." He pinched his eyes to a smoldering look and tilted the chalice with his pinky raised. The floating pinky was another Carolingian burlesque he added to the sham. Andy watched the students snigger as they shoved through the crowd holding hands, moving his still-pursed look to Sam.

"Jesus Christ, does that ever get old?" Sam chafed, half-amused and half-not.

Still sipping, Andy winked and shrugged, lowering the pint and wiping away the creamy mustache from his neatly trimmed goatee. "No." He laughed and pushed the hair from his forehead. "It just gets easier. You really should try it. Become *enchanté* like me."

"How was the weekend?" Sam asked. "You crazy Jew … You know that word isn't … "

"Ah, wild! Yes, yes … Very entertaining." Andy's eyes traveled the room, he grinned at another girl in a booth.

"Oh yeah? What happened?" Sam asked, again shaking his head at his friend.

"Well, Friday night I had a date, went well … very *enchanté*." Andy smirked softly.

Before Sam could even feign an interest in Andy continuing his story, he carried on.

"This administrative assistant from a little tech firm that I moved some units to a while back. I was at home and felt bored and just decided to hit her up. Good thing that I did."

Sam was able to slowly mouth a word that started with 'w', either 'why' or possibly 'what'. Andy had paused for a quick sip and recovered before Sam knew the word he was going to use, only having contracted his lips to pucker an elongated 'w' sound.

"When I met her, she had been seated the whole time at her desk, very sad for her to have to hide her best feature. I kind of took a gamble. When I leaned over her desk she was wearing this pencil skirt and had these thick-ass legs pumping out. When I say thick, I mean *thick*. I could tell she had a nothing-sized waist and I tapped the table to check, like in poker. Seriously, even when sitting down I was pretty sure that I could see her ass rise like a cushion at the sides, the skirt was like an overstuffed crepe. She was small, super short, and built like one of those miniature ponies. You know I like small and tiny. Just so tight. I think she said she used to be a gymnast or a dancer or something. I can't remember. But what I do remember was that she was petite, almost too much, even for me."

Sam quickly burst in while Andy wet his chops. "I don't understand why you, all six-feet plus of you, likes such tiny women.... It just seems ... "

"Oh," Andy laid down a joker-card expression, "I think you do." He moved his hand to his face and left a small space between his thumb and index for his blue eye to radiate through.

"I don't think that height and vagina ... " Sam bemused.

"Sure it does." Andy smacked the table and snapped back to regular posture. "It's human anatomy, plain and simple."

"Yeah, but," Sam said with uncertainty, "in my experience ... "

"Go on." Andy dragged the second syllable.

Sam sighed defeated, shrugged and freed the conch.

"Anyways, I took her to my favourite Italian spot. You know Esposito's, I've taken you there before. You're the only person who hasn't *at least* given me brains after. They treat me like I'm goddamn Sinatra when I go there. 'Andre Blue Eyes' they call me. I don't know if they think that I'm Sicilian or something. They get a kick when I say 'scusa', 'per favore', and 'bella ragazza'. I haven't figured out *enchanté*, yet."

"And ... "

"Right, right ... So I picked her up and, you ever get the feeling that things are going to go your way? I mean that you won't have to try very hard to get what you want? Like it's going to end up *enchanté*?"

"No," Sam stoned.

"Well, I gave her some flowers at her stoop and she invited me in. Truth is, if it wasn't at the Esposito's joint, I would've blown off dinner, but I really wanted cacio e pepe and some of that homemade rosemary bread they make. It's so good, and they serve it with this heavenly infused butter, I have no idea what it's infused with, maybe duck fat? Maybe some other animal ... Either way, it's amazing. So I was hungry and I won't break a reservation, I'd prefer my reputation than pussy. Well, depends on the ..."

Sam rotated his extended index finger in circles at the wrist.

"Yes. So. We went to dinner and could only get through the appetizers. A couple bites into a caprese salad she said to meet her in the bathroom. We had already downed a bottle and a half of wine and I was getting to that 'down for anything' kind of mood. The bathrooms are just like the ones in the Godfather scene where Michael has to shoot the Mick cop and the Turk. Solazzo was the Turk. Who gives a shit about the Irish…"

Andy at once turned to the bartender, who was ignoring his customers and listening-in to the story. "No offence, Kenny … Out of context."

"I'm Welsh." Kenny tilted his head indifferently.

"Cool." Andy continued, "So open the door and this chick has already cuffed herself to the pipe that ran from the tank above the toilet bowl close to the roof with one of those chains that dangles around face level. She had her skirt hiked up and her panties were down around her ankles. Now, if I wasn't a bottle or so deep on Chianti, then maybe I might've had some questions, like, do you have any rubbers? Or, how clean is this turn of the century bathroom? But, for the life of me, I had nothing. So I did what any good mensch would do and dove right in."

"What did … "

"Pulled out and nutted in the bowl. Is that what you were going to ask?"

"N-no … "

"It didn't take long, I had my favourite dish on the way. And she kept calling me daddy. That's the thing with the young girls these days, they always call you daddy. I have no clue what that means, but it turns me on. I finished up and it turned out that she dropped the key in the toilet. I had just flushed my babies and her handcuffs were legit, real, police joints. So she's panicking, I mean, with good reason. Assed-out and latched to a toilet in a quiet bistro. There were kids, man! And parents out for a nice family dinner! Quite the scene. I asked her what she expected me to do. I didn't bring any handcuff keys, why would I?"

"Then what?" Kenny leaned in.

"I did the only thing that I could do. I had them box up the food and cork the last bit of wine and called 9-1-1. I thought about leaving right there, but stayed, I'm a pretty good guy. The fire department came and sawed through the chain. She was quite embarrassed. I thought it was pretty funny. The owner, Frankie Esposito, gave the old 'boys will be boys' rub."

Andy mimicked an older Italian man's accent. "Ah, Andre the blue eyes, you cheeky *bastardo*, you making with the woman inside of my *bagno*? Only you, ha-ha. *Piccollo monello*."

"He wasn't mad?" Kenny asked as his queue for drinks proliferated.

"Nah, we go back pretty far," Andy responded.

"What about the girl?" Kenny hunched forward.

"She was shy now. She asked if she could come over to maybe finish up on dinner. I figured because she probably didn't want the last visual to be herself dogged-over a shitter. I felt bad and said we couldn't go to my place...."

"Cause you live with mom?" Sam taunted.

"Yes, and I have told you a thousand times over that I am proud of that. Jewish mothers are protective and I couldn't move out if I wanted to."

"But your pops is the Jewish one!"

"Yeah, but Mom had to go extra hard to prove herself and now she is way more Jewish than Dad ever could be. He's only half anyways. And I ain't about to complain about not having to cook or do my laundry. I love my mom. She's a nice lady."

"I thought you were French?" Kenny mused.

Sam squinted and shook his head and hands.

"Yeah, I am a lot of things...." Andy grinned. "So, I said my place was dirty, why don't we drive out to the beach and have dinner there. So we had a nice little picnic by the water. I had my pasta, she her cannelloni, then we banged on the beach beside a cute little fire I made with newspaper and driftwood."

Andy sipped again. "Problem is, no open liquor or fires are allowed on the beach. Someone called the one-time and they showed up ready to read the riot act to our sweaty, sand-covered asses."

"How much was the fine?"

"I knew the cop! You believe that?" Sam nodded frankly: yes.

Andy finished. "An old buddy, we used to ski together. He laughed it off, kind of the way old man Esposito did and even took off the handcuff bracelets. Ha-ha, she had been wearing them the whole time! It all worked out! *En-fucking-chanté!*"

"That was just Friday?" Sam asked, jealousy was the wind that blew his bitterness.

"Yeah! Then I joined the guys at the stag on Saturday afternoon which ran until Sunday night, absolute debauchery. Strippers, gambling, blow, way too much booze. Too much of everything. Way too much. Spent like a grand on that son of a bastard. Goddamn degenerates, all of them. Hope he has a herpes flare-up on the wedding night, cheap-ass. I'm kidding. It was a blast, good to see the lads again. Don't know if we should get together all that often, might die within the decade if we did. Took this morning off and interviewed with another company. They made it sound like they want to make me a tasty offer. Told them it had to shoot the sun out of the sky because my current contract and bonus incentives are massive. But, who knows? Here today, gone tomorrow. I've been fired for less than screwing a secretary, but that was a lay-up! Finished up about an hour ago with a 25K contract from a lead that I was given from that other secretary I banged a month ago. I think the sales outweigh the methods in which I reach them. She was so hot, so small … I would've done it for no leads, no sales! Nice lady. Today was a good day." Andy drained half his pint after flitting his pinky with a little greeting gesture at another girl in another booth.

"Who's stag? Who's getting married?"

Kenny was yanked away by a server to fulfill the endless ribbon of chits.

"Oh," Andy's face dropped slightly, "uh, Dimitri Jones. You didn't know? I guess … "

"Nah." Sam bled with disappointment.

"Well, I guess you kind of lost touch with … "

"Everyone."

"Yeah," Andy affirmed, downcast. "Except me!"

"True." Sam bobbed his head. "Who needs them, anyways?"

"Yeah." Andy creased his lips downward. "Who needs life-long pals, chums, and buddies to go and have stupid-fun awesome adventures with, male bonding time, new and old memories, wedding parties, and keeping mum on all the shenanigans with a closed circle of secrecy. You know, *friendship*."

Sam's face twisted. He was silent, sipped his beer and cleared his throat. "What hap … "

"Chloe, you fool!" Andy pounced, awaiting Sam's easily telegraphed pondering.

"Oh," Sam mumbled, "right."

"We've been through this, what … fifty million times? You keep digging this hole for yourself and at the bottom is her. *She is the devil!* Guess what? You hate her! She hates you! Why are you even together? I feel like this moment keeps repeating…."

"We actually fought this morning…."

"No shit! You fight every goddamn day! She has all the control over you in the world and you have none, nothing for yourself. You single yet? You *promised.*"

"No … not just yet, I wanted to sit down and talk to her, I tried to invite her out…." A look of terror loomed over Andy's face as he glanced over his shoulder. "But she wasn't home. Left a note, and when I called her, she hung up."

"She's probably with her sugar-daddy, or a stevia-xylitol-agave-daddy. Some granola eating pus … "

"Hey … "

"Well?"

"Yeah … the coffee shop girl said she's probably cheating on me."

"I been saying that for … "

"Years, I know. I said that to her." Sam chewed his thumbnail. "You really think so?"

"I am not saying it to be mean. I wouldn't try to hurt you. I am saying it because she is mean, she has changed, and she is the one hurting you, and it's getting to be the only language you know. She is obsessed with herself and all that self-improvement bullshit. Don't get me wrong, sex with her is probably ridiculous, but you ain't the one having it with her, buckaroo. And yes, I definitely think she is cheating on you. But, since you pay the rent and she has that joint bank account that you let her use, it's like living with her parents. Trust me, it's sweet. She gets her own room, food, roof, and just has to find somewhere to get it on without you knowing."

"She *has* changed a lot."

"So have *you!*"

"Me?"

"Oh my god, yeah. You are so shy and broken now. So defeated. Back in the day, man, you would have jumped in as my wing-man with those chicks instead of sitting back and just watching…. Your confidence is in Chloe's purse with your bank card and your balls. Get your balls back! I love you, Sammy. I hate watching you like this. I hate having to sit here and listen to you bitch week after week after month after year about the same shit with the same woman. Remember? You used to slay. Hell, you used to talk to people besides me and barflies here." He leaned into Glen or Frank: "No offence old-timer."

"None taken, son," replied Glen or Frank.

"Anyways." Andy leaned in a put his hand around the back of Sam's head. "I don't want to drag this on. It's depressing the shit out of me. Your depressing life is bumming me out. That's not fair. Let's just, for one time, say that you have your nuts firmly twisted back into your sack and you can chat up some young, not-as-smart-as-they-think-they-are college girls. Call it spring training for when you break free from the demon-woman."

"She's not all bad, Andy." Sam advanced his pawn reactively, tritely.

"Maybe, but probably not. You are my friend. Not her. I owe her nothing. I'm Team Sammy. And if she is cheating on you, which she most definitely is, then to *hell* with her."

"To *hell*." Sam toasted Andy. They plunked down their glasses.

"Two more for me and the Spaniard, and a couple of shots of Jameson … make it four," Andy said to Kenny as the girls emerged through the crowd.

"I'm Mexican, not Spanish, you punk bastard."

"I know…. But we're selling on Mexican, buying high on Spanish. Spain is hot this year. Hey, who's the salesman, here? Say you're from Barcelona and don't say another word after. Say Barcelona with that stupid 'th' sound, chicks eat that up. I know you haven't been but I bet these spoiled debutants have. Let them tell you about Gaudi and Parc Guell and that half-cola half-wine swill. Do it for me, *Monsieur Lambert.*"

"Fine." Sam crossed, then uncrossed his arms. They hung loosely at his side, unnaturally. He could feel a tiny bubble of malcontent manifest somewhere deep beneath the surface.

The blueprint that the two friends had relied on throughout their years was theoretically simple, but hinged on Andy as the greaseman. His extroversion was magnified tenfold when he was next to Sam, who played the quiet voice of reason. Andy spoke a lot, sober. When in the cups, his tongue was a beast with no leash. His looks and charm allowed him to infiltrate any group, but his hotfooted rambling could upset the neck-buttons with an offside comment. Still, his delivery and energy swooned more than it stung. People gravitated towards Andy; ugly and desolate lands are not the trophies sought by conquering kings and queens.

Andy could generally have his choice of mate. Sam was content to sift through the rubble for silver, or use his dichotomic personality to woo the girls rebuffed in earnest by Andy's outspokenness. That is how he met Chloe, nearly ten years ago.

In a bar.

In this bar.

At the same spot at the same wood. She had been there with a girlfriend, helping her mate drink away the memory of a recent break-up. A younger, equally predatory Andy was more than willing to assist Chloe's friend in the most therapeutic of ways. Watching Andy with a jilted lover is watching a surgeon with the grace of a maestro and the instinct of a shark. This left a more confident Sam and a shyer, less confident, homesick undergrad named Chloe, alone together. She complained about gaining weight, Sam told her she was beautiful. She complained about being not smart enough for calculus, Sam told her she was brilliant. She said she was broke and miserable, Sam told her not to worry. Unlike his friends, Sam was not spinning lines to bed the young woman, he saw dignity in her vulnerability and strength in her stress. She was pretty and he felt her smile in his bones, like something Sam was missing.

Time moved like sandpaper against Sam. He left college with a diploma, a girlfriend and an inspired attitude. He'd had fun with Andy and his friends in college, but was ready to hit the real world. Day-by-day Sam began to make concessions; a stop-gap job here, a pricey rent for better location there. He was tired from the grind and loved Chloe. She was exhausted and overwhelmed in her final years of college and Sam made it his mission to help her with her anxieties. He opened his heart and his bank account, he made his life about keeping her happy. Andy would never leave, but his friends did not share the same feelings for Chloe that he did. "She's taking advantage of you, man!" they'd say, though Sam assumed they were just jealous of his happiness. Chloe pursued other means of advancing herself after graduation. Sam would not vacate his position, which was becoming increasingly frustrating, and she was leaving her promises to help with rent, groceries, and the bills unfulfilled.

"Hey babe," Sam would say, "you know how much I love and would do anything for you.… I know you're stressed out from school and taking some time off work, but the new place, which I love, is expensive and the groceries and bills are piling up."

"I can't even right now Sammy." Chloe always started in that way, "I love you too and I am so thankful for your support. This is so hard and I don't understand anything sometimes. It makes me so anxious and angry. I couldn't do it without you, It's just a draining, frustrating process. I'm almost done with the program and then you can look for a better job, I'll get a better job, and we can travel and be happy like we always wanted."

"Chloe, you are the smartest, most beautiful and talented person that I know. You can do anything you want and I will be there to lift you up when you fall."

"I love you," they told each other with lengthy embraces.

They did not have a lot of extra funds so Sam stayed in with Chloe to watch movies or step-out on simple, pleasant dates. The monotony slowly began to breach like a thick treacly flood. Sam had always been a shy, somewhat nervous person, but cheerful and even effervescent. Chloe decided that she didn't want to follow her college-directed career path and shifted gears by taking an array of courses on health and fitness.

"Hey babe," Sam would say. "You know I love you more than anything and will stand by you no matter what you do. But, I am starting to feel boxed-in at work. I don't think I like working in an office and I can't look for anything else while you're taking all these classes. They're expensive and so is all the equipment and certifications. I'm just a little lost and I want to explore some options, maybe travel and do some cool things, but we need more money."

"I can't even right now, Sammy," she would say. "You know I love you, but I need to do this. I feel so unfulfilled. I'm mad that I feel like I wasted my college years in something that I wasn't interested in. You want me to follow my passion don't you? You said you would always stand by me.

Well, this is where I found my passion. Spirituality and fitness. I know it seems like a lot, but it's way harder on me. After this, I will be able to get an awesome teaching gig and we won't have to worry about anything!"

They informed each other that they loved the other, a hand pat or a peck on the cheek if they were close enough.

His life and lack of amusement was losing carbonation, his cheeriness eroded slowly and his optimistic view of the future was narrowing to its current pinprick of tunnel-light. Andy voiced this a little, then more, until now where it was a chorus during their infrequent outings. Sam was loyal; he helped Chloe battle with her frustration in college, then existentially in the post-graduation vacuum, then in her conquest for personal betterment. If anything, she had always been the pessimist and he the source of inspirational words. Until, one day, it seemed to him like it was out of the blue, she no longer needed him and his words of praise and support.

"Hey babe," Sam would say, "we've both been working a lot lately and I feel pretty stressed out with Chen and him hiring new people for jobs that I had asked for. I want to quit. I want to travel. We should just pack our bags and go to India or Costa Rica like you've been talking about. I know I have been a little down and not jazzed about the meditating and tantric stuff. I'm just starting to feel the drag of this routine. I think that I need a reset. I … I love you a lot and want to … well, I want us to … I don't know, we should try to reconnect because I also feel like we're drifting apart a little bit and it makes my stomach hurt really bad."

"I can't even right now, Sam," Chloe would say, interrupted from meditating, practicing a yoga position or texting. "I love you and all that stuff but I need to focus on my form and the universal dharma. Thanks for you support but you're getting in the way. You have to stop complaining about Chen and whoever else, the negative attitude won't get you anywhere and you drag me away from nirvana, that's not a good vibe. I meant to tell you, I'm going on a yoga retreat in Costa Rica in a couple weeks, must have slipped my mind. It's for advanced yogis, so maybe while I'm gone you can take Andy and do some road trip or something."

"Oh," Sam's head dropped, "sounds fun … is it expensive?"

"Money, money, money … always about the money, Sam. You can't put a price on healing your chakras. Especially when you are the one damaging them."

"I guess you're right." Sam caressed his arm. "I just wanted to say you look beautiful and I love you."

"Me too," Chloe said, moving into warrior's pose.

She no longer needed him, wanted him or even loved him. She had sought self-improvement and gained independence, but had failed to return the favour. Sam now felt he was inescapably confined to his dead-end job, detached from his friend group and falling deep into depression. She had consistently progressed while he had stayed back to help her reach the next rung. He felt as though she had made her way to the top and kicked over the ladder, leaving him in the darkness alone. He had become meek and obstinately miserable with complete resignation. At a time when he needed a hand to get him out of the quicksand, she distanced herself; he felt abandoned.

"Hey babe," Sam would say, "can we talk?"

"Sam." Chloe was always in a hurry now. "I can't fucking even right now. I have such a busy day and another instructor called in sick."

"O-okay. Well I just wanted to talk about us. I don't think I'm happy."

"Wow ... news flash, Sam Florin is unhappy. What a story. Read it before."

"I-I mean; I don't want to ... "

"Look. My therapist says that you are toxic for me, but not to change my environment right now. He says that I need to focus on me and not making any major changes yet."

"What does that mean? What about me?"

"All about you. huh. Sam is the sun of his own galaxy. Everyone revolves around you."

"I didn't say that, I just feel so down and depressed and I miss ... "
"Shit! I'm going to miss the start. Thanks a lot Sam."

"I love you." Sam sighed to the slammed front door of the apartment.

Those negative feelings snowballed and created the Sam of today: a woebegone, resentful and ineffectual shell of the buoyant and caring spirit he once was. He was tired and too weak to even call things off with her; he lost his motivation and replaced it with a feedback-loop of begrudgement.

The memory, with the ales and whiskey, made Sam wistful. Andy jostled him from his plaintive pauses and forced him back to the conversations, to the weak and shallow dialogue which had in turn forced him to dwell upon ancient history.

The girls led the conversation by talking about university, further elaborating on their future goals, internships, and opportunities. As was his custom, Andy threw slight, almost imperceptible sexual references. Each drink made Andy's hair-trigger vocal delivery hasten, become more difficult to comprehend, and wax carnally. Andy began to pile on the innuendo; testing the waters, planting little seeds of erotic imagery, lubricating the discourse.

Sam allowed the dialogue to waft around him like foul-smelling smoke. He found the girls to be "spoiled millennial brats", which he commented to Andy, who in turn did not seem to care.

It bothered Sam that the girls spoke of the future as a return on an investment they paid nothing towards. They were born white and rich. The social climate was at its most fertile, ever. Opportunities would hang like ripe fruit on a sagging branch that stooped within grasp. Sam could not pin down what pricked him as especially confounding about the girls, but lay somewhere between the success they envisioned for themselves and the certitude of which they were sure to attain it.

"So, bachelors, then masters, then PhD? Sounds like you've got it all mapped out," Andy remarked.

"Indeed," replied Beck. "It's a lot of work, but you have to go for your dreams."

"Sounds expensive," Sam added.

"Uh, I guess? I don't know, my parents pay for my school."

"Do you have a job?" Sam contemned. "Have you ever worked a day?"

"Oh god *no!*" Beck answered nonplussed. "School *and* work? You'd have to be crazy."

"We did." Sam pointed to Andy and himself stoically.

"I volunteered at the doggy shelter a couple of times," Steph added.

"I bet you do a great doggy," Andy added, Steph laughed.

"So," Sam pinched the bridge of his nose, "*you* don't work. *You* volunteer at a pound. Don't you need experience to get the jobs you want?"

"I'm not worried," Beck responded confidently.

"Why?" Sam asked, confused.

"Because things will work out. You have to focus on your dreams. Half the battle is envisioning success."

"But, reality is so much different."

"I don't know. Most of the people I know are in the careers they wanted. Almost all my friends, in fact."

"Sounds pretty lucky," Sam added.

"Yeah, I guess … maybe it is lucky." Beck repeated the word as if she was unsure of the meaning.

After a slight pause Sam downed his beer, requested another and spoke as if to a forum. "How are all these kids getting jobs without experience? I don't get it?"

"It's about who you know these days, Sam," Andy said as one would trying physically to calm the first tremor of an impending earthquake.

"Bullshit! Where has hard work gone? Where has working your way up the ladder gone? Where has loyalty and … "

"Easy there, old man," Steph said. "It's all about networking, it *is* about who you know. Lots of people get jobs through family, school networks, and organizational ties. There is no shame in that. You can work as hard as you want, but, and not to be a bitch, I shouldn't say that word, but, every person in here wearing blue and gold knows someone who knows someone who will get them a job. That's the reality. It's not luck. It's just how it works."

"What about him," Sam said reflexively, pointing at Andy. "He sells snake oil and gets offered jobs fist over fist!"

"He's hot, like super-hot … " Beck stated factually. "He's gorgeous and can probably work a room."

"I got a few rooms we can work." Andy wrapped his arm around Beck.

"Look," Sam raised his palms in defeat, "I'm sorry, I'm just … "

"He's just tired from the flight," Andy added. "Booze is hitting him because of the jet-lag."

"Where from?" Steph asked.

"El Salvador," Andy carried on. "He's salty because he works for a non-profit that helps reform kids lured into the gangs and he takes it very personal. On top of that, he met his *ex*-girlfriend at this very spot."

The girls looked at Sam under half-moon lids, reassessing his demeanour in the new light of his chivalrous backstory. .

"He just sees so many talented, smart and caring young children, not given the chance to shine and it wrenches his heart. Right, Sammy?"

" … yeah." Sam shook his head, exasperated and thirsty. He twisted his trunk on the bar and ordered another beer.

"You should draw a clover on his beer!" one of the girls yelled at Kenny who blinked drably at Sam before turning his back. "Oh! You know what? I bet it's still sunny out, we should find a patio!"

Sam made an acidic frown. Andy toyed with the suggestion before issuing another round of shots, lifting four fingers to the barman.

"You shouldn't!" Beck said. "We owe you for the other rounds, it's not fair!"

"Don't worry about it, *ma chère*," Andy said. "It's my treat, *enchanté*." The girls both giggled. "Sammy there, me and him used to come here back in *our* undergrad days." The girls giggled again. "Yup, these have been our stools for as long as I can remember. Second most comfortable thing in the world."

"What's the first?" Beck asked.

"Well that is my bed, I have an amazing *duvet*," Andy said with his put-on French accent. Beck snuggled in to him like a kitten.

"And what's your bed like?" Steph turned with wet, drunk eyes to the silent Sam.

"Well, my bed as of this moment is a fucking, godforsaken couch." Sam belched.

The girls laughed but Andy shot Sam a fierce glare. "He means he prefers the couch for intimacy, right?"

Sam took a sip to wash away the taste of resentment, like whipping snowballs into the mouth of a volcano. He used to be so good at playing along with Andy's rolling gambits, what happened? Sam could not soothe the negativity that was grabbing hold of him; he felt every sole that tread on his shoe, every handbag and elbow bounce off his body, and each droplet of alcohol that accidentally rained down on him.

The female population in the bar had begun to dwindle slightly, leaving the fellas looking the way fellas do when the ratio lacks a feminine presence. Twice the friends had to dismiss drunkards from corralling Steph and Beck. Neither Andy nor Sam cared to quarrel, but the countenances of the college boys were becoming more amphibian and their comportment more belligerent.

"Hello, Sam," a rich and magnificent voice slid beneath the high-pitch fight between caterwauling students and the straining music-speakers.

"Yes … " Sam was suddenly tasked with knowing if it was indeed Glen or Frank.

"Oh!" Sam surprised. "Well, hello … you're not … "

"No," an older, but hard to say how old, man responded. "No, Sam. I am not Frank *or* Glen." He chuckled slowly.

"Where did they, I mean, he go?" Sam quizzed. "He's always here until he gets the boots."

The older man, staring straight ahead, his finger crossed in front of a glass of neat brown liquor. He barely moved his lips, but his low voice seemed to cut beneath all the distortion and background noises. "Bob, is his name, young man. And Bob has some tasks that need tending." The old man made the slightest of facial movements beneath a greyed beard, allowing a smile to naturally extend across his calm, unwrinkled face.

"Bob, huh," Sam whirred. "How did you know my name?"

The old man cut a throat-contained laugh. "This is far from my inaugural visit to this pub. Also, your friend, *Monsieur Lambert* there, has been saying it all night. The way mothers do when they want their offspring to learn self-identification. The way that seeks inclusion within the foreignness of a group."

"Ah." Sam nodded with extra-wide eyes. "Well, I should, uh … yeah." Sam turned to the group and was met by Steph, pushing up against him.

"Join me for a drink after, young man," the man said, laying a hand on Sam's shoulder that he could not see, but felt keenly.

"You're funny and cute…." Steph poked his stomach. "I like this whole belly thing … it's like my dad."

"Is that a compliment?" Sam asked as he took a sip of beer. "I've heard that today, something about dad-bod."

"It's *so* in right now, girls don't want a guy that tries."

Sam, taken aback, responded, "I thought the business of fathering just went to shit or something. Like you all have daddy issues. Trying to replace him with another underachieving slob."

"Ha-ha!" Andy laughed with nervous embellishment and slid in, "Don't we all!"

"What happened to the righteous little student from an hour ago? The high and mighty one? Gone dumpster diving for dick?" Sam asked, surprised by his own words. Andy fired another stern look across the bow. Sam responded with a baffled shrug.

"The best freedom is making your own choices or not making any," Steph responded, swaying on the balls of her feet, inching closer to Sam, seeming to ignore his slight. "That's empowerment."

"So … Empowerment is doing, or not doing, anything? Anything or nothing? Is there any … thing, or action, that you can't twist into being called 'empowering'? That doesn't make any sense! Where is the consistency? I don't get it! It's all about having your cake and eating it, too!"

"Sam, I say this with love, shut up." Andy chuckled without any trace of humour. "What else do you do with cake? Let it … "

"No, man … I'm sorry, but … " Sam searched for what he wanted to say. "Doing something only because you can isn't empowering, it's just power! It's still just dick swinging! Only … "

"Only you don't need a dick to do it," the old man leaned in and said to Sam. "Seems more even to me."

Sam shook his head. "Look," he focused in on Steph, "if you weren't drunk, you wouldn't be into me and I wouldn't talk to you. I don't respect you. You seem like the type of person who has abandoned her status and privilege, her entire ideology, and the next morning will just blame it on alcohol. Maybe call the police!" Sam felt the same sour feeling from the girl on the bus that morning. "Stuck-up little princes and princesses, like, all of you can afford to make mistakes, sober up and pretend they never happened. Life is just a game with unlimited extra lives. Bullshit! You are all so entitled! You're all so …"

"Were you born a grumpy old man, Sam?" Beck snickered and rolled her eyes. "You sound exactly like my dad."

Steph smiled at Sam. Sam did not feel like smiling. She leaned in to kiss Sam. Sam moved backwards and found himself buttressed against the wood.

He looked down at the shorter girl pushing her mouth slowly at him. Her closed eyelids were painted smoky bronze that led to impossibly thick, fanned-out eyelashes. Her pink-slathered lips were struggling to flatten out and move naturally up towards his.

"Easy," Sam started, finding no space to back himself farther. "Andy … " He craned his neck back like a disenchanted cobra.

Andy was in a full-on embrace with Beck, his thumb raised up to his friend before wrapping his arms around the girl. Sam saw him whispering something to Beck. She bit his ear and said something back.

"Night cap at the beach!" Andy triumphed. "I have a few towels and some gin in my trunk."

Steph's eyes opened and she spun to face Andy, holding Sam by the sleeve. "Great Idea!"

"*Enchanté!*" Andy again exclaimed. "Sammy, let's go!" The tenderness in his smile was defrauded by fiendish coiling of his upper lip.

"Yeah Sammy," Steph pulled the collar of his shirt, "tell me how much you hate me while you fuck me, daddy."

"What?!" Sam strained with absolute perplexity. "You have got to be kidding me…."

"Choke me, daddy, call me a … " She stood on her toes to get closer to his ear.

"Young miss," the old man interjected, moving his hand between the two, "Sammy here is my nephew, well great-nephew, even though sometimes he isn't so great." Beck giggled. "I'm Uncle Domino and I'm visiting from the old country. I need just a few minutes of his time, would that be all right?"

"Yes sir," the girl responded mechanically.

"So, what you're not coming?" Andy moaned.

"You will see Sam later, *jeune Andre*." The supposed Uncle Domino turned to Andy.

"You got it," Andy enthused, pointing his finger at the old man.

Andy and the college girls immediately filed out of the bar. Sam watched them exit and looked at his watch. It was not sinfully late.

Uncle Domino grinned wryly.

"They just left like that?" Sam muttered. "Fucking Andy. Always thinking with his dick. He just … "

"Takes orders very well." Uncle Domino maintained his unctuous demeanour.

"Huh?" Sam turned to the uncle. "Orders?"

Uncle Domino waved off Sam's comment. "I'm not keeping you, am I young man?"

"I'm not that young, sir." Sam moved the glass from his face and shot a burst of air through his nose sardonically.

"I suppose not at this venue, on this particular evening. Though I am sure my years push the median tremendously." The man squinted and nodded. "Even still, you act like an infant in the grand scheme of it all." Still staring ahead, Uncle Domino shook his head. "Yes, an overgrown boy in the guise of a man."

Sam, trying to get a better look at the stranger's face, pulled back. He sat back on his stool, thought about contesting the comment, but shook off the slight. "Listen, *uncle* … can I get you a drink, I … "

"Have no idea how people work." The man interrupted with his calm, charcoal timbre. "Verily you misunderstand the human species, especially women, *especially women*, and the younger generation, to what I would consider a comedic extent. Comedy, which it would be, if it was not so unnervingly pathetic."

"Hey!" Sam sneered indignantly. *Who does this guy think he is?*

The old man turned his entire profile to allow Sam rebuttal.

Sam looked at the man, he was older, but striking. He wore a bespoke suit that made Chan's and Chen's wardrobe seem cheap. His swarthy face was symmetrical and unblemished. The grey in his flow-back hair betrayed his buoyant olive cheek and taut orbital skin. The beard was long enough to add wisdom, but short enough to not seem pontifical.

Sam met eyes with the stranger.

They were deep and perilously dark with bands of dazzling, inimitable colour woven beneath, only apparent when the light smuggled in. He waited patiently on Sam. An inextricable confidence was infused within his eyes. Sam found it impossible to manufacture thought when they locked on to his. Sam saw, and felt, an inhuman poise, with no hint of anger or threat, somehow intimidate him, cowing the air from his lungs and causing his knees to tremble.

Sam snapped out of it, scratched the back of his head, flattened out his hand and smoothed his palm over his head and face. "No, I don't get people. But there's no need to insult me." The man said nothing. He pulled out the stool to the left of him and tapped it. Sam slowly swung his legs over the cushion and settled into his coveted slouch.

"So," Sam tapped his fingertips against the wood, "your name is Domino?"

The stranger smirked. "Luciano Domino." He held his hand out towards Sam. A fine hand, robust and full of colour.

"Sam Florin." He shook Luciano Domino's hand. The silkiness of his hand made the tightness of the grip seem preternatural. It did not hurt, but it felt like Luciano could squeeze a planet to bread crumbs. "That's a different kind of name. Is that an accent, sir?"

"No, no … Just the language without any cleavers or mallets to spit the blood of delicacy on the chef's apron," he responded with sincerity.

"Please, call me Lucy."

Sam reclined on his stool. "You don't look like any Lucy I've ever seen before, man … sir, I mean."

"Samuel, you have never in your life been introduced a Lucy, male or female." His response did not deviate from his urbane bearing. "By your estimation, I should at least have curly red hair, no? Maybe I should be reclined in the atmosphere surrounded by pixels of effervescence? A sky of diamonds?"

Sam pinched his chin, then moved his thumb mouthward to nibble on his nail, "Well, you're not wrong, I guess."

"Enough of this tiresome ado regarding my name." Lucy wawed his hand peacefully. "I am sitting beside you, Sam, because I want to speak with you on an explicitly intimate level."

"Look, Lucy …" Sam sympathized, "I'm really flattered, but … "

"Sam," Lucy tilted his head frankly, "with the utmost pity and reluctance I must inform you that intimate has manifold definitions, and, not wishing to not further desiccate the choking gills of your floundering, beached ego, I am not interested in any form of tryst with a lumpy, laggardly layabout, such as yourself."

"Of course." Sam constricted his brow to conceal the blow of rejection and disorientation at the palaver. That he felt dismayed at the repudiation, did however, befuddle him. "But, please don't insult…"

"Sam. You are a *coward*," Lucy broke in, factually.

"Excuse me?" Sam tore the pint away from his lip.

Each man stilled; Sam's incredulity was mirrored by Lucy's unblinking calm.

"I can repeat it for you, one time more, if that is what your rhetorical flush has petitioned for. Samuel Oscar Florin Tejada, you are a *perfect* coward. That is why you have not told me 'good day' and left after I disrespected you, almost immediately."

Sam, noticeably agitated, began fingering through the files in his mind, again falling silent. Lucy raised two fingers to Kenny who nodded and began filling a glass.

"Look man," the stool squeaked beneath Sam as he pushed himself from the bar-top, "thanks for bailing me out, but … "

"Sit down Samuel." Sam did. Lucy placed his hand on Sam's forearm. "I know you better than you know yourself. How is not important. I know about Chloe, Harry, Kayoko … I even know about the girl on the bus who accused you of perversion like the peeping Tom of Coventry."

"What the hell," Sam quivered.

"Please, do me the honour, willingly, of sitting with me. I have other methods but I can verily assure you Samuel Oscar Florin Tejada, my time is worth infinitely more than yours.

Sam felt strangely at ease with a counter-intuitive calmness.

"Allow me to explain, as I can espouse that your amazement *should only* be evinced by being spoken to with boldness by a hitherto unfamiliar interlocutor, and not the ingredients of his utterance therein."

"Why do you talk so funny? Why am I listening to you?" Sam crinkled his face. "Weird name, weird words … and you're just ripping on me."

"In due time, my boy." Lucy smirked. "You may not believe me, but I mean no disrespect. However, it is impossible to remove a malignant tumor without first producing some gore."

Lucy nodded at Kenny after he plunked down a beer in front of Sam. "I have heard you speak, I have witnessed your actions and, furthermore, I can read the nature of your intrinsic qualities in the sum of your idiosyncrasies. If you would be so kind and patient as to let me dissect you beyond the fatty tissue of your physicality and press my fingers to the innards of your soul, I can vow to assist you in being less of a, how you might colloquially define, a pussy."

Sam's hand was still gripping the empty glass. His jaw, candlewax warmed to a languorous pliability, was powerless to occlude. *Why am I still listening to this guy?* Sam thought. *I want to get up and leave. Maybe I'm just drunk. Maybe …*

"Where oh where to begin." Lucy narrowed his eyes, using the back of his hand to slide the freshly filled chalice closer to Sam.

He licked his top lip salamander-like as Sam nodded morosely at his beer.

"Cowardice is simply an anthological term that I have chosen to describe the many inhibitions that I have remarked in your conduct. You are, and this is without rehearsal: jealous of all those around you; fearful to execute or even propose within yourself any form of change, whether exorbitant or minimal; angry, with neither the backbone nor bravura to negotiate all the rage, repressed but unmastered, that feasts upon your psyche like piranhas; you lack pride, whereas hubris is a sin and your comrade Andre has a damnable proportion of it, your destitute confidence is humiliating and deplorable, not humbling and altruistic, as you may tell yourself; your laziness triumphs over any inborn talent or learned ability you could nurture and cultivate to a prowess- acres upon acres of trampled-upon and unwatered seeds; finally, because my throat is demanding hydration, you are irresponsible, you recognize all these disabilities with eagle-eyed clarity, the way your defective emotional and mental constitution has impaired the prongs that you are even too timid to even *pretend* to stab at the fugacious shadows of 'happiness', deceiving yourself that every moving force in existence is to be held responsible for your mediocracy, when it is you, executioner of your own dreams: formless, shapeless opioid reveries that cannot even contour a silhouette, never mind a fully developed image.”

“Well …” Sam cleared his throat. He took a big sip of his beer, looking up, fighting what felt like tears. The soft bulbs of the overhead lamps were enough to threaten a trickle from the dyke. He knew that he should be angry, but somehow, he was not.

“You do not have to feel ashamed to sob in my presence, young man, the cleansing properties of such an expulsion may be a better panacea than another, more radical aftereffect.”

“I’m not crying.” Sam quavered with the pint still pressed to his mouth, his voice suppressed hollowly within the glass.

“Of course you’re not,” Lucy replied with empathy in his voice. “Because all those attributes that I have adroitly prescribed, would never allow you to weep, let alone blubber in public. You’re too scared.”

Sam ran his wrist over his eye. “Why is that?”

“Excellent, my boy!” Lucy clapped. “A question! A simple, rudimentary, open-ended question that permits a further excavation of your ailing fettle.”

“Listen … you speak very … well, I guess… but I am having a hard time following.”

“Have you ever read the novel A Clockwork Orange?”

“Seen the movie,” Sam replied stiffly, sniffling.

“The movie employs an argot for the characters which Burgess, a linguist, coined as Nadsat. It is a Russian-influenced slang which the teenagers speak all throughout the novel. While no one could possibly have been exposed to the language before, aside from Anglophones with a Russian pedigree, most are quite capable of recognizing the vocabulary by the conclusion of the novel, or film, if you prefer.”

“And?”

“And. I am only speaking *one* language, *one* dialect: your language. Free of patois or bastardized jargon.”

“So?”

“So: listen, and you may increase your lexicon as an ancillary dividend, while we mend you of your deleterious insipidity.” Lucy sighed. “I may have committed to the erroneous notion of over-budgeting my trust in your intellect."

"No ... " He shook his head slowly. "I'm smarter than I look, assuming I look like an idiot."

Lucy lifted his chin. "Very well, young man," he said with a gentle rumble.

"Now, Sam, I have given you an analysis, though briskly recanted, of the pathologies and behaviours that maintain a scourging grip upon your character. A plague that coughs no bile, but a pestilence that resides deeply within you."

"Hold up." Sam raised his hand. "Are you like a doctor, or something? A shrink? A psychologist? A Freud?"

"No, Sam," Lucy patted his eyebrow, "just a compassionate man who sees a hog limping about the thicket with a fractured femur and an arrow lodged in his side. A friend."

Sam assented. Lucy ordered another round.

"But like a doctor, I do find the aspect inquiry to be of paramount, in both importance and interest. Certainly, you act and react in such a way that denies you the elementary luxury of simple joys. However, in exposing the root, you cannot rebuke that the onus rests like a yoke, bridled on your own sloping, endomorphic shoulders."

Sam thanked Kenny for the beer. "It's *my* fault?" He turned back to Lucy.

"Indeed. The unhappiness, the lack of success, the stress and anxieties you carry with you, all of these are sequestered inside of you with miraculous efficiency. It is quite impressive. You are, almost as a reflex, able to offload your problems as being the products of extraneous forces; the luck or shortcomings of others."

"Maybe I just suffer from a bad case of bad luck," Sam proffered limply.

"It is fascinating.... The infelicitous misanthropy that you exhibit is predominantly a symptom of genius. The curse of the intellectually superior. A gift of cognitive primacy that is in tandem a curse of mortal insight. A venomous claw that breaks its own flesh but spares the vein. You, however, Samuel ... You are not at an advantage of thought or wit. The instance that you have somehow tunneled to the same subterranean trove of restless irritation with humanity as those tormented by their brilliance is salivating. Whereas the gifted isolate themselves with erudite divertissement until they inevitably determine their existence to be as incomplete and invaluable as their years of academic pursuit. You have buried your head and wormed beneath the soil to a similar depth out of sheer cowardice. The gifted realize that they are nothing in a greater nothingness and their actions are meaningless. You achieve the same melancholy and cynicism without the romance and sophistication of wisdom, crudely trying to bend shapes out of the wind."

Sam went to speak but was hushed by the calmed raising of two fingers by Lucy.

"You have arrived at a juncture whereby you no longer feel it vital, no longer give validation or even consent to the birth of critical thought, which could expose you to a situation where change, for the better or worse, could occur. You are not exceptional, Sam. You know this. You are ignorant enough to chase a carrot with simple elation. However, you eliminate yourself from the race and blame it on the superiority of the other competitors. You blame the competitors for being faster and stronger, or conversely, for being unworthy of sharing your little oval with, but despise them all the same."

"You have even created a belief system, and I use the word 'belief' with a surrender of rationality, akin to that of cultic ceremonial obedience, to justify a dismal rationalization for surrendering."

"You're talking about my …"

"Yes, that foolish approach to life that you blindly wave like a little red missal."

"What's wrong with doing to others as others should do unto you?"

"You mean aside from zipping-up your own cadaver-pouch?"

"Y-Yeah …"

"You are pacifying the virility of your own biology to show your neck to anyone whose own system of negotiating reality does not align with yours. And Sam … There are few humans in this modern time that would any longer remove their jacket and lay it over a puddle, let alone follow the remaining, unenforced aspects of your dogmatic system of failure."

"People are shit." Sam closed his eyes and shook his head, feeling woozy streaks follow his side-to-side head movement. "Is it so hard for people to just, you know, have consideration for others? Is that so much to ask?"

"In theory, no," Lucy affirmed. "But when you are the only who is struggling with this, believing himself to be the only sane man in an asylum full of crazies … Well, I think you see what I am insinuating."

"I think so," Sam stretched his back, "but why should I change? Society, that's the sick patient."

"I cannot refute that claim. Without reasonable doubt the entire social clime, in its current condition, is composed to castrate, bludgeon and cremate. The drones buzz like bulbs and are equivocal when the anthill is flattened. The people driving the steamrollers are congratulated publicly, while the queens are plump and potent far beneath the topsoil." Lucy rimmed his glass with his index finger. "Apologies, that is an anecdote for another time. For now, micro-incisions are the best course of action.

"What we are getting to, in a roundabout way, is change, Sam. You need to change. You need to change your milksop approach from half-to-full-measure. You need to acknowledge and remedy your defects and deficiencies and annihilate the part of you that, at the same time, blames others for your downfalls and then pursues justification for forgiveness."

"How?" Sam choked on a prevaricating belch. He pushed his pint away. "How do you expect me to shirk all my instincts and change overnight?"

"I have to admit an admiration for the doughtiness of your words. You assume that you could grow a pair in one heft stroke?"

"You are either making it sound easy, or impossible, I don't know.…"

Lucy scratched his chin. Sam observed that this was the first time his counterpart was marinating in deep thought.

"Well," Lucy pointed at Sam's chalice, "can I stand you another drink young man?"

"I don't know, sir … I am feeling pretty torched," Sam bubbled. "I've got work tomorrow and …"

"A job you do not care for, around people who are indifferent, overlooked for a position that you only proposed to yourself when it was hinted that it would be set upon your lap."

"How did … I didn't mention that.…"

"Little matter." Lucy stared at Sam, wagging his fingers again at Kenny.

The bartender robotically poured another round. He turned to Sam. "Do not worry, I have absorbed your check."

"Thank you, I guess." Sam felt his nerves vibrating. A shadowy knot spread along out from his stomach. He thought, only maybe, it was the yogurt. "I have to go to the bathroom."

Sam excused himself, holding his stomach and shuffled through the diminished, incredibly masculine clientele, to the bathroom. He wiped the toilet seat and hovered above the rim. *What the fuck is going on?* he wondered as he drove his palm into his forehead. *Who is this man? Why does he know me so well? Is he trying to …? Nah.* Sam concluded his thought without a bowel movement, only a handicapped urine.

He emerged from the stall and began to wash his hands, cupping water onto his face. "Tomorrow is going to be rough," he had begun to say aloud as three men entered the bathroom.

"That's him," one of three men said, pointing at Sam.

"Hey, you!" Another raised his voice. Sam lifted his head to see the reflection of the men through the mirror.

"Me?" whimpered Sam.

"Where is Stephanie?" demanded one.

"And Rebecca," the third sounded.

"Beats me, fellas," Sam responded.

"He's full of shit, him and some guy were chatting them up at the bar all night."

Sam shrugged. "That was a while ago, I've been with … my uncle since then."

"Bullshit!" the second man said, he cocked back his right to launch at Sam.

Sam raised his fists, in defence only, as he shrunk against the sink. His eyes responded to the threat by closing.

Nothing happened. Not even a noise, save for the drip leaking from the faucet head.

Sam opened his eyes to see that two of the men who entered and demanded the whereabouts of Steph and Beck were lying on the ground. Lucy was standing between Sam and the third man, the canary as it were.

"Young man," Lucy said softly. "This other young man … he put you in a vulnerable position to be assaulted, without witnesses, without fair trial or any tangible system of defence."

The snitch stood against the wall shaking.

"Sam, what would you like to do to this human being? Would you like to strike him? Scream at him? Put him in a cheap pine box?"

The stranger shook fiercely, he stared imploringly at Sam.

Sam wiped the remaining tap water from his face and stared at the man. He felt steam shoot from his nostrils. He felt his knuckles crest like nascent mountains. He took a step closer.

"Act now, Sam. This might as well be the foul young woman on the bus. Michelle. Harry. The faceless member who is roosting within Chloe's eggs in a nest that is not yours."

Sam could feel his fist unwind, loosen, then his fingers surrender and sway from his wrists like a wind chime.

"All of you. Leave," Lucy said dispassionately.

The standing man, and the two who were lying unconscious, immediately vacated the bathroom on their heels, without word or thought. They did not even turn their faces towards Sam.

"I-I don't know …" Sam began. Lucy waited patiently to finish his rambling. "I can't … I've never been in a real fight … Why couldn't I? I wanted to … I just …"

"You did exactly what I had assumed you would do," Lucy said with hands folded behind his back. "Come," he patted Sam's shoulder, "one more for the road."

Lucy followed Sam back to the barstool, hand still on his shoulder. A fresh pint awaited Sam. The bar was now virtually empty aside from staff and some randoms.

"Assumed?" Sam finally said with startle. "Did you set me up?"

"Of course not," Lucy said. "But if I did have a hypothesis worth testing, those young rogues certainly helped me confirm my bias."

"Which was?"

"You are a worse coward than I feared," Lucy uttered. "Your emotional and mental blocks even hinder your ability to react in the most barbaric, natural way. Even facing the barrel, you would lay down your arms. You did not even taunt, insult or hurl saliva on the man. Any of the men. You had carte-blanche for savagery, justified and warranted bodily harm, yet you shriveled away from the opportunity for revenge."

"They didn't do anything by that point."

"And at which point would your more atavistic instincts have usurped control? As they shoved you? Caved in your skull? Squeezed the ghost from your shell?"

"I'm sure I would have done something at some point."

"But you do not know, nor are you certain."

"You're right, I guess."

"I'm aware." Lucy tapped his fingers. An ashtray was brought over.

"Dude, sir, you can't smoke in bars."

"Samuel, we are in the guts of the night and about to flesh out the intestines of your cowardice. No inspector will step foot." Lucy plucked a cigarette from the pack, leaving one elevated and gestured for Sam to take it. He then struck a match to light them both.

"It is not the jealousy, the envy, a lack of manhood or any fear that is the main symptom of your ailment. It is your anger, an over-controlling and transference of wrath. A misappropriation and compartmentalization of blind fury. Like manure, the fresh piled on the old and acidic, fermenting with misled and uninformed attempts to vindicate with vacuous and pitiful empathy. Empathy that is both fraudulent and so utterly misdirected that it vanquishes the stock that you should have in stores for yourself. That's why you hate yourself."

"I can believe that." Sam curled his fingers around the mouthed cigarette while Lucy lit it with the match.

"You are an untripped landmine, a relic from a long-lost war, jack-booted time and again by enemies and non-combatants, until one day, you will detonate, more than likely taking the leg of some innocent village child with you."

"Oh god," Sam dismayed, "that sounds awful."

Lucy hemmed. "It does. You will otherwise battle invisible monsters like Don Quixote, claiming shadows are conspirators and having all the self-determination of a roulette pearl."

Sam did not even stir on his stool, his head down, cigarette burning between his lips.

"There is no celestial judge or tribunal that is clicking the stones of an abacus in your favour. There are unseen laws that transcend the decorum of society and culture. The meek inherit nothing but the weakling genes of their ancestors. Power does not come from strength but from the imposition of will, the manipulation of rules and the riddance of fear."

Sam was drunk. Lucy's words were bouncing in his head with the lightness of newly-hatched mayflies. "Yup," he hiccupped. Balling his fist and swallowing with stubbornness.

"Samuel," Lucy parentally toned.

"Sorry, I am …"

"What do you want?" Lucy stated rather than asked.

"I want a …"

"No, relating to your evident problems, your inability to …"

"I just want people to follow the fucking rules, man…." Sam blurted with half-open eyes. "I just want people to be nice and good."

"Understand that they cannot, and they will not."

"Then I want to be able to *be* the judge, the jury and the executioner. I want to have the courage or the power to filter out the pieces of shit. I want to …"

"Yes?" Lucy sat up.

"I wish that I could just take all the people that make me angry, that make me feel all that wrath and fury, and just blink them out of existence, you know?" Sam lifted his head, as if feeling the gravity of his words. "Sorry, I'm hammered. That was a little harsh."

"I do know." Lucy nodded. "Kenny, I lied, one more round." He waved as the barman reached for another empty Guinness glass. "No, no, my boy. We'll each have a splash of the *good stuff.*"

Kenny knelt and, after much bottle clinging and shuffling sounds of displacement, rose and coughed. He brushed off a dusty, antique-looking bottle and poured the reddish-brownish, thick liquor into two rocks glasses.

Lucy accepted the drinks. He removed the half-full pint lightly crocheted in Sam's lax grip and shook him to attention.

"One last hoist, young man," Lucy said. Sam raised his borderline comatose head and lassoed his fingers around the glass.

"To Samuel Florin," Lucy started, then paused. "To a new day, to a new Sam … to *Hell* with them."

Sam grumbled what sounded like a mutilated refrain of Lucy's toast.

They muzzled the liquor and set the glasses down.

Lucy sighed with onsen-like content.

Sam thrashed his tongue around his mouth like the studded tail of a wounded crocodile as he tried to mesh the cough-syrup like substance with the scant sputum left in his jaw.

The taste was a mixture of Tawney Port and Oban. The feeling, however, hit him as if he was unknowingly fitted with a jet-pack and flung towards the cosmos without warning. It braced him for a few seconds; he became aware of every disparate molecule which huddled together to comprise his being. His eyes soon forced themselves open, a blinding glare of pure nothingness. His ears dinned with a fizzing, screeching clamour. A fleeting tizzy shot through his appendages, feeling his libido surge like a bell-sounding high strike at a carnival. Even his naval felt like it had prolapsed and had begun to take flight.

"Damn." Sam shook, then felt the incapacitation of drowsiness flood back into the recesses and folds from where the energy had torrentially gushed a moment prior.

"Sweet dreams, young man." Lucy smiled and scraped a match to light up another cigarette.

PART 3

THE JARRING FEELING of waking up on a week day at one's own volition, unaware of the hour, but certain of having caught a surplus of winks, is an anxiety that spreads quicker than cracks on a frozen pond in a boilerplate movie climax.

Sam awoke with this exact punch of panic, from standstill to super-sonic, to discover he had spent the night sleeping on his stool at the bar. Not at Mahoney's, but the bar-top in his apartment and the stool belonging to a set of three he and Chloe had purchased to adorn their settlement.

Sam allowed his eyes to shutter naturally; he felt the soft breeze that whisked the budding leaves on the velociously greening trees tickle his face.

The first thought that struck Sam, preluding the rabbit-punch of real-ity, was that trees reminded him of showgirls, slowly allowing their foliage to slide off. The truest beauty and the crux of the performance was the burlesque teasing that occurred between a fully verdant and nude, fully stripped branches. The life slowly draining Rothko harvest colours that people take road trips to witness. The yuppies sip their ciders and admire the transcendence of trees: clothed to unclothed. Interest, a fickle caliper, wanes once the tree is bare, the disheveled brown leaves left to smear and crunch underfoot. The tree, surprisingly, is less an attraction and more an object. Once spring arrives, when the last song of winter fades, the tree acts with great celerity to cover its limbs, reclothing itself, settling back amongst the all-season pines and needles.

That would be the most philosophic thought Sam would achieve that day. Possibly ever.

He felt the germ of hunger. He was confused at his sleeping scholar's hunch at the table. Then, not hearing the tumult of his alarm, an immediate pang of catastrophe plunged him into frozen waters.

"Oh fuck." He had already kicked the chair out and begun to disrobe, nearly tripping over his fettering slacks as he stumbled towards the shower.

He was already late. Technically, he should be smoking a cigarette, smiling dumbly while replaying a conversation with Kay in his head. There was no time to eat. He thought about taking a taxi, but Sam was cheap enough to argue that five minutes or thirty minutes, late is late.

He slowed down and swallowed the hysteria that had propelled his mind at a speed that his body could not match, a horse-drawn chariot with unoiled spokes.

Sam knocked on the closed bedroom door and entered after hearing no response. He rarely pierced the doorway, only to grab fresh clothes, which he now washed and kept in a drawer in the living room, and to steal the odd nap when he was certain not to be caught. He did not see Chloe and was not surprised. It was not uncommon for her to stay at a friend's place, even on a week day. She might have been home and not said anything, though his sleeping on the counter would at least have given her a reason to harp on him.

He threw his phone-charger, a nutrition bar of Chloe's he scrounged, and a few Tylenol capsules in his bag. Sam did not know if he was groggy, hungry or still drunk, but felt the slightest of pulling sensations tug at the base of his skull and pit of his stomach.

Wrapped in Sam's fingers was a yin and yang of placidity and anxiety. His mobile was an inert device that slept while all kinds of data were left in the ether. Far from a Luddite, but Sam did not have the insisting probe built within him to be cognizant of everything all the time. Conversely, if he was being called and told not to bother coming in or another emergency, he would prefer to know before wedging into his formal attire.

It was not until his walk to the bus stop, deciding that he would not spend twenty on a cab when he could spend two-half on transit that he began to think about the previous night.

"I must have got blackout," he mused, "though I feel pretty good now."

The sun was as it had been the day before, as was Sam's lack of sunglasses. He thought he saw a man, a man who he had seen before, spraying down the sidewalk. A talkative and annoying man, also Mexican, who would undoubtedly make the greatest attempts to sidetrack Sam on his hurried gallop to the boulevard. Sam breathed heavily, already ruing the man for asking him questions about the motherland that Sam was so distant from, in mind and body.

Sam cupped his hand over his head, he caught one ferocious beam in the unprotected corner of his eye. He blinked and gasped.

"Huh," Sam starched his lips, "guess I was seeing things." He carried on, noticing an unattended hose dribbling into the street. "Maybe I am still pinned."

Sam wondered what came of Andy and the moronic girls he had brought into their sanctum. "Ugh," he grumped vocally. "Stupid college pub crawl." He scowled. "I just wanted a few draughts and a chat, is that so much to ask? Kids these days, they think they have it all figured out...."

"Spare a dollar?" A youngish Caucasian with bare, black feet ran up to Sam.

"No, sorry man." Sam snapped from his thought.

"Come on, man? Buy me a slice of pie? A burger?" The man followed alongside Sam.

"Nah, I can't, I'm running late," Sam said with trace amounts of sympathy, noticing the shoeless hooves.

Sam began to walk faster, hearing the slapping of callouses against pavement.

"All you rich business types are the same with your Gucci loafers and Honduran maids...." The man raised his squelch, trailing Sam by a few paces. "In your ivory towers and, and ... one-percenter."

"Hey ..." Sam huffed, screwed his eyes closed and began to turn around to show the man his shoes.

"Where'd he ... ?" Sam scratched the back of his head. *I guess he thought I was going to hit him,* Sam thought with a slight profusion of pride. He looked up and down the boulevard. "Where did he run to so fast? What the hell?"

One benefit of running late was that buses were no longer stuffed like a bulge in chino twill. Sam easily boarded the platform and sauntered to the rear, careful not to ease his pore-glistening back against the seat.

He marinated about the encounter he had after Andy left, with a strange, older by his alabaster quills, man.

What was that guy's name? Sam thought. *Lucy!* Sam remembered the man had taken his whole bill. He contemplated if he was a therapist or maybe was hitting on him. *How'd he know me? Was he mean to me?* Sam massaged his temples, wondering if they'd gotten in a fight. And if so, why had he stuck around the bar so long. He scratched his chin and couldn't shake the feeling that he'd promised the strange man he'd do something.

Sam's train of thought was tipped off the rails by the irritating sound of an incoming call to a younger-looking girl seated against the window to his left.

"Hola," she chirruped in a tone that was not Spanish.

She continued to speak in what he concluded must have been Portuguese. Even in a crowded bus her voice would have risen above, but they were the only two passengers in the rear section of the depleted post-rush hour bus. He tried to regain the momentum of his memory but could not concentrate. The girl, around twenty, pulled a candy bar from her backpack, and began to unpeel the wrapper with an acetic crackle. She began chewing aloud and laughing, spraying pieces of chocolate and nougat, visible into the fissures of sunlight.

Sam pushed his eyebrows to his hairline, rubbing his temples in a circular motion. The crinkling of packaging, the flamboyant mirth, the sloshing bronco-like champs which floated the smell of junk food; Sam grumbled and moved his fingers to rub his temples. He was too tired to even care right then, so he just shut his eyes.

He removed his hands and was blinded for a moment by the pressure he had placed on them. When the glowing palpitates of inner-eye light and darkness subsided, it was dead quiet.

He stared at the spot the girl was, had been, gabbing on the phone while eating her snack. Had been, was the ingredient that startled Sam stiff as a stainless steel screw.

"What the … " Sam peered owlishly.

He froze, blinked in disbelief, and continued to perch motionlessly.

"Maybe she got off," he tried to convince himself amidst a flush of terror. "No, no … the bus didn't stop."

He stood up on disposable chopstick legs and wobbled to where she had been sitting, where he had seen her seated. There was no backpack, no cell phone, and no candy-bar wrapper: *nada*.

He skulked headlong up the aisle, nervously looking through the rows of plastic seats: *nada ainda*.

"Oh jeez, oh jeez, oh jeez," Sam whispered, grabbing the pole for stability with eyes-wide like a bamboo-clutching tarsier. His chest expanded and sunk, faster and faster. His entire body was instantly covered with dew. Even his nails were sweating.

His hand shot up and pulled the cord to call for the stop. His body, now working at a greater level than his brain, recognized the bus was about to wheel past his stop. His eyes were peeled open but he saw virtually nothing.

Sam was frozen in place. The bus driver had to less-than-politely remind Sam over the intercom it was a fine-worthy offence to request a stop and fail to vacate. He silently dragged his feet down the steps. The door closed with truculence behind him. He had yet to blink.

Sam marched the beat without recognition for any other soul as he crossed the pavilion, he cut people off and some yelped indignantly. He moved on auto-pilot, allowed the elevator doors to passively ease together in front of him, and pressed his finger against the numbered button to his floor, until a buzzer sounded, withdrawing his finger with a scare. Yet to blink, yet to look up, yet to form a full thought. Numb with shock.

"Am I going insane?" he asked himself, alone in the elevator after the doors closed. *Did I see a ghost?* He massaged his temples and growled, his body turning to a pair of bellows.

As the elevator doors contentedly abstained, Sam burped.

"What's that taste?" Sam felt a smoky, saccharine wash thickly tickle the back of his throat with acid fingers.

Sam was lumped upside the head with the memory of drinking and toasting some unregistered liquor with Lucy. He swallowed down whatever elixir was currently trying to writhe its way back up.

Lucy ... Sam thought. *Maybe he did want to have sex with me.* He nodded. *Want, or...* He shook his head.

The panic of lateness washed Sam's delusions to the back of his mind, barely and momentarily. He entered the office to hear the usual sounds of 'go', post 'ready' and 'set' at this point in the day. Keyboard and mouse clicking, paper shuffling, chatter which was both idle and vocational.

Sam lurched and walked with haste to his desk. Michelle's seat was unoccupied and pushed into her desk. Chen's door was closed.

"Oh jeez," he plopped his bag on the desk, "they're talking about firing me."

Everyone was consumed with some species of task. He looked around, noticing little out of the ordinary. No ghosts, no phantoms, no out-of-place chimeras.

He removed the charger from his bag and plugged in his phone. He grabbed the bar he brought from home and walked to the little break room. A fresh pot of coffee was percolating, dripping bronze water into the clear pot with an orange plastic handle. Sam undressed the health bar and closed his teeth around the chalky, unyielding skin.

"Luck day for you Sammy," co-worker Linda said.

"Why's that?" Sam coughed a piece of food from surprise. He covered his full mouth to answer, sweaty hand upon sweaty lips.

"Harry and girl-Harry, Harriet, get it? They are at some training thing in the big office. Sent the email out that they would be out for the day, maybe two. Is that why you took the liberty of being late? You saw the email?"

"Really?" Sam nearly leapt with relief, "No, I, uh, yeah, I mean ... I had some trouble with my phone and at home, I ... "

"Got to leave the house issues back at the ranch, Sam." Linda smiled the way a turkey might.

"N-No worries." Sam took another wrenching bite; the bar became more obstinate the farther he got. His jaw began to feel the reps. He was quivering beneath his damp clothes.

Sam eyed the coffee and decided to check his phone while it brewed. It mattered little what he did today, he could probably even leave. He probably should, he thought, something fishy was happening.

He turned on his phone to find a few missed texts, calls and unopened emails. He read the email from Chen, indicating he and Michelle were off to a retreat that would focus on managerial team-building. Cute.

The calls were from Andy, unanswered and unnoticed the night before. A few texts indicated the girls were ready. The girls were not waiting. The girls were gone. Andy was tired. Andy was going to sleep. *Enchanté*. What happened to Sam last night? Is Sam alive? Andy has a story to tell Sam. The usual.

There was a text from Chloe, sent this morning, quite recent, ten minutes ago. "Did you eat my fucking yogurt asshole?" Another read "I can't find my protein bar!" "The fucking sink is acting up, what's the super's number." And: "Asshole."

Sam had had enough. He gripped his phone to fire a response to back to her when his line rang. "Hello?" he answered unsurely.

"Sammy, what the hell happened to you last night?"

"N-not much, I stayed at the bar and went home."

"Who was that guy? Your uncle, I think he said? Never heard you mention him."

"O-Oh yeah, he … "

"My man! You missed quite the time last night. Me and … I can't remember their names.… Oh man we … "

"Andy, it's not a good time now.…"

"Huh? Lame. Okay, well … let me just say, you have to try better at being single.… I can't have threesomes all the time."

"Yeah, yeah … I know.… Gotta go."

"Love you."

"Love you too."

Sam pulled a stack of folders out of his bag. Even when he had taken them he knew he was not going to look them over at home. His mind quickly shifted to getting a cuppa. His mind was in primal, goldfish mode now. He dropped the papers and motored towards the breakroom again.

The pot was nearly empty. *Fucking Linda and her stupid travel mug*, he thought spitefully.

Sam poured the light brown water into a mug and frowned as the visible speckles of ground infused stream struggled to fill the cup halfway.

"No hoity-toity coffee for Sam today?" Linda asked sitting at a table leafing through a newspaper.

"No time," Sam replied absently.

"You know," she stirred the powdered creamer into her big, metal insulated mug, "my son is in university and opened a coffee shop on campus."

"Banging, Linda," Sam muttered.

"He said that the mark-up on coffee is astronomical, that you're better off brewing coffee at home and bringing it in a reusable mug." She held up her own and slide her hand under it like a home shopping network model.

"Ah, yeah, I bet that's a good idea. Listen Linda, I can't talk…." Sam hastily stirred some cream in the coffee.

"It is! My other son, well, he has that ADHD." She shook her head. "He is having a heck of a time in high-school."

Sam's head slowly rose as he thought about cussing that he did not care. He simply said, "That's really too bad, it can … "

"But this semester, he got straight As!" She beamed

"That's great, Linda. I'm not really … "

"You should meet my sons." She smiled down at the spoon, rattling off the sides of her cup, echoing with magnificent amplitude in Sam's ears. "You could learn a lot from them."

Sam had it.

"The older one had to get over a big fear of success and … "

"You know what, Linda?" Sam turned with a slightly raised voice. Not a yell, but more aggressive than anyone in the office had heard him speak. He closed his eyes and tried to soften it. "I'm not feeling great today… You … " He opened his eyes to commence his diatribe.

Linda was gone.

She had been sitting at the farthest corner from the door. She would have had to pass Sam, at such speeds that the clippings on the walls and papers on the desks would have been carried off by the spiralling vacuum.

Everything was still as smog.

Sam went pale. He dropped his cup and felt the coffee splash against his socks. He did not imagine Linda. He had worked with her and her nasally stories since his first day. He put up with her candy-floss perfume and shitty baking at pot lucks. He had the taste of her fruit cake barrelling up from his stomach. His hair and neck were soaked with sweat.

"Oh man," Prashad, another co-worker said. "Linda drank the coffee again. Oh, a little spill." He looked at Sam, bracing himself with a seen-a-ghost expression. "I'll call the janitor." He briskly exited the room.

Sam was tensing his arms against the counter, petrified and staring at Linda's mug as he had been at the student girl's empty seat in the bus.

Sam tried to pluck at thoughts like hundred notes floating around him in a whirlwind. None were tenable.

"Sam?" a mousey voice had seemed to get louder with each repeat.

"What!" He moved his head, still aghast.

"Um," Fatima his co-worker limped on, "I'm sorry, um, I was looking for the Benning files and found this."

She was holding a business card.

"Are you leaving us?" Her eyes became soft.

He grabbed the card with jitters that shook his whole arm and looked at it: Luciano Domino: Agent. It had a phone number and the address of an office building in the business district.

He looked at it, vibrating throughout his body.

"N-No, um, maybe … Just playing the field?" he squeaked.

"It'd be a real loss." Fatima smiled faintly and apologized again for looking through his files.

He eventually answered, "No problem." But she had turned-foot and already left the area. He hoped.

Sam bulleted through the corridor. He sighed with reprieve as he saw Fatima at her cluster and carried on to his own.

He scrutinized the card again. It was thick and unbending. Black-matte with gilded lettering. It was either, or both, the grandiosity of wealth or the flaunting of something sinister.

He picked up the phone. He was shaking so bad that he had to put the receiver down and guide his pointer with two hands after several failed attempts.

It rang.

"Luciano Domino's office please hold," a female voice said with sprite courtesy.

He waited.

He gritted his teeth as Le Badinage drifted from the earpiece.

"Young Sam," an unmercifully smooth voice interrupted the viola hold-music, "your call is slightly later than predicted." Sam had the same feeling when he heard the voice as he did recalling the charred sweetness of the liquor. "You must have overslept. You have to maintain vigilance with those pesky mobile battery cartridges, they fall like some kind of ... well, they die."

"L-Lucy?"

"Yes, Sam, you recognize my timbre, for also, you called me. I have you scheduled for a summoning at noon. A meeting, Sam. If I am not mistaken, I believe that your superiors are absent this day, so you should find no encumbrance tip-toeing past the hounds."

"You ha ... "

"And Sam, please do stop for a coffee, a cuppa joe in your slavish derivative-speak, you have ample term, and I desire your full attention, my boy. I will explain everything and answer your every question. See you soon."

Click.

It was a Carib minute before Sam eked out an incomplete farewell and minutes more until the jagged stabbing of the off-hook tone became distinct enough for him to hear.

Sam thought about explaining his departure. He instead clutched his bag against his breast like a wounded puppy and flew down the staircase, his knees seemed to fail sporadically and steps randomly ducked from his heels like moles.

He did stop for coffee. The café was an empty shell of its rush hour bustle. A few people snapped away on laptop keys or thumbed through novels.

"Hey Kay." Sam's head was tilted down, watching his fingers play ragtime on the counter.

"Sam ... Are you all right?" Kay's head tilted sideways.

Sam's head moved around dartingly. "Yeah, crazy morning, uh, the usual, I guess." He continued to tap his fingers and sway his head, abstaining from eye contact.

Kay eyed him and grabbed a cup from the stack and spun towards the coffee pot. Sam looked over to see Krys watching him narrowly. He ceased tapping his digits. He nodded and resumed a looking around the counter with aimless distraction.

"Here you go," Kay smiled, "it's on me. I double-charged some douche earlier on, and it looks like you could use a cuppa.... Seriously man, are you okay? You look like you're going to throw-up."

"I'm ... " He looked up and forgot about his morning and arguably everything until that moment. "I'm not sure."

"You have time for a smoke?" Kay asked, motioning to Krys that she would be right back.

Outside the café, Sam and Kay leaned against the planter.

"What's wrong, Sam? Is it your job? Is it your girlfriend?" Kay's tempo sped up. "Did you guys break it off? Oh man, I was only kind of serious about that cheating stuff. I was just trying to be a bit of a bitch. Well?" She jostled him

Sam was staring at the blue sky with his eyes hanging half-open, mentally exhausted, his mouth agape. "No, no ... Well, she didn't come home last night, but ... " A new feeling snaked through him and crawled out of his mouth. "Yeah, we're done."

Kay steamed a sympathetic sound, she placed her hand softly on his arm. "I'm sorry."

"Huh?" Sam snapped his head towards her. He noticed the hand placement and her compassionate expression, "Oh ... right ... thank you ... I'll be okay."

"Anything else?"

"Yeah, well ... I have this appointment that I am nervous about."

"Like a job interview?"

"Maybe? I think that's why I'm nervous. It's ... it's been a very strange morning."

"I didn't catch you this morning. Your routine is off, you must be tortured." She poked his ribs.

Sam's face softened. He smiled back, flattered that she'd noticed his absence. "Cheeky."

"Pinch them." She grinned, jutting her face towards his.

They met eyes and remained quiet for a second.

"So, big day for change … " She tapped the ash from her cigarette. "You on the rebound?" She bumped her hip against his.

A medley of emotions minced across Sam's face. Poker was not one of them. He grew nervous that he was taking too long to flesh out a response.

"If it's too soon … " Kay's neck lowered lightly.

"No!" Sam jerked upright. "Not at all. I just haven't planned a date for … forever."

"That's okay, and sad, but more okay.… Why don't you meet me out here, tomorrow at … when are you done? Oh right nine-to-*fiver*." She feigned pushing glasses up the bridge of her nose, nasally pinching the last word in jest. "At five then, and we'll figure something out from there."

"Y-Yup … " Sam tried to unstiffen his lip and unwrinkle his brow, only finding success with one at a time.

"Don't be nervous Sam, you're totally going to get laid, and it better be good." Kay patted him. "Kidding, you goddamn pervert." She cupped a rotating hand to Sam and flicked her cigarette.

Sam stared at the smoldering butt on the ground, then watched her lope back to the door in a high black skirt, easily letting go of the littered cigarette.

"Fuck." He smiled to himself, impressed and harrowed by the same lie. "Fuck." He looked at his watch, deciding it might not be a good idea to be late for Lucy.

Sam arrived at a building he hadn't recalled ever seeing. He shrugged off its never-seen qualities with the dopey splendor of commuters who satisfyingly say 'always drive by, never stop in.'

Domino Tower read the gilded lettering, the same font as the business card.

"Holy shit." Sam craned his neck like his toothbrush reaching for his rearmost molar. A fog of incredulousness cleared for him to capture one thought first. *Bull-fucking-shit he's a regular at Mahoney's.*

He was captivated by the lifelike gargoyles that stared threateningly at the street. There were figures of war, angels, a three-headed dog, and a sea monster bundled around a ship. All were in such a detail and immaculateness that Sam could not stop from gawking at their graphic features.

A man bumped Sam. "Watch out you fucking tourist," the man growled. A growl that did not sound human, more monster than man.

Sam was startled by the supernatural tone and jumped back when the man spun and grunted. The grunt of a warthog. Sam shuddered when he saw the guttural man's face, a stout head with protruding, for lack of a greater accuracy, tusks. The man was squat and built like a hockey puck, dressed in a fine pin-striped suit. He turned to face forward and slapped a cellphone against his cauliflowered ear.

Sam continued to stare.

"Are you entering, young sir?" a doorman atop a feasible staircase asked Sam. "Right this way."

Sam nodded and stared into the man's somehow pleasantly yet malevolent black eyes.

A honeyed-blond in reading classes sat photogenically at the grand, black-granite reception desk. She flicked her head towards Sam. "Samuel Florin." She stood and bowed politely. "Take the elevator to 1600."

Sam stuttered in thanking the woman, already having resumed her devoirs. He twisted his neck to leer at the uncommonly arresting secretary. "Knock-out," he said to himself.

"Oh, sir, you have to sign in." She handed him a heavy clipboard, the same granite as the desk, with a page clipped in by a golden buckle. Sam signed, peering up twice to theft a gaze at the secretary. He penned his signature and then had to pause to remember how to spell his name. She did not descry his peeking.

An elevator attendant tipped his cap to Sam and said nothing. Sam leaned to press the button but was beaten by the attendant's swiftly mechanic movement. His white gloved hand remained on the button a few seconds longer, staring with the same ominous enthusiasm as the identically dressed doorman.

Sam nervously broke off eye contact as the attendant failed to return a nod. A shiver unfurled down his spine. He was all too happy to blame it on the air conditioning. It was set to summer, or some overblowing notch that was too rich for the mild spring day.

Expecting to see a hallway, the doors instead opened to a room girdled by rich, buttery wood. A chandelier was a glorious cherry-blossom tree that grew from the Versailles ceiling. A path of burgundy carpet led to a closed pair of massive wooden doors like a serpent's tongue leads to its mouth. He marveled at the room, the feeling of standing in an enormous coffin, the living smell of dead nature, and another receptionist just left of the door.

He felt the assertive softness of the carpet fibres through his shoe bottoms, stiff but allowing, like the waters of the Dead Sea.

"Hello Samuel," said a criminally attractive girl, the kind that could be any mix of ethnicities but, at least one of them can dance better than you.

Before Sam could open his mouth to stutter, the woman followed up, "Mr. Domino's eleven-thirty is running a tad late." Sam was captivated by her posh British accent. "Please have a seat and he will be with you shortly." She smiled and Sam coughed on his spit.

The wait was brief. Not brief enough for Sam to riffle through the bizarre stacks of reading material.

On the circular table to his left were old National Geographic and Time magazines that had title pages with headlines about Genghis Kahn, Armenian genocide, Reagan's second term, the bombing of Hiroshima, Idi Amin, and the Yankees' murderer's row winning the 1927 World Series.

The pile on the table to his right was stranger. A colouring book that was half-completed by various people, given the dramatic differences in style and signatures in crayon. Some appeared to belong to historical figures.

One looked like the Walt Disney logo, scrawled beside a picture of a dinosaur that was filled in with bright colours. Another was Charlemagne who had filled in the cell of a horse with all green. John Lennon's nosey self-portrait beside a picture of a mountain range that paid no respect to the lines and expected colour scheme. A disorganized mess of hard-pressed spots of shiny wax and wrinkled tears in the paper from attempting to cross out the page had the name Picasso. The initials O.V.B. had added additional lines to a picture of a frog leaping from a lily pad, meticulously adding to the design with a black felt marker. A hot-air balloon with one hurried streak of red crayon was left by Thomas Edison.

"Mr. Florin," the secretary said softly as the large doors opened slowly, creaking from the displacement of their immense thickness.

"Sammy my boy," Lucy said in boxers, undershirt and calf-high dress socks. His arms spread in a Christ on the crucifix pose atop a footstool in front of the room-large window overlooking city and sea. A small bald man in a white dress shirt scurried about him with a ribbon of measuring tape.

Sam entered as the doors hissed closed. The grandeur of the room carried the same motif of wood from the waiting area, with bookshelves on each side with an uncountable numbers of tomes. "Thirty-six thousand," Lucy laughed, "books, you were wondering."

"A-Am I … "

"Intruding? Not at all," Lucy said. He then spoke in a foreign tongue to the small, kneeling man. Sweat penetrated his bare dome. "It's difficult to find time for a fitting, a truly lost art, but the best are still as talented as their ancestry advocates." He lowered his arms and winked at the man, "Si, Giuseppe?"

"Ah, si … " The man nodded rapidly in agreement. "Si signore."

"Bene," Lucy clapped his hands, "you may go."

The man shirked away bowing profusely and then shuffled to pick up a ledger and bundled rolls of fabric sitting on a wooden stand with brass seraphim supporting the tabletop. He had the shifty gait of a tardy beetle carrying the day's scrounge between his mandibles. At the doors he paced nervously in situ waiting for them to open, laboriously ventilating, and invocating something to himself under strained breath.

Sam caught the word *padre*.

"Sam," Lucy verved, whipping Sam's head around from the tailor's distracting excitability. Sam shook disbelieving at the sight of Lucy already fully-suited; shrugging as he tugged at the lapels of a light-cream blazer, then patting out the sleeves, finally flattening out a black tie in the foreground of a white shirt. He gestured Sam towards a chair, tucking the tie behind a three-button vest of the same cloth as the suit. Sam pulled the walnut caquetoire away from its already respectable distance from the black marble desk, he wondered why he moved it, and decided to place it back in the same spot. The goddess Venus was carved into the wooden backing, standing as on the half-shell of an oyster, her hair billowing over her discretion. Sam lowered himself on to the plush padding and placed his arms on the rest. Then on his lap. Back on the rests. The chair was agreeable but he could not find comfort.

Lucy surveyed Sam through the entire procedure, grinning even as he sank into his own opulent Chesterfield wingback, black leather with a golden 'L' insignia on the headrest. His expression like those of the same guiled glee that his attendant's portrayed. An additional sense of gamesmanship when he joined his fingers together with his elbows tented on the armrests.

The silence, even with the roar of the air conditioner, made Sam sense a dampness behind his lobes.

"Well?" Lucy finally broke, separating his fingers and meeting them back together.

Sam was at a loss, his mouth rigged open by a tanker bar.

Lucy cleared his throat, patiently adding, "What do you make of your *gift?*"

"G-Gift? You … "

"Of course I did, Samuel, you asked … well, practically pleaded for it."

Sam shifted his hands from the rest to his lap, finally grabbing the bottom-most part or the chair as if it would rocket upwards. "Asked you for what?"

Lucy pressed a button on an intercom with smug satisfaction. A moment later his assistant emerged with a dossier. Sam nearly fell to a tranced state watching the incomprehensibly attractive woman move lithely to the desk and out of the door.

"Pound of flesh," Lucy hemmed, unfastening the string around the folio. He pulled a manuscript sized packet of papers out and began whisking through them.

"Here it is: '*I wish that I could just take all the people that made me angry, that made me feel all that wrath and fury, just blink them out of existence, you know?*'"

Sam's jaw still received no electricity, without rounding a legible word he made a negative sound: no without the 'n'.

"Yes, genuine article. Word for word." Lucy slid the script towards Sam.

Sam looked down and saw only the page which had each of the two, and Kenny, as speaking characters in a screenplay.

Sam made sounds, like deaf-speak, shaking his head.

"*Intelligenti Pauca*." The corners of Lucy's mouth extended towards his ear.

After another silence, Sam sputtered to himself with enough capacity, "What does this all mean?"

"Mean?" Lucy repeated rhetorically. "It means you are most gracious and thankful to me, who is only most humble in my munificence."

"I meant … "

"Yes, yes … I will abate you." Lucy pushed himself from the chair and turned to face the window with his hands locked behind his back. A heavy exhale dropped his shoulders. "I do so hate exposition. But I fear your inability to negotiate context requires me to expose you to the fulcrum of the matter."

"I take it you're not a head-doctor," Sam shakily remarked.

"No Sam. You should really take a few moments to revisit our inter-action in order to save yourself the embarrassment of stating questions to answers that have already been explained."

Sam flipped the document to the first page which contained dialogue between himself, Andy, and the two sorority girls.

Lucy turned to face Sam. "You were in a worse condition than I could have anticipated, young man. It was not until you had declined so much as to strike an adversary, one with no reason to feel compassion for or to fear recrimination from, that it became palpable."

Lucy took the lid from a crystal whiskey decanter and poured two glasses of liquor. "It's just a horn of peat I assure you." He placed a glass in front of Sam and a pearl ashtray with a medusa head inlayed with gold in the centre. He opened a gator skin cigarette case and offered a stick to Sam.

Sam accepted the cigarette and a light, breathing in a long, atwittered pull.

Then a trilled release.

"Good. Relax. Sit back. Listen." Lucy tapped a cigarette against the case and proceeded to light it. "Such cowardice is beyond hindrance. Such inability to broker theme or topic in either vernacular or social setting is astounding. Sam, congratulations, I have lived a long time, longer than my influence on the Bohemian and avant-gardiste. I have seen coups replace kings, juntas oust coups, and the same cabals succumb to a crown to lead a headless state. I have seen the world sliced up and stitched together so often that it now appears to me as a ceramic sculpture that was once a tea-pot pot, glued and mended to an oeuvre that Kandinsky would be crippled to whimpers. I have eaten roasted dodo and auk stew with cutlery made from mammoth ivory and Irish elk, then scoured my palette with the Sun King's pinot from the elusive grail."

He lightly twisted a long ash from the tip of his cigarette.

"And yet, in spite of my life, full of glib and frippery, I felt pity when I saw you. I felt sorry for you. I saw a chubby, negative, eighth-of-a-man. A man who lacks courage and capital. A life that has no reason but to live because it is too cowardly to end itself."

"T-thank you?" Sam pinched his eyes curiously.

Lucy scoffed. "It's supposed to be sympathy for, not sympathy from." He cleared his throat. "At any rate, I am who I am. No good deed goes unrewarded and the devil is in the details."

"I'm confused, am I seeing ghosts? Are you a ghost? Am I a … "

Sam felt a stiff slap against his cheek. Dealt without enmity. He rubbed his face and took a sip from the glass, watching the legs of the whiskey slowly descend. It was just a normal glass of probably-expensive, maybe priceless, single malt scotch.

"To put things very simple, I could have given you the power to erad-icate your foes with a trigger or a button. I could have armed you with a weapon to dismiss those who have wronged you. But, alas, you would have never used any of it. Left to your own accord, you would have found a reason, even if I had sworn to you no reprisal of law or harm, to allow dust to collect on your musket.

"So I eliminated free-will."

Sam reeled back in his seat, "What?"

"Not entirely." Lucy retook his seat. "Anger is a misunderstood creature, like a snake. Destructive and beautiful. The poison and the anti-dote. All in the same fang."

"You turned me into a snake?"

"My word Sam, I hope that is the vertiginous effects of shock controlling your speech." Lucy screwed out his cigarette and rubbed his hands. "No, I fulfilled your request, to blink those who slight you out of existence. It is a power. A great and devastating power. But, a power that, with effort and prudence, you can wield like the turned thumb of a Roman emperor."

"How?"

"Well you have been busy already." Lucy took a smaller stack of papers from the portfolio. "Arturro Carrera. Benjamin Sharpe. Carolina Gomes. Linda Hawerchuk."

It was the final name that stung Sam. "Linda?"

"Oh yes. She is gone." Lucy's candor was natural as spring water.

"Gone? What do you mean gone?"

"She is wiped from the atlas, young man, as she drew your ire. Probably, if I know Linda, for her holier-than-bromide about her sons. You know, one is … "

"Did I murder Linda?"

"If it looks like a murder, and quacks like a murder … "

Sam's face went pale and dropped.

"No, you did not *kill* her," Lucy franked. "She is simply gone."

"I-I didn't want to … I mean, I didn't … "

"Of course, of course … Though you don't seem so concerned about the gardener with whom you share heritage, the vagabond or the Brazilian girl."

Sam rubbed his stomach, a knot was evolving somewhere.

"You can see, this power is terrific. A sceptre for most human beings. The matter of importance is that you must learn to mediate that slumbering coil of animosity and dispose your mind as a flute to serenade it suitably."

"I thought the music meant nothing to the snake and the snake just focused on the instrument itself, not the sound…. In fact they maintain it's unclear if snakes can actually hear or just feel vibration," Sam rattled-off, looking down at his feet.

Lucy shook his head with surprise. "And this you know?"

"I saw it on a documentary in the dentist's office once," Sam nearly sobbed.

"How curiously esoteric." Lucy smiled as Sam nodded dolefully against his chin-flab. "Our time is concluding." Lucy looked at his watch. "But realize, this may be the best, and definitely the most life-changing gift you will ever receive. A benefaction, if you can adapt. At no cost. Pro bono. I am waving my usual fee of … well, I ask for not a hair nor denarius in return."

Silence.

"Now you may thank me." Lucy smiled and rose to his feet.

"T-thanks?" Sam also stood and began to walk to the door.

With his hand on Sam's shoulder, he said, "Face or heel, young Sam. Look where life in the middle has taken you. Be the starfish and grow back the phallus that society has castrated you from. Harness the power and ride the steed like a war horse. This is merely a teaching tool." Lucy pumped his fist energetically. "I will see you soon, Sam."

Already outside of the door, the secretary smiled and pointed him to the elevator. He turned to see that the door to the office was secured and the receptionist was working away without any difference.

The gold-coloured doors to the elevator were bordered by oaken sculptures of angelic variants. They opened and a woman knocked his shoulder as she exited. Her face was bandaged beneath big, Onassis sunglasses like Wells' invisible man. Sam only knew she was a woman by the physique beneath her skin-tight jumpsuit. He could not make out her muffled utterances but they sounded frantic, pleading and tearful. The receptionist's rejoinder of "Please have a seat and he will be with you shortly" was cordially cold.

Sam arrived at his street. He was unsure of how long it had taken or by what route he had arrived. Confined to his thoughts, which could be described as a confused scramble at best, left him in a blur of relative darkness as soon as he felt the carriage of the elevator lilt under the weight of his feet. From discreet sound of the doors allaying, eclipsing the palatial waiting room, Sam only saw and felt blurs of reality. An empty-skulled captain had brought his aircraft to where he could make out the runway from the surrounding terrain.

"Sam!" Chloe pipped, surprised to see him return to his own den.

"Oh, hi Chloe," Sam said absently. His head was down and his eyes strained open.

"You're off work early, aren't you?" The way she spoke seemed unfamiliar to Sam. Without the incisors she usually bit with.

"Yeah," he groaned, "it's been a strange day.... Strange, strange week so far."

"Are you okay?" She sounded concerned. "You're so pale, are you sick?" Her tone shifted to one of self-preservation as she covered her mouth and nose with her hand.

"No, no … Just work stuff and … well I got passed up on a promotion. I guess that's the big news. I know we don't really talk much, but there was a job up for grabs that I didn't even know about and I didn't get it."

"Why didn't you know about it?" she asked. "If you didn't know about it how can you be disappointed about it? They probably weren't considering you for the offer anyways, otherwise they would have told you something about it, am I wrong?"

He stamped his palm into his face and dropped his bag on the counter where he'd been asleep hours ago. "I know, I know … But … What are all these boxes?" He looked around, distracted.

As his hand slid down his face, Sam noticed myriad boxes; some deflated and flat, others taped into cube-form, others that were full of stuff. Sam's stuff. "And why is my stuff in them?"

"Ugh, look." Chloe slid out a stool opposite Sam at the counter. "This obviously isn't working. It hasn't worked for a long time. This isn't easy for me and will probably be less easy for you."

"But … *My stuff?*" He glanced over to see a few boxes of clothes and some pictures, interrupted from being wrapped with newspaper. "I pay the rent! My name is on the lease! This is my place!"

"Our place or it was … I have already spoken to the super and signed a new contract. Yours was a month-to-month and I offered a year-long commitment."

"Is this about the yogurt?" Sam's blurted.

"Typical." Chloe folded her arms. "Typical small picture Sammy. Typical blind, unable to look at the big picture, idiotic Sam. This is not about the yogurt, which might have been past the best before date. This is about you stagnating and being stuck in a dead-end job with no prospects and no … anything. You have one friend and little else. You let yourself go, look at you! You're miserable and sad. The only things you ever feel are worth talking about are the negative things about your job, your bosses and coworkers, all the strangers that act like normal people and don't fit into your stupid way of looking at the world. It's shit Sam. It's all shit. You aren't shit and haven't been shit for years. I used to remember how sweet and kind you were. How thoughtful and out-going you used to be. But those memories, the good times, they've dried up. I get angry when I see you as a fatter, dumber version of yourself than when we met."

Sam nodded mournfully.

"I, on the other hand, have tried to better myself. The courses and classes, the programs and activities … Not once did you ask to come along. Never ever did you try to include yourself or take an interest in what I do. Remember? I asked you so many times, millions of times, if you wanted to come to the gym, go to the store and meal plan, meditate and do yoga … you even shrugged when I asked about tantric sex, getting another person in or going to get some toys."

Sam could only crack his throat. He knew it was true.

"I feel like you blame me for all of your stubbornness and bad luck. It's not bad luck, Sam! It's lack of effort and lack of trying to grow!" Chloe seemed as though she would cry but a soaring rage held back any tears.

"I've moved on Sam." She looked away. "Moved away from you and on to better things. I'm taking the apartment because, well, you have no fight and won't push me back. You pussy."

Sam, with his head down, felt flagellated: weak and beaten.

"See?" She stood. "That's all you have to say? A lowered head and nothing else? I was hoping to have all your stuff packed and in the lobby by the time you got home from work. You can come back for the couch, it's ugly and smells like you anyways."

Sam finally broke his silence, "Chloe, are you cheating on me?"

She laughed. A cackle that escalated to maniacal hilarity as she responded. "When things first started going downhill, I fought it. Then it happened once. I hated myself but I felt alive. As my pity started to become hate it happened more often. Sam, you fucking fool, I have gone on vacations with my lovers and met their families. I have had full relationships behind your stupid back."

Before he could speak she continued through her lunatic's fit. "I've fucked in every part of this house. Look." She disappeared into the bedroom, and the returned. "I left condom wrappers and beads out hoping you'd find them and just step up and be a man."

Sam was still too shocked to get angry. Her abdomen muscles clenched and softened as she roared. A muddy feeling washed inside him, finding her more attractive in this moment than he had for years, betrayed by his next words that were disloyal to his sad, true feelings.

"Are you sure that you want to do this?"

She pushed her hair back and laughed, used an elastic around her wrist to secure a ponytail and continued to pack boxes. In her active wear, tight Lycra-spandex bottoms and sports-bra, Sam watched her bend over and only requited himself with a painful longing of never getting to fornicate with the newer, fitter, happier Chloe.

A key rustled in the dead bolt.

"Oh hey!" A man, tall and striated, entered with an armful of depressed boxes.

"Chandra." Chloe erected quickly and moved to the door, kissing the man in a tank top and sporty shorts.

"Is this your roommate?" the man asked with a hollow yet nasally voice.

"Was … yeah." She placed the boxes on the counter, brushing Sam's bag to the ground. "This is Sam, Sam this is Chandra."

"Namaste." The man joined his palms, fingers to the forehead and bowed.

"Is he being a problem like you said he might?" Chandra asked, slapping Chloe's taut buttocks. "I thought he was at work."

"No," she scoffed. "But I don't expect him to help, he is as lazy as he is closed-minded."

Sam was standing in relative non-comprehension; a cartoon character struck by a thunderbolt, the cinders piling below like hourglass sand with only a nonorganic accoutrement stranded in place.

"Chandra, can you watch him?" Chloe pointed abjectly at Sam with a boxcutter, "I have to freshen and … I don't trust him."

"You got it baby," the man responded as he proceeded to tape together the bottommost folds of corrugated squares.

"So where you moving?" Chandra asked Sam. His voice struck Sam as dumb but friendly.

"I don't know."

"Oh man, you should have a plan. How long have you lived with Chloe?"

"We've been together for eight years," Sam said numbly.

"Wow! That's like a relationship." Chandra laughed. "Sorry that me moving in is breaking y'all up."

Sam sighed contemplatively.

"I'm surprised I've never seen you before," Chandra said through the shriek of packing tape. "Super weird."

Sam stared at the man, feeling a tension in his neck and jaw. He nibbled his thumbnail, and seared at the wavy-haired, admittedly handsome man with a glare.

Through the whine of tape, he continued. "I'm here like every other day, but we always sleep at my place. You never heard us in the bedroom? Are you the one using my shampoo? It's all family, man. It's good isn't it? I still think we should move to mine, but … well … she is right, this apartment is in a sick lo … "

Sam blinked.

Sam smirked.

"So I was thinking with all this extra …" Chloe trailed off as she emerged from the bathroom, the sound of the old plumbing still wresting the water through its pipes.

"Where's Chandra?"

Sam's smirk thinned, then thickened to a diabolic smile.

"Chandra?" She raised her voice and scampered to the bedroom and back. "Sam … where did Chandra go?"

"He's gone."

"Gone? What do you mean gone? Did you say something? You little prick."

"Chloe." Sam nibbled his nail, looked at it, then lowered his hand and placed it on hers lying flat on the counter. "Thank you for this, I really mean it. I appreciate hearing what a loser I am from such an awful human being. It means a lot to know that this is what self-improvement looks like, a cruel and arrogant woman. I am truly and honestly sorry for putting you through some bad years, and I hope wherever you end up is worse."

Sam stared at Chloe. By the time he reached his final word, his voice had lowered to a gritty, sword dragged over cobblestone flint. A simple flick of the lashes had done what years of unsatisfactory protest and trite cavilling could not.

He blinked.

Lucy was right, Sam thought, taking a seat on the couch as he swatted an empty box to the floor. "If he had given me any power that I had to use, that I had to press a button or pull a trigger, I don't think I would have ever worked up the balls."

What did I just do?!

Thinking was like trying to get blood to a numb, sleeping leg. It was pins and needles for him to achieve an earnest reflection through the shocking events of his day and his most recent action.

He sat contemplatively and analyzed a haphazard, shallow list of pros and cons to his new ability. A pinching nervousness was quelled by the giddiness of riddance, Moving between assuagement and hyperventilating. Did the ends justified the means, even if those means were abstract and facile?

Chloe... could we have worked it out? Was it so bad I that I had to... blink her?

He felt this accomplishment bounce between reluctant highs and lows, each diminishing with affect as time passed. He refused the entry of negative thoughts concerning where exactly they disappeared to, what species of magic this was, what would have happened if he did not wield this gift on this day, or if he was still a chicken-livered coward with a cheat code. He ignored all these thoughts for a moment and decided that he had a few others he would like answers from, and if he did not like those answers ...

No, I have to try and not use this... thing, this power. This is evil, not good. I'm a good guy, right?

He lay back and fought to retain the self-imposed status of good guy. *Good guys don't blink their girlfriends away.* He thought about Chandra. *Well fuck that guy.* But that was fleeting. *Damn it, he did nothing wrong, she did. But no one deserves that. Do they?*

This rumination of inner-conflict proved too much for Sam's simplistic two-category purview. Something felt off. There was an element of wickedness and he knew it.

Sam casually flipped on the stereo and let the station play uninterrupted. He unpacked the boxes containing his meagre possessions and began to fill them with his new-ex's clothing, trinkets and quasi-Eastern talismans. He first ransacked the closet and dressers in the bedroom, finding men's drawers that were not his and plugs and rings he had never used. There was a photo album in the nightstand with pictures of her and Chandra on patios, in exotic locations, and kissing while performing difficult acro-yoga poses. He emptied the bathroom medicine cabinet of her tonics and creams, keeping the shampoo that smelled of cedarwood bark and juniper berry. Her foodstuffs with all their living bacterium was exported from the fridge to a garbage bag. The walls were purged of inspirational pictures and framed clichés.

Sam was hit with a mixture of emotions. "I really was an absent boyfriend, I didn't even notice these," he said. A moment of forlorn, then anger. "She did this shit without telling me! Letting me play the fool?" More anger that the two lovers were unable to suffer further wrath. "I wish they were here so I could ... " And he concluded with acceptance, "It's done ... I hope they burn."

The following morning, sobered by a sleep in the freshly washed sheets atop the turned and rotated mattress he had purchased six years ago and had not graced in more than two, Sam shrank beneath the sheets and stared at his roostering mobile.

"I can't do this, I can't ... I can't believe that I ... "

Sam experienced doubt which could not claw with much success against the engraining of his routine. He fought the idea of leaving his apartment, exposing himself to the public and the potential of a godforsaken massacre. The kicker, the lining of a medusa-head on a pearl ashtray, was that he was supposed to meet Kay in front of his office around five.

Given the previous forty-eight hours, she could likely shed her mortal carapace and divulge her identity as a humanoid preying-mantis with elongated, serrated limbs, truncated lace-woven wings, and a forejaw that widens and collapses around his neck and takes his head clean off.

"Unlikely, but ... "

Sam, out of character, chose to walk to work.

Chloe had always remarked that it was, at most, a five-minute difference and ultimately healthier, though her choice of words was more castigating than motivational. Sam was nervous about the trek, feeling he did not fully understand how to properly ordain his giftedness.

He threw on a pair of sunglasses. Chandra's glasses were left with their arms pleated on the table and were more fashionable than his, especially without the crack in the lens they earned tumbling from his pocket. He unfolded the plastic arm and read '*365 days with my Moon.*' Cute. He put them on set off with headphones knitted tightly to his eardrums.

A cyclist ripped by. Objectively speaking, the rider had more than enough room to veer from Sam, whose only infiltrate on the path were the toes of his knobby wing-tips. The man swore and lifted his finger with hostility. Sam was startled and stepped back, lifting his hand and dropping his neck with remorse. The man, for some reason, unsaddled himself and perambulated up the sidewalk, guiding his bike, berating Sam the entire slog.

"You idiot, you fucking dumb fucking idiot. This is the bike lane," the man with wraparound glasses and a sleek helmet shouted. "You know it's *illegal* to block the lane? What's wrong with you?"

"I-I'm sorry I ... "

"Y-You're new to walking?" The man imitated Sam's stutter. "You could've broken my ... "

Sam's startle and repentance diminished and his fatigue of the public harangue replaced apology with anger. When it did, a simple shuttering evaporated the cyclist. His bike clanged against the ground.

Fuck! Sam thought. *That guy barely did anything. No one is safe.* He kept his eyes on the pavement as he walked and thought about the family who would never see that guy again.

He buried a hand in his pocket. Quick side-glances were enhanced to a full panoramic appraisal. There was no one around. He paced around the bicycle, laying on its side like a tipped cow. *Shit. Shit. Shit. I have to learn how to control this thing.*

Sam locked the expensive-looking bicycle to a stand at the corner of his street and pocketed the key.

Sam arrived to meet Kay very closely to the same time as he would have had he taken the bus. The anarchy of queuing not only spent the savings of Sam's psyche, but the bus wasted a considerable dime with its stop-start movement and traffic congestion that made the trip feel like pyramid construction. Surprised to find himself far less prickly than normal, he thought he could start riding that bike he found, when he learned how to ride one properly.

A lady held the door open for Sam at the café, he said 'thank you' and the lady replied with 'you're welcome'. Healthy. He buttoned into the rear of the line and saw Kay stretch out from ahead of the line and wave. He smiled, waved back, and worked to erase his stupid grin.

He was behind the same man as he had been on Monday. The big-headed fella had his glasses now sitting backwards on his head. He was speaking with someone on the other end of his headset about mergers or acquisitions or something. Sam was too immersed in a peek-a-boo game of brief glances with Kay to pay full mind.

The man approached Kay to order. Krys was steaming and creaming a large take-away order, stacking tiers of to-go cups on four-point paper trays, leaving only one register open.

"Hey," he started, "so, uh, you never called."

"What can I get you?" she replied with a put-on Japanese accent.

"That thing you made me last time, I guess," he said, continuing as she wrote on a cup. "Seriously though … I thought we hit it off, why didn't you take me up on my offer?"

"Oh." She pulled her eyes from the cup to his and spoke in her normal cadence. "Because I didn't want to."

The man scoffed. "Whatever, just the coffee then." He clicked the button on his earpiece. "Steve, you there?"

She took his money and doled out the change. "It'll be a little bit, we have a big take-away order to get through."

The man scoffed again and waved his hand condescendingly at her.

Sam approached next and smiled. "Hi."

"Hey." She smiled back. She wore less noticeable make-up which meant she probably wore just as much to make it look that way. Her hair was wavier than usual and hung past her shoulders. "I'm really excited about today!"

"Me too, so five? Or just after five? Five-ish?" Sam cleared his throat. "I like your hair."

"This old muff?" She stroked it with her fingers. "I thought something different … Kind of got me in trouble with the manager."

"I thought you were the manager," Sam puzzled.

"Ha-ha, nah … I don't want the responsibility," she said. "Turns out Krys there, was brought into be a key holder. Gave me shit about not tying my hair back. I couldn't care any less."

Sam nodded with a stiff chin. "Well, that is … "

"Hey, Yuki, where's my coffee?" the big-headed man interrupted. "Instead of flirting with Pedro here, why don't *you* make it."

"Absolutely, sir. Your well-being is of the utmost concern to the café. Please feel free to submit any opinions, comments and suggestions to the company website at www … " she said colourlessly.

"Bitch." He sneered and continued to wait.

She smiled at Sam. "Actual handbook instructions."

Sam smirked at Kay between disparaging glances at the man. "I'll let you get to it then." He grabbed his cuppa.

"See you soon!" She ran her fingers through her hair, straightening the curls before they sprung back to helixes.

Sam went for milk, deciding on skim, mostly because the others were bone dry and he did not want to further burden the two employees.

He overheard the man's phone-call. "Yea Steve fly out tomorrow morning. Yea. No. Yea, not this time. Yea. Some little Jap broad. I know! They are my bread and butter. Right? Obviously didn't know who I am and all the cake I get. Stupid little twat."

Sam assumed correctly he was lamenting his rejection by Kay. He missed his cuppa with milk and squeezed the thermos, which was more resilient than Sam. The thermos slipped from his hands, hit the counter with a bang and splashed a drop of dairy on the man's shoes.

"What the fuck?" the man shot, pointing at the single bead of milk. "These are calfskin you retard."

"Then this is good for it … Moo?" Sam joked prior to grabbing a napkin and holding in front of Steve's friend.

"Bro? You still there?" He pressed his finger to the button on his receiver. "I'll call you back, some loser got milk on my loafers and I have to rock a piss."

Sam squinted and rubbed his knuckles together. He secured a lid around his cuppa and decided that he too had to use the lavatory. He entered behind the man whose head was angled up to the ceiling. Groaning from liberation, Sam huddled into the urinal beside him.

"Hey," Sam whispered unsurely, his eye darting about.

"What?" The man focused on the tiles in front of him, returning their warmth.

"Sorry about your kicks," Sam said.

"Whatever, hombre." The man shook, zipped and went to grab a piece of paper towel.

Sam also zipped and moved to wash his hands beside the man with his shoe on the counter. "I said sorry."

"And I said whatever. Hombre. Chico. Whatever you people call each other." The man ran the tips of his fingers under the water and slid them over his coif.

"You should use soap, and wash your hands," Sam said with a stone in his belly, staring down. "That beautiful girl, well no one, wants to touch your dick. First or second hand."

"The fuck did you say?" The man squared to Sam who peered at the situation from the reflection of the mirror. "Do you know who I am?"

Sam shook. Some fear, some disbelief at his status of instigator. "No, do you know me?"

The man righted his stance, his chest like a barrel of nitrate. "You're some little fucker about to get smashed in a public bathroom."

Sam's body went frigid. "Well, at least the barista can bandage me up. The one who didn't call you back."

The man brushed his suit-jacket. "That worthless little slut?" He moved closer.

Sam watched in the mirror as the man raised his leg-sized arm, then he blinked to brace the impact. Between his movement and Sam's blink, the words he used for Kay defrosted his nerves and boiled him instantly. Perhaps a latent aggression which had been hiding when he had first seen the man was unleashed and needed only a mite of anger to ignite the powder keg.

Sam's strategy, a veritable Kieninger Trap with a Budapest rook, felt to him like just vigilantism. He peeped under the stalls finding no dropped trousers. He was alone in the washroom.

He splashed a bit of water on his face and winked to himself in the mirror.

"Shit," he said to his reflection. *That was too easy, it's already happening.* He held his upturned palms beneath the hand drier, thinking that that guy shouldn't have messed with Kay. She was too much of an angel for that garbage.

He grabbed his cuppa and heard Krys crossly yell out, "Derek! I have a to-go for a Derek!" He smiled as he pulled out a cigarette and took his first after-sex pull in quite some time.

The chatter in the office was the whereabouts of one Linda Hawerchuk. People were not yet concerned, but it was not in her character to peel out early and refrain from draining the coffee pot as a first act of the work day.

Sam shrugged. "I saw her yesterday, but, then I didn't." Not technically a lie.

The workplace made Sam nervous. Anger was never the over-arching sentiment he lumbered around, but was wary of how easy he had been able to foster it recently. Perhaps knowing the consequences of his wrath could make him calm down easier. Maybe.

An email stated that Michelle and Chen may be absent for another day with the retreat, thusly comforting him that the two lighting rods for his most impure cerebrations would be 'safe'. The test would surely be administered upon their return, he thought, in much simpler terminology.

The day was a success. Sam was left to his lonesomeness to be productive and worthy of his pay. More so, he was approaching five o'clock with anticipation and queasiness. He thought about how to approach his date; Kay seemed of the newer breed that did not inherently require the pomp and magnitude of masculine chivalry, but one can never know.

The steam-whistle frothed. Sam had been a window-shopper for years while he was with Chloe. His nose, which had been bent to an aquiline hook from being pressed against the storefront, was pulled by the lowering façade, like the partition in a limousine. He descended the staircase with the restraint of a nihilistic pre-teen on December 25th: Cool to the touch, but still very much a child.

Sam offered to grab them a cuppa which made Kay laugh. He played it off as a joke and they set to the seaside to ramble along the boardwalk. Some of the food stands were primping up their business to capitalize on the chance that the early spring weather would continue. Hawkers of the same breed as the clothing companies that are effective at using cheap fabrics to quickly cash in on faddish slogans with simple graphics. The deep fryer baskets crackled as they were lifted from vats of oil; the charcoal briquettes crouped from the drippings of kebabs, fuming workmanlike towards the atmosphere; and the hotdogs lapped in the cooker with an endless, squeaking carousel of revolutions.

"How long do you think they let them sit for?" Kay wondered, staring through the glass of the Ferris-wheeling broiler. "Like, how do you know if this guy was left for dead, and let to ride for the whole day because he's wearing sunglasses." She followed one sweaty wiener with her finger.

"How can you?" Sam replied. "I always look at the sauces." He swirled the plastic spoons in the condiments. "See, the ketchup and mustard has a skin, and the mayonnaise … "

"What kind of sociopath puts mayo on a hot dog?" Kay sneered, "Relish and onions." She stirred the relish, less a green than brown. "I'm gonna pass."

Sam agreed. The man at the stand offered to cook them one fresh. They declined the offer and instead approached an old man pushing an ice-cream cart.

"One or two scoops," the man asked in a thick Mediterranean accent.

"Two!" Kay smiled. Sam also grabbed a pair of sweet iced spheres lumped on top of one another, plumped into a waffle cone with a little paper strip to keep the hands from getting sticky.

The two of them leaned against the wall that divided the path from the beach, staring into the sea.

"It's crazy," Kay began. "It's crazy how there are already people who are so aching to be seen that they are shivering on the beach right now."

Sam had been coming to the same thought as she spoke. "Beats me. I blame it on all the young ones wanting the perfect picture for profiles and bragging rights."

"Easy there, old man … " She laughed. "My generation certainly sucks, but yours isn't much better."

"And why is that?"

"Well, you guys started something that will probably be your downfall, if you can't adapt."

"Go on … "

"All the equality business, rights for everybody, all the positive social movements, and your generation was pretty influential, it has to be said. But you guys, especially on the older side, are fucked." She nonchalantly licked the top scoop, strawberry.

"Why are *we* fucked?"

"Because, things are moving way faster. I grew up with the internet. And porn. Did you? My older cousin always complains that he had to steal his dad's nudie mags and catch a beating for jerking off. Gave him some weird dominatrix fetish, or something. Anyways, your age group started to get these benefits and now mine is making a crazy dash. Take Krys, you know Krys, the *anager*."

"I'm sorry, *anager?*"

"Yeah, turns out they don't just scare you, but the bosses. Krys kind of bullied his or her way to be the manager, and decided that the word 'manager' was a form of bigotry. Made a big fuss about being called he or she, and boom, made *anager* a thing. Fast, too huh? The bathrooms are now both boy and girl, all documentation must contain the word 'they' and Krys basically bullied their way to the top.… In a day. Do you know how long it takes me to try and drop the pronouns? Like I said you guys are fucked."

"I mean, there's nothing wrong with that, I just ask that whomever I speak to understands that it is outside of the box that I'm used to."

"But isn't that weird? That the people who want the special designations are the ones with the least amount of patience? I'll be honest, I was perfectly fine, maybe even a tad militant before I met Krys. They made *me* feel kind of like a sexist, and I'm a woman! It kind of made me look at it like a farce. At the same time, I want equality and respect. On the other, I watch the way they act guerilla towards the customers and it makes me feel bad for them. Still on the other, it's impressive what a strong will gets you. But then, on the other-other hand … "

"Long day?" Sam patted her shoulder.

"Yeah," Kay licked the streak of pink cream that melted on to her hand, "don't mean to talk shop, but it's screwing with my morals. How do you see it?"

"It's like something that I have no idea. Kind of like … If you listen to music and you find a genre that suits you, or a style of pants that you like the most. That might be the soundtrack and slacks you wear for the rest of your life. I guess you kind of have to update your music selection and follow the trends. For me … well … it's something that I have to try and figure out as I go along. Understand the *context*. Try not to get mad when I don't understand and just try to educate my … "

"Can I lick your cone?" Kay smiled.

Sam stiffened with an accidental look of pseudo-disgust.

"Is it because it's milk?" Kay asked.

Sam nodded. "I blame it on breast-feeding. Sure there are two breasts, but I ain't never seen … "

"Then come on." She moved in with her tongue out, teasing her head closer and closer to his ice cream. "Don't be shy, I wanna try." She grabbed his hand and scraped her tongue from his hand to the topmost scoop, making eye contact the whole time. "See, old man? Not so bad."

The top scoop fell and splatted against the path. They both laughed. Kay pulled her top scoop and plunked it on to Sam's.

"There," she smirked, "baptism by fire." She licked her finger and winked at Sam.

A jogger was screaming 'on your left' and 'on you right' as he barrelled down the boardwalk. Kay and Sam had begun to walk slowly together, bumping together with prolonged, incidental contact that became a flirtatious canter where they took turns putting weight on the other. Her head dipped against his arm and his hand grazed hers. The jogger cried 'left' but struck Kay's arm, sending her ice cream to the ground.

"Damn," she muttered. "The cone is like the best part."

"Watch it," the jogger said.

Kay bent down to pick up the sopping mess and Sam blinked. The jogger was no more.

"Where did he go?" asked Kay.

"He's really fast." Sam shrugged and gave Kay his cone. Pliable, prior to mushy, and still crunchy at the vertex. She kissed his cheek and grabbed his hand with her sticky palm. Sam could feel her tacky fingers wriggle between his.

A feeling of instant remorse crept up the walls of Sam's purposeful ignorance. *For her, you did it for her, he was a jerk and she is innocent. Fuck him, don't disrespect a lady like that.* A bubble of anxiety erupted around Sam's belly button like an overtaxed water cooler.

"This is gross to you, isn't it?" She laughed. "I can feel your hand get stiff…. Makes it all the better and funnier." She bit the top of the cone. "Serious though, where did that running-man go? He's not Barry Gordon."

They walked past dusk until the still-early moon let its tail wag tremulously over the rippling tide. Sam was more nervous now than before. He learned a few things about the girl, especially her fascination with dogs. She stopped and asked to pet every dog that walked by except for small goblin-faced ones, having been bitten by a French bulldog as a youngster.

He learned pot was cool again. He learned guys with Asian fetishes are something to be handled with caution. He learned that university is still a bloated form of coitus interruptus. He learned that roommates are a necessary evil in such an expensive city. He learned that she really liked the colour black and wore it almost exclusively unless the heat demanded something lighter. He learned that her favourite food was pizza and her favourite music was British downtempo, trip-hop. He learned she was twice bitten but reticent to become shy. He learned that sexuality is fluid and that every girl her age had been with another girl. He learned that she enjoyed books. He learned that she did want to settle down. He learned that Kay was past the one-night-stand period of her life.

"It's fine," she said. "I don't want to make it sound like I'm some sort of slut.... Because I don't like that word and shut your brain up for thinking it." She laughed. "But it just ... I don't know. It takes a piece of your soul.... Like it just becomes something to do. I don't care about reputations or anything like that. I kind of want to find someone who I don't hate after cumming and don't get frustrated by when I don't."

"Yeah, I ... have no idea what you mean."

"You never had your time in the sun? Sexually speaking of course."

"Yeah, sure, but not like my friend Andy. He's got a new girl every other day. I have been, had been, with the same woman for eight years. I haven't had actual, two-human sex for maybe three years? Maybe we drunkenly slept together, but, nothing really."

"You poor baby," Kay sympathized. "On top, having to watch your tomcat friend. Maybe he's insecure...."

"Nope!"

"Lonely?"

"Doubt it."

"Megalomaniac?"

"Eh." Sam tilted his head. "He's attractive, I guess.... If you like that type: Tall, dark, you know the rest.... Can't really blame a guy for shooting the shot. He's a great guy. For all it's worth, he's been my best friend for as long as I can remember."

"Opportunistic then," she said. "He sounds really nice, I'd love to meet him!"

"Yeah, that's more like it. A real killer's instinct on him. He says that's my problem; that I overthink.... Even before Chl ... my ex. I just never picked up on the signs. Couldn't read the writing on the wall. Doubted myself. Get a bad case of the jitters."

Kay disengaged from Sam's sticky mitt and pulled him in for a kiss. Balancing on her toes she pulled his head down and forced his lips on hers.

"Shut up," she said when they finished, slapping his chest. "Stop being so cute, you fidgety bum."

"I-I mean, I can try to n-not be such a … " Sam chewed his thumb, stuttering.

"I said stop." She kissed him again.

The following morning Kay's alarm chimed before Sam's. He looked at his mobile and watched her slide her skirt over her waist and tuck in her shirt. She turned to notice him awake and crawled atop his torso.

"Morning." She kissed his chin.

"Hey." Sam smiled, oozing confidence, at the very least. "I thought you weren't into one-night-stands?"

"Who said I'm done with you?" She dropped her head on his chest. "Um … That being said … "

"You don't ever have to leave." He felt her cheeks lift and tighten against his chest.

"I swear," she rose to an equestrian's mount, "I would go lesbian if a nice guy like you chucked me, Christ. I've had some real assholes in my life."

Sam stroked the outside of her arm.

She spun her head around the bedroom. "How fresh is your break-up?"

"Recent enough, why?"

"The boxes," she pointed, "the garbage bags, the random little chick shit left in here. And your walls make it look like a serial killer's apartment, ha-ha. I didn't notice it in the dark."

"It spiralled fast." Sam laughed with taut nerves. "Slow, slow, slow, and then fast! Like a pop fly in the sun that you only saw just in time." He acted the increase of speed with his hands.

"And the serial killer part?" She rocked on his lap.

"I'm very dangerous." Sam winked.

Sam hummed to himself the entire walk to work. Kay had taken her leave to get ready for a day of work and then school, while Sam had earned a bowl of honey-glazed cereal. He was drained but in fine spirits. His spoon swamped about pulling up big mounds of damp circles with the centres poked-out. He was even up earlier than usual and could comfortably make the distance, surrounded by enchanting figments hovering around him like a baby-mobile.

He saw Kay at the café. The interaction was less coy and more comfortable than he would have guessed. Sam could read the on *anager's* face that their displeasure was apparent. "Who cares," scoffed Kay. "There's no line and you're just my customer," she punctuated with a smile.

Sam was long-removed from the game. He did not know whether to ask her out again, how soon, or how unconcerned he should act. He did not want her to think this was a rebound deal, though he was fully unsure what it was. He wanted to blow off work and hang out together. He felt his palms moisten and the stuttering imperil his speech.

"Sam?" she said, "I think I left something at your place, can I grab it tonight?"

"Y-yeah, s-sure … " Sam had not realized that he had not spoken a word in several minutes.

"You like pizza?" Her eyes flickered like yarn in a kitten's paw.

"Y-Yeah."

"I'll be over at seven with some pizza. Maybe pick out a movie you don't really want to watch and really get into, and has background noise that doesn't dry or soften the … you know."

"Yeah." Sam grinned.

Sam casually waited for the elevator. His heart was still pumping too much juice for him to test his mettle on the stairs. He might be a few minutes later than Michelle, if she was there, and she might want to gnaw him out while threatening a full chewing when she captured the throne, but Sam did not care.

He undersold his patience.

He arrived at his desk to find Michelle in a well-rehearsed pose, a glass smile and braided fingers resting placidly on her desk. She was painted and robed glossily. Eyelash extensions, an airless business skirt and even her lips seemed zaftig.

"My-oh-my," she began, "I hope this hasn't been the case while Harry and I have been away. I will have to let people know what a stickler I am for punctuality." She tilted her head and cut an eye that pinched her new lashes together but did not alter the straight-lipped smile she contrived.

"Yeah, I don't know," Sam said cavaliered. "You should do that."

"I will be having one-on-ones to assess who is most valued and whose values line up best with my own vision for the office." She kept staring at

Sam, who was rummaging through his bag. "What is your goal within the company? How do you expect to drive the brand? What … "

"Michelle," Sam sensed annoyance percolating, "why not leave the serious stuff for when you have your own room." He felt the first bubbles in a heated cauldron, burping as they surfaced. "How was your retreat?"

She adjusted to a gossiper's pose; her chair slid out and her back arched, she leaned in, her hands rose neck-level and her elbows pillared with engagement. "Well … "

Sam periodically hummed with ascent or surprise or placatory. He listened to the inflections and adjusted his chorus accordingly. Easy. Calm. Annoying but amenable.

Sam's phone rang.

"How's things, babe?" Andy asked.

"Oh you know, pretty swell, pretty good, pretty … "

"Holy shit, you broke up with Chloe?"

Sam snickered. "Yeah, how did you know?"

"You didn't start off with a sigh, the kind an old tradesman sighs whenever he has to use his knees."

"Yea, she's gone!" Sam cheered. "Cheating ass bitch!"

Michelle glared at Sam.

"Awesome! Congratulations! She told you she was? Knew it. Trifling … So, we hitting the town tonight? I've got the paint."

"I think I might be out on that."

"What? How?"

"Well, you know that coffee shop girl?"

"You fucked her?" Andy shrieked.

Sam covered the earpiece, noticing Michelle look up. "Yeah, well, umm … we're hanging out tonight and … "

"Don't."

"Don't what?"

"Don't go getting yourself tied down, what, a day after you ended it? It's called a rebound and you need to get it out of your system and then a few dozen more and then, just then, maybe you can think about … "

"I know what a rebound is, and that's not it. She's cool and funny and hip and … "

"Just for saying the word hip means she's too cool or too young for you."

"Shut up." Sam laughed. "Anyways, I have had a thing for her for a while and, for once, things just went my way."

"Well, as long as you don't catch yourself in your own net, I'm happy for you. So you're busy tonight? Victory pints at Mahoney's?"

"Can't. She forgot something at my place and we're going to have pizza. You should meet her, give her a once over for me."

"Like, when the king bangs his subjects' brides to be?" Andy asked with an air of innocent inquiry.

"No, you dick," Sam scoffed. "To meet her and see what I'm talking about."

"Maybe on the weekend, if it lasts that long."

"Prick."

"Love you."

"Love you, too."

Sam hung up and shook his head. Andy was kind of a dick. Though, underrated in his astuteness thanks to his boorishly outspoken way of barraging opinion and advice.

"Personal calls," Michelle frowned, "another facet I will look to clamp down on. Thank you Sam, sitting across from you has given me so many bad habits to iron out of this place."

Sam shot her a glance, but ended up staring at her with a hate-based sexual-attraction look that scared him out of anger.

Sam was informed that Chen would be a ghost after Friday. He was taking his owed week of vacation for his final five work days. Sam was sore, but more interested in knowing why he was overlooked for the promotion. Overlooked in the way you can trip on your shoelaces staring into the infinity of the horizon. He knocked on the door. He was told to come in but found Chen pacing, laughing into his headset. Chen raised a flippant index finger to hold Sam at the door.

Why would he say to come in if he was going to do that? Sam unnerved.

He was gestured to grab a seat. He complied. He waited. Chen was still talking about whatever, practicing his golf swing with an imaginary club and ball, over and over. A stand-up mirror beside his desk seemed to give him great satisfaction as he watched his fingers overlap his thumb, his shoulders square and his hips swivel with the rotation of his torso. He watched the imaginary ball sail far over Sam's head and then beamed with the ball's supposed distance to the flagstick.

Sam pondered if this was some kind of new managerial technique. Sweat the proletariat out of his resolve and let him iron out his own will.

"Okay, okay … Ciao." Chen pressed a button on his earpiece and plopped the contraption on the table. "Sorry, Sam, that was business." He sat down. "What can I … "

The phone rang again.

"Harry Chen," he answered, "no, no of course it's a good time…. No, nothing important. Give me one second."

Sam was already outside the office.

At Sam's apartment, he and Kay ate pizza and she informed him that he did not know good pizza when Sam mentioned that it was delicious.

"This is okay, just okay … But really, where do you buy pizza? Those slices in the business district? The cardboard with goop they sell at the chains? Honey, I will show you good pizza … the best pizza." She held out her hand to list off: "There's Leonardo's, Napoli Pizzeria, Mama Guilia's, The Del Piero Brothers, even Alberto's Pizza by the Slice is better than what you would normally order."

"I've heard Esposito's is pretty solid."

"Yeah, it's pretty authentic, but the place itself is kind of mobster-money show-off…. Bad memories of that place."

"Bad memories?" Sam asked, preparing to ask if she had food poison or witnessed a stoolie get hit. Before he could deshell his follow up, her little foot was massaging his crotch with the dexterity of a ragtime pianist.

"I don't mean to be presumptuous," Kay said, lying on Sam's belly vacantly watching the credits of a movie they only saw the opening credits. "But do you want to hang out this weekend?"

"Of course I would." Before he finished she leapt to her knees.

"Do you have a bike?"

"No … oh wait, yes!"

"Let's bike the coastline! It's supposed to stay nice for the weekend and it's not full of tourists yet."

Sam added bashfully, "I don't really know how to ride."

Kay cooed and cawed, "I'll teach you, old man. Didn't you have a penny-farthing or was it still horses when you were a chi … "

He grabbed her and swung her on to her back so fast her hair wrapped around Sam's entire head.

Sam lay on Kay's lap, tired but far from defeated. "What did you forget here, anyway?"

"Oh, nothing, I just wanted to come over."

"I see, very sneaky." His projection was marred by something in his head, which Kay easily sensed.

"What're you thinking?" she asked.

"Well … I want to ask my boss, my soon to be former boss, why he didn't give me a look for his job. I mean, I kind of already know why and I know why he picked his replacement. But, I feel like I should still have a word with him. We've worked together a while and I just want to hear some ideas about what I can do better, you know…. What I can do to not be swept under the carpet for another six years. I don't necessarily want to work there forever, but if I was to look for another job, I feel like they'd ask why I held the same position with the same description and never moved. I'm worried that I'll get angry, he does something to me, I get hot, and … "

"Oh, you do have a mean streak, Mr. nice guy.…" Kay scratched his bare arm. "I knew you had some crazy in you. Would you throw a chair? Hang him out of the window by his feet? Take the office hostage?"

"The windows don't open," he snickered. "They're like the windows in Vegas hotels." He paused. "No, but …"

"Just talk to him, you'll be fine."

Sam awoke and showered with Kay. He thought about his conversation with Andy the day before and toyed with the notion that maybe he was moving too fast. She *had* brought an overnight bag with the intention of crashing and each of them seemed expeditiously cozy with the other. Impulsive or impetuous? Was it premature? Like judging the bounce of a ball on its first wallop against the hardwood, only to watch the next bounces suffer the sophomore languish and peter-off to a roll?

Those thoughts glistened from Sam like the soap he rubbed on Kay's narrow shoulders. *Who cares?* he thought. *I'm happy, I'm getting laid and I feel happier with myself. She likes my gut!*

They walked to work together. Sam showed her the bike he claimed as his own. "Wow!" she exclaimed. "That is a serious piece of equipment for a guy that claims he can't ride. Why is the seat so high? Do you have two sets of knees? Jesus, mine has a basket on the front and a rattrap on the back. This one seems designed for speed, like one for those weird middle-aged guys that wear their full uniforms everywhere they go. Do you have bike shorts? Ha-ha. A little jersey, too?"

Sam answered with nervous laughter. "Ha-ha, no … I was given it.… Haven't taken the girl out for a test ride. We can christen it on the weekend. Maybe meet up with Andy for a drink or something."

"And you can meet my friends, too. They don't sound as suave and cool as your pal, but they're some knuckleheads you'll be sure to despise."

They walked to the office and café. Kay received a chiding from Krys for being a minute late. Sam admitted he had someone like that at his job, too.

He had a while before the office would be free of the Bosnian cleaners playing their traditional folk music that sounded like steel strings on a tin-can guitar. He waited and sipped a cuppa at a table. He could not help but listen as Krys took out their unhappiness on Kay. Another barista was apparently late for the busy Friday rampage and Krys poured aggression into Kay that would blister the palm through a double-cup and snow gloves.

When Sam went to say goodbye, still pre-rush hour Krys shoved between them. "This cisgender is the reason why you're late." They poked Kay. "You may not be paid enough to take this job seriously, but I am. Everything is a joke to you, everything is all unicorns and sunshine, huh? You want to be the person that was fired from a café? Is that what you want?"

Krys' attention found the latecomer who just entered. "Michael, on the floor now!"

Sam shrugged embarrassingly at Kay who returned with an equally prehensile-between-the-knee-highs expression. A little hate and a little humiliation. Sam felt bad. He felt responsible and the source of his lady-friend's chewing out.

He went to use the bathroom before starting his day unprecedentedly early. He sighed at the urinal. A great start to the day appeared to be in jeopardy. He was looking within himself for the fortitude to approach Chen when Krys emerged from the stall, buttoning up their pants.

They rolled their eyes and moved to wash their hands. They turned around to face a zipping Sam who was startled by their approach.

"What?!" Krys barked. "Never seen a transgendered person in the bathroom. Get used to it, criminal. This is the new way of the world. This is progress and you and all your allies and ableists are going to be old news, fast. And don't think that you can … "

Sam blinked and then was faced with his own jumbled expression staring back in the mirror. A stiffly upturned lip, slightly puckered brow and uneasy eyes. The eyes that stared back into his were asking him if what he had just done was a hate crime.

He stood silently in the lavatory a few seconds longer contemplating if any crime was or was not rooted in some kind of hate, or conversely, love. *That was an accident.* Sam pulled his hair. *I gotta get outta here.*

Riding in the in the elevator, Sam's thoughts began to race. *What if I can't get my anger under control. How many 'accidents' will it take?* He feared it would catch up with him. What if he blinked the wrong person out of existence? Sam thought about calling Lucy. He knew the answer, it was on him and only him. *This is bad, this is bad,* he repeated internally. *I'm a land mine, it doesn't matter who steps on me, I could go off!* Sam could have turned dying embers in to a wildfire with his frantic breathing. *It'll be okay. Just calm down, that's the lesson, just chill out, just chill…* Sam was punching away on the keyboard when Chen, a second after him, arrived. Mr. Chen floated into the office carrying a bike wheel and bagged suit. He was immersed in a conversation on his head set gambolling his yacht club chortle. He waved at Sam before screwing his face at his watch and shooting him a look of playful incredulity. He continued laughing to his office. Sam could hear the underwater bass of Chen through the walls; the unzipping of the polyester garment shell and the spraying sounds of antiperspirant.

It was not until he heard the slight groan of Chen's upholstered executive office chair that he moved anxiously. Almost necessitating the old heave-ho to propel himself from his seat to his feet. Sam was not nervous insofar as he knew what Harry Chen would probably say. It was a matter of dealing with the likelihood of his anger getting the better of him. He poured a cuppa sludge and stirred in the creamer.

He began to submit himself to the idea that there would be no consequences to deal with, so to speak. He could veritably take stewardship for his years of jealousy and belittling and choose a method that indulged his sour taste and newfangled acumen. He could speak to Chen however he wanted, treat the man like a speedbag or an inflatable clown with sandbag shoes.

He felt excited. He began to think up adjectives to carve out precisely what he wanted to say, wishing to leave no fat on his rant unless he wanted the marbling to render. He fantasized staring at Chen like a square of filet mignon, skewered at the end of his sterling fork, admiring the blood oozing between the directions of the grain down to his fingers, then shoving the too-big chunk into his mouth and forsaking his detest for porcine chomping, if only because the piece would not allow his mouth to fully close and it tasted too good to spit out.

Sam caught the reflection on his face in the stainless kettle. The bulbous hull reflected his side profile in a way that made his covetous leer look more Dick Dastardly gritting his palms after tying a damsel to the train tracks.

"Be cool," he shook his head, "whatever happens, happens."

Sam knocked and entered Chen's office, not waiting for a reply. Chen replied to Sam's entrance with a pestered glance and the motion for him to grab a seat. Sam remained standing, arms folded his back like a cadet. He moved his arms akimbo, to his pockets, then again at his blindside.

"Sam," Chen raised a finger and signed off from his call, "this is so unlike you. So early! I love it." The boss clapped and smiled handsomely. "Please have a seat."

"No thank you *Mr.* Chen, I'd rather stand."

"Have it your way." Chen rolled his seat closer to the desk, clasping his hands. Each ring finger was dressed, the left with a wedding band and the right with a garish class ring. "What do you want to talk about? I assume that's why you're here so early. My days have been pretty hectic and … "

"Why wasn't I informed about the opening? I didn't, well, no one knew you were leaving. I could've had time to put together a resume, something to demonstrate my worth. What I have done, what I could do."

"Oh Sammy," Chen sighed, "the position was never meant for you, or anyone, but Michelle. She has everything for the optics and the skills the job requires."

"Optics?" Sam repeated perplexed.

Chen looked around as if someone may hear him in the empty office. "Optics being … well … We have moved away from the historically out-dated all-white, all-male management team. I know coming from someone of Asian descent that may seem a little off. But, injecting a newer approach to business only helps, never hinders. *Diversity over adversity.*"

"I thought the optics were bad, her being the fiancée of your best friend."

"That actually lets me vouch for her. I am acquainted with her education, family, personal history and … "

"So she was hired because she is also Asian?"

"No, no, not at all. I mean, the fact it is a 'her' is as important as her … this is hard to say: non-Caucasian heritage. I don't mean to down-play her intelligence, her work ethic, her education, her attitude, her maturity, or anything else. But, Sam, being a white man, you have to work a little bit … "

"I'm Mexican!"

"Oh!" Chen sat back with surprise. "You are rather white for a His-panic. I thought Florin may have been French or Italian. Interesting. I will add that if you were a woman, Latina executives are all the rage. There is probably a good niche for Latin men.…"

"Listen," Sam felt himself letting go of the wheel with unanticipated, invisible trust, allowing an unseen hand guiding the ship, "you spoiled daddy's boy. You fancy, golf-money asshole. You stuffy voice-boxed, insin-cere, pedantic, nepotistic, posturing, jackal. You country-club, silk-tie, opera-going, wine-sniffing bitch-ass." He felt his cherry-sized testicles turn to grapefruits. *That felt amazing. Why have I never done that before?* Sam licked his lips like a freed man rubs his cuff-freed wrists.

Chen's eyebrows leapt up. He was silent.

"Ha-ha!" He clapped. "I wish I had invited you to the sending off dinner. I think they had a roast planned, that stuff is perfect!"

The corners of Sam's lips curled like horns. "You are going to be a streak, a goner, a nothing if I choose." Sam felt frustrated, but comfortable in his words. "You are not even going to be a pile of dust, just nothing. Like, poof! I hate you. I always hated you. You climbed the ladder by stepping on my face. Your daddy gave you everything and you gave everyone else the illusion of merit and fair play. You don't know fair play, you have money to pay the ref and the judges. You cheap, cheating, disingenuous cunt."

He felt the confidence of a man drunk with invulnerability.

"Woah, Sam!" Chen became stern. "I will have to ask you to … "

Sam slowly blinked. "Fuck you, Harry."

Chen remained. His cheeks were crimson and his eyes clinched angrily at Sam.

Um, what? Sam thought. *Why is he still here?*

"You want to know why you didn't get the job." He raised his voice. Sam's confidence drained to anxiety. He nodded. "You asked for it, pal."

Why isn't this working? Sam's confident inner-roar shrank to an impish and cowardly squeak. His hands fidgeted. His head dropped and his eyes raised to peer up at Chen like a disgraced politician.

Chen clicked away on his mouse and rotated the screen towards Sam. "These are performance evaluations." Sam lengthened his neck to see a list of employee names on an aggregated performance score evaluation chart. "You see the upward trends? Yeah? You see the one that shifts maybe a little up, and little down, but stays relatively linear? That's you. Not bad enough to fire, nowhere near exceptional to earn a promotion."

Sam's confidence was a vague memory.

Chen enlarged the window. "You know who made this? Michelle did it to go out of her way, above-and-beyond to prove herself as an asset. See the skyrocket? That's her."

Chen minimized the window. "So, it's not nepotism or favouritism it's you being passed, again, by someone who works harder and better than you, again."

"Well … " Sam started, but was quickly cut-off by a reddening Chen.

"Not only performance, but attitude. Yours has just been slowly declining since day one. Sure, you show up every day. Sure, you are polite, but so are the homeless until you refuse to give them change. Then they are sullen little children who continue to loaf on the sidewalk and hold their hands out. I don't know how to motivate you. You have one set back and it's the end of the world. Where is the confidence?"

Chen adjusted his tie and wiped the spittle cornering his mouth. "You're always either late or just on time. You drag your feet and are unenthusiastic at meetings. You never contribute anything more than 'the same old' as you call it. You are a boring and overpaid employee."

Chen settled himself. "Look, I know we started at the same time and it's probably hard to watch me, and everyone who started after you get promotions, good raises and earn mobility. Don't kid yourself, myself and the others did earn it. You have not gone the extra mile or proven yourself capable of more the duties than those you are currently tasked to fulfill. You have hit your ceiling, it seems. Maybe there are problems at home or whatever. Which is fine, not everyone is equal, my father taught me that."

Sam nodded again. It was all accurate and he did not have to struggle to comprehend.

"However," Chen rolled the mouse on its little sphere and began clicking anew, "you cannot launch personal attacks against your superior. I am the manager, remember. The first part was kind of funny, but the second was hurtful. I will have to send an email here to recommend disciplinary action henceforth."

"Don't do that," Sam snarled.

"Sam, you have left me little choice. I really don't know, with the positions being reallocated if I can … " Chen was typing fastidiously and was fixed on the monitor.

"Don't!" Sam yelled. His vocal cords and lungs felt like an old generator, kicked on for the first time in a long time. He felt the cobwebs break, the sprockets whine, the dry gears spark and churn without viscosity, the grime and soot flush through the fuel cells cough out of the exhaust fan. It was hoarse. A muscle that had lain dormant since infancy.

Chen snapped straight back in his chair. "Florin, do not use that tone or…"

"Fuck you!" Sam yelled again. He felt the bilious propulsive from his stomach to the open air. The vehemence left his mouth with acrimony and mucus.

He spat towards the manager and hit the chair backing where Chen had just been.

Sam's whole body buoyed up and down with fury. He stared at the translucent hock that rolled lightly down the soft chair-back.

"What the hell?" a female voice from the door.

Sam turned slowly. Michelle was aghast, holding the silently door for support against a hurricane of disbelief.

Sam seethed at her; bubbling at the core, shooting sparks of grease like a broiled roast.

"What the … I heard shouting … What did you just … ? What did I just … He just disa…" Michelle's quavering half notes were abrogated instantly.

Oh this is bad. Sam became pale.

He felt a daze blacken his vision. He dizzily held the desk for support and tugged himself in front of Chen's monitor.

"Please be advised. Samuel Florin has made a threatening verbal attack to my well-being. Let it be recommended that termination of said employee … " The memo was cut short. The message was to be sent to the upper-lot of management and cc'd to Michelle.

Sam felt a panic as he highlighted the entire text and pressed delete. He glanced around. He got up and peered outside of the yawning door to Chen's office.

Still alone.

He darted back to Chen's computer and began to compose his own email with the same addressed recipients. He erased Michelle's name in the carbon copy slot and allowed the office-wide correspondence to populate.

He wrote, "To all whom it may concern, as of this day I am regretful in announcing my departure from the company. I have experienced a great deal of success and vanity but wish to abandon my post in favour of love. I will be … ”

Sam was searching for the correct word.

“ … raising my anchor with my soul-mate, my one true companion, my love Michelle Nguyen. Apologies to Channy and … ”

He tried to remember Chen's wife's name.

“ … my wife. I realize this may come as a bit of a shock, but the heart wants what it wants. A suitable replacement should be found within the office itself. I nominate Samuel Florin. We have had our differences, but with me gone, I feel he is the best candidate, with the proper training. Regards, Harold Chen.”

Sam left the keyboard and shut down the terminal by holding the button for three painstaking seconds and darted to his own chair. He sat back and saw the little box that indicated an incoming message float from the bottom right margin.

I wonder if Chloe would've stayed was a thought that he perversely slid under the rug of his subconscious.

People began to fill the office and the coffee-pot chatter was reigned by the despotic analysis of Michelle and Chen. Sam droned about the circles listening and nodding, trying to see if he had succeeded in the nakedness of his technique.

His phone rang before lunch.

“Sam, it's Andy,” he adrenalized. “An assistant I bang here and there at your head office just gave me some news. Did your boss run away with his mistress? That cute little thing in your office? Did he refer you for his job? Is it true?”

“Yeah, man … ” Sam nervously responded. “You have a girl in every office?”

Andy laughed. “Seriously, this is huge! We should celebrate! Hell, I'm in the area, wanna grab a victory lunch beer?”

Sam looked around at the busied office-workers, entirely consumed in the gossip. *Jesus, they are easily distracted,* he thought. “Let's get a cuppa, you can meet the lady! Plus, there is something I have to tell you,” Sam proffered.

“She works with you?”

"Nah, at the café in the lobby."

"Okay well, I have a bit of time and I'm in the area."

"So downstairs from my office? The café in the lobby?"

"I'll see you soon. Love you."

"Love you too."

Sam stood up and brushed his trousers down when his phone sounded again and he answered.

"Luciano Domino's office, please hold." The beautiful secretary, Sam assumed.

Ride of the Valkyries played in the background, an anxious smile crept on Sam's face as the brass introduced themselves.

"Sam," the milk-velvet voice broke the melody, "I did not think that you had the fortitude for such machinations. I assume the ruse was a thoroughgoing audible, young man?" Lucy sounded as though he were grinning.

"I improvised, a bit, maybe," Sam responded.

"Well, felicitations on beginning to appreciate the compass and occasion of your gift."

"Thanks … "

"Sam, I must caution you. I realize that you are going to celebrate at some point. Most likely with your solitary, non-coital playfellow. Yes? Yes, I know that you are agreeing in silence with a jounce of the cervical vertebrae." Sam was indeed nodding. "It would be in your best interest to withhold any information related to the abilities that I have bestowed to you and a knowledge of my identity. The powers of the truly gifted should be the mask donned by fictional protagonists of cartoon strips. Do you understand?"

Lucy did not wait for Sam to answer. "The difficulty in categorizing the paranormal, even the lack of immediate heuristic correlation would bring a systematic misery and persecution on you that I would be unable, no, unwilling to snooker. The choices that you make will determine whether you inherit fortune or something less agreeable."

"So … "

"Leave the integrity of your abilities to yourself. Simple, yes? You may, of course, do as you wish. This is only an insinuation built from experience;

however, the course of actions you take will decide your fate. Call this simply a friendly warning. Good day to you, Sam."

The tone went dead without Sam having the chance to say a word of farewell.

Sam hung up the phone and raised an eyebrow. He did not know if he was a capable secret-holder, any classified material he was given was usually by Andy and to be kept from people that Sam did not hold acquaintance with. There were, of course, plenty of things hushed from him that he had come to learn, but those things no longer existed and formed the contours of a dead, flat galaxy. He had no one to explain his absence to, and at this point of white-hot gossiping, no one would have noticed him gone.

"Hey, are you okay?" Sam asked a visibly flustered Kay.

"Hi, uh, no ... " she started, scratching the counter. "Krys just left! Right after you did. Up and out and stiffed me here with a new guy for the whole day. No 'I'm going to the bank' or 'I'm throwing myself in the ocean holding an anchor'. No nothing! I've called, I've texted, but zilch."

"I thought you hated them?"

"I mean, yeah ... A total bitch; rude and godly and just mean. But, where the fuck did they go? I'll have to probably pull more shifts until they find another new person...."

"I'm sorry," Sam said and he was. Layered and complex.

"It's fine.... What are you doing here?" Kay checked her watch. "You haven't been up there long. Couldn't get enough, huh?" She winked and rubbed his hand lightly with one finger.

"Actually." Sam coughed and felt the vibrating espresso machine do him no favours by sending a tremor through the counter against his zipper. "I'm meeting my best friend for a victory joe." He moved his hips back.

"Andy? Do I get to meet him? I haven't seen any 'beautiful blue-eyed Jews,' as you say, walk in," she teased. "Celebrating what?"

"Well, it's a long story, but both Chen and Michelle are gone and he suggested I take on the leadership role."

"What?! I thought you didn't really like your company? They didn't even offer you the spot before? I thought you were pretty offended, no?"

"Well, I might as well take the office, the raise and see where it takes me," Sam said, feeling his phone vibrate in his pocket. "Sorry, it's Andy."

"Hey man," Andy started, "I'm actually at a bench across the street, and a nice little picnic table, wanna grab me an Americano? Almond milk?"

"Why?" Sam puzzled. "Come in here and meet Kay."

"I can't, I got us a nice spot out in the sun, come on man … "

"Fine."

Sam turned back to Kay. "Guess he's already across the street…. I'll get an Americano and a cuppa to go."

"Drats." She smiled and made the drinks. "Well, he can't hide for long."

After the coffees were poured and sleeved, topped with milks and lids, Kay suggested the two meet up in the evening to celebrate. "We can do a little celebration dinner, sex, and maybe ride bikes tomorrow and meet up with my friends!"

Sam agreed and carried the cups out the door, waited for the little man to illuminate and free the crosswalk and met with Andy.

"Here you go, weirdo." Sam handed Andy a coffee and removed a cigarette from his pack. "Why didn't you want to come in and meet Kay?" He lit the cigarette.

"I don't want to rain on your parade, old pal, but it hasn't been a week. I mean, this week has had more activity than the last however-many-years of your life. But, you should take a step back and take inventory, you know? It's a big deal dropping a long-time girlfriend, getting a new one, wanting to quit your job then maybe getting a huge promotion. You gotta smell the roses, you know?"

Sam nodded, taking a big pull, putting his lighter back in his pocket. "Maybe, but I'm actually feeling happy. Being with Chloe made me miserable. Kay makes me happy, actually happy. And as for the job, I'm owed this. It was a matter of time before they stopped and realized what an asset I am." He took a few drags. "Besides, I have a feeling my luck is only starting to change." Sam smoked with the smug contentment of a rich man, old enough to savour the taste of wealth, conceits a Gran Corona between his grinning teeth, leaving the gold and red band on the cigar so everyone can see.

"Who are you?" Andy laughed, jostling him with a fist. "And what makes you so sure the floor won't fall out?"

Sam thought about Lucy's 'friendly warning' and replied, "Just a feeling that I have. Like any problems I have will be gone. Like magic."

Andy nodded. "Well that's all well and good and I'm happy for you Copperfield." Andy took a sip and sighed delightfully from the caffeine. "So you like this broad, huh?"

"Yeah, she's great," Sam began. "She's young and fun and beautiful as all hell. She is so different from Chloe and, this is going to sound lame.... But she wants to see me. It's not like I'm chasing some butterfly that can float close to me or far above my head. She wants to spend time with me and I want to be with her."

"Maybe she's just not sick of you yet."

"Maybe, maybe not. Like you said, it's early and I don't want to ask those questions."

"So, Chloe was cheating on you then?"

"Yeah, I met her new boyfriend, seemed nice enough, he probably would have gotten fed up with her too."

"Would've?"

"Will," Sam shook his head, "will get sick of her. Who knows? Who cares? They're gone and out of my life."

"I'm surprised she let you keep the apartment. I assumed you'd be hollering at me asking if you could stay at my place."

"Would your mom make my lunch and do my laundry, too?"

"Of course! She loves that shit! Make all the jokes you want but I love my mom and that is one lady that I would never mess around with."

The boys laughed and drained their cups. Sam offered to bring Andy into the café, but again, he declined. He was on his way to a meeting of some variety and had a few dates to prepare for on the weekend.

"You're probably busy on the weekend with your new lady, but I'm going on Dimitri's skiff for a few beers on Sunday. You maybe want to see if he lets me take it out Monday? If it's nice we can grab a case and dawdle in the water instead of Mahoney's for a night?" Sam gave him a questioning glance. "I know, I know, but you and me on a boat, maybe harpoon some females and ... who knows?"

"Yeah, that might be fun actually."

"One more thing." Andy placed his hand on Sam's shoulder.

"What's that?"

"You have got to get some new clothes." Andy tried to pinch the fabric of Sam's shirt. "This thing is like a can of beans cooked on a fire, it's ready to burst. And make sure you get breathable fabric, it feels like dolphin-skin with all your sweating."

Sam returned to his desk where he was greeted by a couple nice surprises. An email to the office that read the rest of the day could be spent at the employee's leisure. The higher-ups were evidently frazzled by the news and assumed a similar sense of fragmentation at the lower-level. Another e-mail was sent to Sam alone; it stated that pending a review with human resources that Sam would be developed into the position of manager that he was recommended for by an outgoing Harry Chen.

There was also a black and gold floral arrangement in a black, urn-like vase with a note sitting on the desk. The note was in a black enveloped and was black with gilt text and edges written in raised cursive font.

"Dear Sam," the note cordially went, "I am happy for you and proud of the growth that you have thus far exhibited. Never look a gift horse in the deus ex machina. A suggestion, however, must be propounded. If you are to use your power and *wish* to not incur the trivialities of question and explanation, *take the girl's bag and remove the DNA from the seat of your former superior's chair.* Regards, Lucy."

Sam felt gut-punched. He waited fretfully. He pretended to work until everyone left. A male colleague said, "First on the field, last off the field, I wish I had it in me, Sam."

"Thanks," Sam responded. The chatter of the outgoing employees was a mix of gossip and relief that their day was cut short on such a beautiful afternoon.

Sam waited until he was certain of the office's emptiness. He grabbed a soapy piece of paper towel and cleaned Chen's entire chair, the keyboard and the spot where he planted his palms earlier that morning. He found a duffle bag, alligator-chestnut. He opened the bag and removed Chen's billfold containing a grand of folding money.

The word 'tax' flashed through his head as he pocketed the wallet.

He looked at Michelle's desk and saw nothing but her work documents and a framed picture of her and her fiancée in front of the monitor.

He pulled her chair out and found a black leather handbag. It had three golden-metal consonant letters overlapping each other on the buckle. It looked and smelled freshly purchased with anticipated manager coin. He opened it and found a matching wallet with more pictures of *them* and crisply minted hundreds, one-hundred of them. It hurt his hand to riffle the count.

For a moment Sam wondered if he had set an early plan in motion by accident. He noted the thousands of dollars he had just rolled into his own thirty-seven. "Maybe I'm telepathic," he quipped to himself. "This feels wrong." He thought about all of his other wrongs. He stopped thinking.

He canvassed the area one more time before leaving. The money belaboured alongside receipts and pointless plastics in his chocolate-brown wallet, a tawnier shade around the fold and seams. The wallets were shoved inside the purse which was nested like a Matryoshka doll within his messenger bag.

There were few errands or chores that needed tending, but Sam did not wish to putter aimlessly around his neighbourhood or apartment. He thought it a reasonable activity to invest his recent windfall of big faced banknotes on Andy's suggestion: clothes that fit.

Sam entered a big department store, the crown jewel of the shopping district, with its regal, stone façade and impeccably clean windows. There were pompous door men that vetted entrants with either warm silent nods or deriding snorts, Sam received the latter. The first-floor staff, the fragrance pistoleros and the beauty-product clinicians in stagy, pharmaceutical lab-tech coats, smiled affectedly beneath their thick, shiny polymers. The bright lights rebounded from the sterile showcases and the myriad oils and perfumes which gave Sam a headache.

He took the escalator to the men's clothing floor. He passed floors of women's wear, shoes, hosiery, and intimates. The mannequins comported themselves with an air of primacy, the reflective, featureless faces enhanced the superiority these statues exhibited, whether the hands-on-hips with the pelvis jutted out model; a less-intimidating but sassy one hand on the hip one hand turned up, as if saying 'what's your fucking point, Michael?'; even the friendlier, young-girl poses, hands behind the back with the knee curved inwards, came off as daunting. They wore outfits that cost a better rent than Sam's and those emotionless faces seemed to carry much sentiment, but not a one being kind.

If the female mannequins struck Sam as intimidating, the male mannequins were entirely unlikeable. Sam was greeted by a suave inanimate with an open poet's shirt and long thin legs that stood relaxed in leather boots, staring off without noticing a soul from under its dignified non-face. A casual-business plastic-man holding a sport coat over his back and hand in his pocket struck Sam as the kind of guy who bragged about stocks and bench presses and blowjobs and abortions. The tuxedo wearing mannequin, his outstretched hand groping for a martini would undoubtedly regale the gents club with his extra-marital affairs, how a few lashes made his son the best running-back in the county, and how lawn-care was in the blood of his Latino groundskeepers.

Sam hated all of them. Their expressionless debonair and physiques made Sam wonder if all the mannequins, though black in composition, were still the purest representation of white dominance that he had ever seen. Somewhere, deep in his brain, he yearned to hear Krys' critique of the gallery.

An equally expressionless man who strived for the same self-possessed debonair as the mannequins approached Sam. "Can I help you, sir?" He folded his arm behind his back and floated his chin towards the skylight.

"Y-Yeah," Sam said awoken from his thoughts. "I need some new clothes … work and maybe play."

"Yes, well, this location offers the premium service of personal shopping by trained styling professionals such as myself," the man whose name-tag read Gregory said without eye-contact.

"Well," Sam started, "I know what I like, just sizing … "

"Clearly what you like is doing you no favours, sir," Gregory said without appearing to move his levelled lips.

Sam shook his head. "I know, I know, I have gained a few pounds," the rep smirked, "but I am getting a promotion and need to look the part."

"Well, you said work and 'play'." Gregory slowly created air-brackets with his long digits to recapitulate Sam's previous statement with mockery.

"Yea, well, I … " Sam began, stuttering from nerves. "I just need a few shirts, pants, maybe a jacket and maybe some casual wear."

"Follow me," Gregory said and turned sharply on the inches of heel beneath his boots. "You may also want to consider getting some newer footwear ... it is the first thing people tend to notice."

Sam followed as the man grabbed randomly from racks. He seemed to know his sport, plunging his fingers into rows of similar garments and plucking the precise piece he searched. Sam also grabbed things that he saw fit to try on, things that he took as being casualwear.

They passed another employee, a pretty young man with a t-shirt that appeared normal in the front, but fell to the backs of his knees like coattails. He wore skinny black jeans and a heather-grey wool cap that sat above the wire arms of his circular-lensed readers. Sam knew at that moment he had become not young, though remained uncool.

The clothes that Gregory chose for Sam were apt. The shirts were darker colours than Sam's usual cornflower blues and daffodil yellows. The pants were weightless, breathable and he could bend over without fearing an eruption at the seams. The apparel hid his gut and allowed room for his arms to extend fully. Even the shoes were comfortable enough, though it was recommended he only wear them inside and use mink oil and a brush for prolonging the leather. An additional plastic cap could be cobbled on the heel and toe to prevent wear.

Though overbearing and a tad snippy, Gregory had done well. He even allowed Sam to try on some contemporary clothing and gave him an honest opinion. "Too tight. Too baggy. Too short. Too long. Too bright."

It annoyed Sam but he persevered. Until. Until.

The other salesman, Remy read his tag, approached and struck a conversation with Gregory as Sam exited in an outfit similar to what he was wearing. They were talking about Remy's last client who was 'too Euro for his own good'.

Sam exited to see only Remy standing in front of the dressing room with his arms at his hips: "Oh god, you can't be serious, you are *not* able to wear that.... We should burn those pants, ugh, my god, have you no shame?" His accent was not quite British

"A simple no is ... " Sam was cut-off.

"A simple *no* is what you came in wearing, this is a quantum physics no.... This is a figuring out who killed JFK no, this is ... "

Sam blinked. That was all for Remy.

"Where did Remy go?" Gregory asked.

"I don't know, he's gone." Sam smiled.

"If I can make a suggestion … "

"Yeah, yeah, I know, I'm not getting this." Sam waved his hand.

Sam tried on a few more casual sets of shirts and pants; shorts and light jackets; whatever he was offered. Gregory rang up everything. He removed ink-dye security tags and wrapped the clothes in tissue paper. Sam paid the majority with folding and the rest on credit.

"That's an awful lot of cash you were carrying," Gregory said as he counted out the notes. "Give me a moment to check the authenticity."

Sam waited. Gregory ran a pen over the bills and then shined an ultra-violet light over the mark he made.

"All good." Gregory sniffed with surprise.

"Why wouldn't they be?" Sam asked as he was given the first of two bloated bags.

"Well, if I may," Sam knew that he would without clearance, "when you came in here, wearing those clothes … I mean a turquoise shirt? It's not the nineties and I don't think you run a dive club at the end of the beach. Anyways, I could see your skin through the shirt buttons and your pants look … well, they look uncomfortably tight."

"Like I said, I have gained a few pounds…."

"Not since your ensemble would have been in style, ha-ha."

Sam was silent.

"I was like 'whoa, I have to entertain this bum until I price him out, I am going to lose commission….' But I was pleasantly surprised. You people normally just come here to take a few pictures with the mannequins or try on the shoes, pose for a gangster picture and …"

Sam blinked and thought, *Looks like the commission is still up for grabs you prick.*

He hummed a song against the grain of the light pop: "*There are plenty of ways that you can hurt a man and bring him to the ground….*"

PART 4

"IT'S BOUND TO rain soon." Kay stared at the sky as she and Sam locked their bikes together on the boardwalk and took off their shoes to walk in the sand. "It's way too early for this kind of weather and when it does rain … well, I don't mind staying indoors for a while." She grabbed his arm.

"Me neither." He smiled and lightly stroked her hand. "So your friends are meeting us here?"

"A couple, but the rest we will meet at a bar. Nothing crazy, just a few drinks."

Sam was introduced to some of Kay's friends who were lounging on the beach. They were friendly. They asked Sam dozens of questions about work as if they had never done a day in their life. But, more specifically how one deals with a formal, office-type setting. Is it boring? Is it stuffy? Does it make him want to kill himself? Does he feel like a sell-out? What kind of vacation and benefits packages are included?

Kay even had a transgendered friend named Mitch.

Sam asked how Mitch preferred to be called and they responded quite eloquently, "Mitch is the best. Beyond that I don't even know. I'm kind of in the air, so if someone calls me 'he' or 'she' technically they're both right.

Why am I going to put others through the same insanity I have felt all my life? Just ... you know ... don't be a dick."

"Do you like boys or girls?" Sam asked bashfully with the naivete of a four-year-old.

"I dunno, I like everything. Like the animals that eat plants and other animals. I like nice people. Down people, you know?"

Mitch was perfectly androgynous with a handsome yet comely face with compelling features. Deep, large dark eyes. Full, pouty lips and apparent cheekbones that had neither a liar's height nor a sluggard's lowness. The makeup made their face appear as one radiant gestalt that contoured and blended triangularly to their Greek nose. Mitch's hair was a short, not quite pixie, a bowl with bangs and faded in the back. Their loose shirt and baggy shorts made the gender even more impossible to assume, but Sam found himself, by the end of the night, with no further care to conceive questions or categorize.

There was a sickly-white couple who shared a towel and bag of salt and vinegar potato chips. It was the first pair of redheads that Sam had ever seen in close quarters who were not related. They were quiet, kept mostly to themselves and applied sunscreen every quarter of the hour.

There was another couple which contrasted the pale ones in every way. They greased each other with oil and could not sit still, posing and photographing each other in candidly staged pictures with their mobiles' cameras. It bemused Sam to watch them contrive 'natural' poses, having to hold an air of impromptu insouciance while the other rolled around snapping flicks. "Right there, right there!" could be heard as they frolicked on the beach and in the waters, sat on nearby rocks, sipped icy beverages and held, or did, basically, anything, whatsoever. Priorities.

There was a lad who Sam had an immediate distaste for. A very cool, slender, tattooed dread who went by Savoy. Even Sam thought the man, who seemed too young for his weathered tattoos, was a complete dreamboat. He had an endearing smile, adorable dimples and inclusive disposition. One of those people who touched you when he spoke and his touch seemed like Teresa of Calcutta's deified fingers to a leper. He strummed a guitar, shot-gunned beer the quickest, did Capoeira acrobatics on the sand to applause from his circle and strangers, and he gave all the girls intricately woven French braids while rolling perfect joints of his own hefty stash. Sam reckoned he could throw a Frisbee to Hawaii and had a vine you could swing on. The more genial and simpatico he was towards Sam, the more Sam resented it. When he welcomed his 'old friend' Kay on to his lap to teach her guitar, guiding his hands around hers, pressing her fingers on the frets, draping his dreadlocks over her and cheering her progress, Sam buried his toes in the sand until they wiggled in cool dirt.

"Sam," Savoy spoke as he massaged Kay's sand-clung feet, "you just got a promotion? That's rad!" Kay fluttered a moan from the pressure of his thumbs on her heel.

Sam shook his head from the distraction. "Yeah, well, more than likely. I have a meeting on Monday...." Kay moaned again, grabbing the beach towel like silk bed sheets.

"That's far out, man!" Savoy said without noticing Kay's groans, his thumbs moved like he was hand-counting cash Singaporean style. "You said you had been there for six years? That's crazy, I've never had a job for more than a couple of months." He swooped the dreadlocks from his face. "Wanderlust, know what I mean?"

"No." Sam blanked, acknowledging to himself that the Rastafarian hair on a white guy might be the grandest contributor for a hate Sam did not wish to feel.

"Ha-ha." Savoy laughed, it was beautiful. "Yeah, I moved out of my folks' place at eighteen and just took a duffle. Went around the continent and worked here and there, for some scratch to survive. Flew to Australia and traveled the South Pacific and Asia, did some work there. Spent a lot of time in Essaouira in Morocco, like Bob and Jimi. I get a tattoo from everywhere I've been in the traditional style. Bamboo, stick and poke, some scarification in Polynesia."

Kay tilted on to her side with her elbow on the sand and head in her hand, facing away from Sam and beamed towards Savoy disciple-like.

"I tried the school thing, that's where I met Kayoko, here," Savoy said with Japanese pronunciation. "But that was the route of our elders. Sometimes you have to surf your own path, bro."

"What do you do for money?" Sam asked.

Savoy tilted his head back. "Ha-ha, I get by. My old man is a corporate lawyer and sets a bit aside for me. I have no shame in saying that. My folks agree with my outlook, be a slave to the oceans and the skies instead of a boardroom with a shirt and tie. Blessed!" The group cooed like chicklets awaiting regurgitated tree ants.

"Other than that I've had some modeling gigs, some of my art has sold. I volunteer a lot or just work to live. I picked beans in Cuba, fielded coffee in Ethiopia and stayed with the mayor of a small town in Uruguay while we rebuilt their city. Anything to *really* know and understand the culture."

"Cool." Sam did not even wait for the group's chorus of palm-leaf fanning and ovarian trills to subside.

"Sav's art is so inspiring...." Kay began dreamily.

"I'll be right back," Sam said as he lifted himself to his feet and dusted the sand from his shorts.

He stood and marched straight to the bunker-styled toilets a few hundred meters away. He lit a cigarette, which had been evil-eyed on the beach by the surrounding crowd. Somehow, the illegal marijuana smoking and fineable open containers of booze were permissible and ubiquitous, but his legal, white-filtered hand-busier was grounds for melodramatic coughing and snide whispers. Sam was already the only guy still wearing a t-shirt and still dry from his light brown feet to his dark black head, so the attention was less than welcome.

"Hey!" Kay ran to catch him, her whole body dripping with water. "Sav threw me in the water and my smokes got wet, can I have a puff?"

Her dark hair dripped and clung to her chest and the makeup around her eyes blotted boldly. Her bikini top shifted down slightly and Sam remarked on the tan-line already formed halfway on the slope of her breasts.

"Yeah," she giggled, "my tits popped out." She wrestled her hand in the brazier and readjusted her top.

"Like, out-out?"

"Yeah, it isn't like Savoy hasn't seen my nipples before."

Sam's face pinched. "W-what?"

"Oh yeah, I never mentioned?" She passed the cigarette back, wet and bent. "We dated on again off again for a while." Before Sam could interject, she said, "He is too loose, too much of a journeyer.... It would never have worked and never would work. Just a really nice guy. One of my best friends. Who says you can't be friends with your exes? Maybe you and yours will bury the hatchet one day."

Sam chewed his thumbnail. "Doubt it."

The group moved from the beach to a dive-bar that sold three-dollar cans of piss-yellow lager and three-for-one shots of Irish whiskey. The kind of whiskey that had an added sweetness to mask its over-proofed and under-aged distillation. The bar that had a scarred pool table with a dip in the middle, pinball machines that got humped like make-up sex on the kitchen table, black lights that brought out the psychedelic neon colours on concert posters, red-baskets with red gingham checkered fry-wrappers stuffed with cheap-fried mozzarella sticks and chicken wings, bartenders with long beards and hair and face-piercings and black black-metal t-shirts with names like Stig and Gorb, and of course a few suits that stumbled into lure girls half their age with the mind that a twenty-spot buys them a guiltless and gullible young piece of ass for a night.

Sam drank his metallic beer and nibbled on grease-infused French fries, shaking the oil of each individually scorched fry with a wiggle the way a wet dog sprays water from wagging its tail. The nuked and fried food carried a taste and smell not dissimilar to the sebum of the damp, matted fur of a rain-soaked dog. He did his best to push away the shots. The strain on his nerves from being the outside man was already plenty. Plus, watching Savoy dance and cradle and laugh with Kay, he knew that injections of high percentage whiskey seemed a bad idea.

To his credit, Sam made quick work of the two suits with their loafers on the raised wood beneath the bar-top as if they were captains of the ship. They needed no telescope to ogle the young, dancing girls. Any young woman who approached the bar for a refreshment felt their grappling hooks dig into her shoulders and aggressively request for boarding. The drunker the girls were, the more difficult their allies found it to cut free the Hermione from the smarmy salarymen. The jocular braggadocio was enough for Sam who twice saw them point and curl their fingers at Kay, once when he and she were in full-embrace.

A song full of power chords that Sam enjoyed in his teen years came on. It was perhaps one of the first rock songs the younger friends were ever exposed to as children to which made him feel old but not venerated. It caused everyone to flood the dance floor. Sam noticed the men trying to pull at the hips of girls into theirs like tendrils, and …

It was easy for Sam. In all the commotion, somehow, no one seemed to notice their disappearance. Though he did think for a moment that it could have been him and Andy, drunk and playful, but it was not. Simple. Easy. Sam's stomach tightened when one of the bartenders came onto the floor visibly searching for the men who had racked up a hundred-dollar tab, a sizeable investment in a cheap shithole. He hunted like conquistadors for their El Dorado, apprehensive of returning to their king with pockets turned out and having to foot the bill. As soon as the server returned to his post, Sam relaxed. The bar was probably used to patrons drinking and ditching.

Sam congratulated himself with accepting a shot from Kay, who took the ounce of whiskey into her mouth and transferred it to Sam with a kiss. He did not love it, but he did glance at Savoy with a mischievous glare.

"Ha-ha, rock on Sam!" He swept his dreads behind his back and pumped his fist. "I knew you could party!" He grabbed a shot. "Do one with me?"

Any mischief was washed away, Sam shook his head quickly and stepped back. Savoy took the shot and looked at Sam friskily with his dark eyes, his cheeks teeming like a can with botulism. Sam forced a timorous laugh. Kay grabbed him by the back of the head and allowed the liquor to drain into her mouth, without their lips pressing. They both laughed raucously and wiped their mouths which trickled with streams of sweet whiskey.

"We used to do that with whole joints." She laughed and squeezed Sam. He felt the sticky residue on his check after she pecked him.

"Still got it," Savoy said, pulling his thicket of dreadlocked hair over his right shoulder.

"I need a smoke," Sam started. "Wanna come with?" he asked Kay.

"Umm," her ears visibly raised as a song came on, "not yet, I love this song! It's so old school!"

Another song from Sam's middle-school days. He did not know it was old school. He already had the cigarette twisted into his bloodless lips before he stepped out the door.

Around the right side of the bar's front doors was an alleyway. Sam turned just around the corner and leaned back against the black film patina of a brick wall with his knee raised and foot resting on the squidgy surface. Down the alley some junkies were heating spoons and fiddling through the windfall of purses and backpacks and the fruits of their bin-diving efforts.

He's a nice guy, Sam thought. He clearly meant a lot to Kay. Sam knew they dated. Sure they banged. But it was over now. Sam tried not to think that Savoy probably had a dick for days that could probably swallow a mouse. That's probably why he was so cool. He was cool. He was a cool son of a bitch. He'd been all over, done lots, volunteered, played music, did backflips, danced, and was a caring and a good conversationalist. So why did Sam hate him. *All those things,* Sam thought. But why did Sam hate him so much?"

Sam was carried away from reality by his self-referential questioning. He nibbled his thumb and smoked his cigarette slowly. He kept the puffs buttoned in his chest for long bouts and breathed them out funereally.

"I don't want to, I can control it, I don't … " He pressed his eyes and sighed. He could beat this, he could fight it, he could …

"Hey! Sam! Got a ciggy?' Savoy floated from around the corner and …

Sam did not even have the chance to react. He blinked and Savoy was gone.

He felt bad. But not that bad. Not bad in the way he prematurely ended the existence of a gorgeous specimen of well-liked and good-natured architecture. He felt like a child with austerely religious parents who is addicted to his own body. So much is the shame that he hides the Playboy in plain sight. The tissues are hilled dejectedly in an easily-seen mound outside the little plastic dustbin in his room. He already has his bottoms down and hands out in front of him ready for a cuffing. But just as he hears the hollow thud of footsteps winding up the staircase, he hides the magazine, kicks the pile of soiled papyrus and hitches his trousers. 'What's wrong, my boy? Why are you sweating?' The father of the boy, a preacher, hardens his wiry and unkempt grey eyebrows. And he will reply, 'Nothing, Papa. I have done nothing to displease you or Mother or the Holy Ghost that sees all and says aught'.

Sam rejoined the group. He was quiet, but there was nothing strange when held to the light of his actions daylong. The whereabouts of Savoy was not asked until nearly an hour later.

"He always runs off," the sickly-white boy with red hair said as if he had a cold.

"Yeah, he could very well be on a freighter to Taiwan by now," the red haired girl contributed.

"Sam did you see Savoy?" Kay asked in earnest, without a tremor of apprehension.

Dead-faced, dead-eyed with the dry throat of a dead-man, Sam responded: "Nope."

"Hmm, weird." Kay grabbed his jacket from a hook under the bar. "He somehow never loses this! He has had it since we dated. I'll bring it." She grabbed the denim coat with tears and patches, smears of dark colours either paint or motor-oil, frays at the sleeve and the bottom hem, and a few anti-establishment buttons, scuffed and scratched from wear.

"C-Can you call him?" Sam feigned concern.

"Ha-ha, no … The guy doesn't keep a cell and refuses to plug in a landline. He says that if he wants to be found, people can find him. If he doesn't then they won't." There was a dreaminess in Kay's upwards-to-the-right eye movement. "Well, I'll hold on to it until I see him." She threw it on and inched towards Sam's ear on her toes. "Fuck?"

Kay's nonchalance about Savoy morphed into her dragging Sam to his door the next morning to check if he was home. One of his seven room-mates, shirtless with a bedraggled mop, mentioned that he had no idea if he had returned or not, that he had a hangover that could kill, and that they could come in and knock on his door if they please.

Kay had been there before. Past the living room where bodies lay on couches, recliners and other bodies on the badly damaged shag carpet, was a hallway with four doors. Kay motioned to the last door on the right, placed her finger on her mouth and opened the door slowly. She flung herself on the visible lump of raised Afghan and shrieked.

"Who are you?" she asked.

"I'm Ashleigh," replied a man's voice.

"I'm Ashley." A girl's followed.

"Aww cute." Kay straightened herself. "Sorry to interrupt, but isn't this Sav's room?"

"Yeah, yeah, totally it is," Ashleigh responded. "But he didn't come home. Probably shacked up with someone and stayed at his or her house."

"Makes sense." Kay nodded and rose to her feet. "Okay … Ashley, Ashleigh … I have to ask, is it weird?"

"Well it's our first time … well last night was… but not as much as you'd think," Ashley responded as they both tittered.

"It *did* feel a little boastful," Ashleigh said as they continued kissing. "I kept wanting to say 'jinx, you owe me a coke.'" They both laughed, then sighed, then moaned.

Sam was already backed out of the doorway, taking in the musty odor of stale booze and tobacco, sweat-caked walls and some kind of organic rancidity. "You gonna leave the coat?" he asked Kay, who had the jacket folded over her arm and a raised thumb to the couple of same-named lovers as she backed out closing the door.

"Nah. I'll play a prank on him, make him think he lost it and surprise him by wearing it." She put it on. "What do you think?"

Sam thought that she had probably already worn it many times, but he bit his tongue and muttered, "Good" and "Okay, then," before heading to the front door.

Sam and Kay walked around the eastern part of the city. Away from the ocean and the adjacent downtown core, but the centre-point of watered-down subculture whose historically cheap real estate and blue-collar grittiness had been diluted by the gentrifying force of upper-middle class men and women requiring bungalows and heritage homes to raise their 1.25 offspring. Gen-X gaining access to their trust funds. Trading their plaids for white-collars and grunge music for lullabies. Aging hipsters listening to post-punk on their walk to the train to ride to their offices downtown. Farmers markets and baby stores replaced bodegas and corner stores. In pretentious memoriam there was an overpriced diner called Bodega and an haute couture retailer named the Corner Store. Graffiti went from territorial piss-markings to community-funded art commissions. Immigrant *manteros* that sold fake sunglasses and pirated movies on quickly bundled bedsheets were shuffled away by craftsmen with inflexible prices and a permit to operate on the sidewalk.

The couple had ventured to this side of town for the brunch and breakfast spots that catered to all sorts of farm-to-table fetishists and enthusiasts of the quaint. Kay had decided that the baskets of nuked lard and fatty snacks had given her a tiny red pimple on her forehead and wanted something healthier. Sam was easy.

Kay's hunger had left her indecisive. They strode by the same boutique eateries with the same plastic-covered menus at the same host-stands like a record skip. Sam felt impatience brewing, he was hungry as well and his hunger was making him crabby. He fought the crankiness; Kay was well-meaning and endearing by the way she raced and weighed menu versus menu, whittling down her choices, albeit painfully slow.

A man with a puppy made her decision no easier. He had posted himself up near a café that seemed especially popular with women. The patio was replete with mimosas, bloody marys and pellucid, Easter-coloured cocktails which hit as hard as they were soft in hue. Sam did not like the look of the man, though it was impossible not adore his yellow-fuzzed golden retriever pup. Something about the toothy grin on the man's face was unsettling; a rapacious wanting that was partially obscured and enhanced by reflective mirror-lensed aviators. Not being able to locate his eyes added depth to his deviant smirk. He had a queue longer than any restaurant, all women, all fawning over the darling dog.

It may have been the way he smiled crookedly and stared at the cleavage in the women's tops. It may have been the double-entendres that were not clever or hidden, but earned thoughtless smiles owing to the stupefaction of the women's attention on the dog. It may have been that he got them to pose for pictures on his own camera, which in and of itself was creepily methodical. It may have been that he was jotting down numbers to walk the dog, pet the dog at his place, dates in general, and that his invitations were consistently accepted. Alas, Sam's leading objection was the way he held the leash, directly at his crotch like an extension of his genitalia. He jostled the leash when people pet the dog like he was jerking off. A slow, sensual tug. The waitresses from all restaurants came by to fill the dog's water dish, offer little treats and donate their numbers to the man. Who, then, wagged his imaginary cock with tractable gratification.

"He's doing a bit! It's a goddamn ruse!" Sam shook his head at Kay who waited for her third go-around with the pooch. "He has a cute little puppy-dog and knows that all these girls will line-up and do whatever, lose their better mind, to pet this fucker."

"Don't call the dog a fucker!" Kay slapped Sam on the arm, but not hard. "Whatever, who cares? So he has a key and knows how to use it. You don't give props to a plan like that?"

"You're saying this guy," Sam pointed to the man who snapped a picture on his phone, down a girl's blouse when she was not looking, "is a goddamn mastermind?"

Kay scoffed. "You're just mad *you* didn't get an adorable little puppy and parade it for dates. Are you jealous?"

"That's like cheating, though. Like compensating with a roadster or a fancy watch," Sam grumbled, then sighed. "Depends, would you leave me for a guy with a dog?"

Kay appeared to deliberate internally. To what extent the dramatizing of her fingers scratching against her chin were genuine, Sam could only wonder.

"No," she said, "but two puppies … "

Kay got her chance and crouched down to let the puppy's little satin tongue scratch her hand.

"Oh! He likes you, he's glad you came back again," the man said. "That makes two of us, sunshine."

"Dude." Sam folded his arms and looked at the man. The man did not reciprocate.

"Ha-ha, no sweat hombre." The man arched his back and thrust his hips, leash in hand. "I think he likes you more than the others. Mac's his name. Little Mackie. He's so popular." He looked smugly at Sam. "You want to pet him."

"No." Sam did not move an inch.

"He's so soft and his little muscles are so tight and tender," Kay baby-voiced. "I can't stop petting him and his little tummy."

The man moaned agreeably without moving his lips. "Tight and tender, I love that."

"You know … he's always looking for mommies and walkies," the man said in a voice too gentle to be trustworthy. "My name is Theo. I can take your number … Miss?"

"Name's Kayoko," she said and made a peace sign.

He made and throaty sound of approval. "What a lovely name. Well, Kayoko, I can shoot you a line if you want to … "

"Florin. Table for two!" a voice shot out.

"Let's go!" Sam grabbed Kay by the arm and swung her into the restaurant.

"He wasn't hitting on me, he seemed like he genuinely wanted me to be a dog-walker! What human alive doesn't want to walk a cute, little, living stuffed animal on the beach or at a park?"

Sam eyed the man, now in the park across the small one-way street. The dog was tethered around a bench and the man sat with a couple women in a semi-circle, moving into massage one girl's shoulders. "You're being naïve." He tasted his coffee.

"You're being jealous." Kay sipped her daiquiri. "Is that the real you? A jealous guy? I've dealt with jealous guys and let me tell you, they are no fun."

"I … " Sam sighed. "I'm not jealous. Or maybe I am. Maybe I had a girlfriend for almost half your life and maybe she had actual boyfriends, vacations, family dinners and holidays with men, right under my nose. Maybe I'm a little sensitive, still … The wound would still steam if it was winter. I just … "

"I'm sorry, I'm sorry … I was being a kind of a cock-tease in front of you now that I think about it." She slid off her shoe and ran it up his thigh. "I just … I love dogs! There. A dog wouldn't cheat on you. A dog wouldn't hump your best friend while you fell asleep eating pizza and watching a Tarantino movie on the couch. A dog wouldn't abandon all technology and grow dreads and move to Las Canarias and bring you back the clap from Ibiza and … "

Sam chewed his thumbs as he rested his elbow on the table.

"Yup," she said abruptly, "point taken."

He removed his thumb and grabbed her hand. Kay kissed his on the back and laced her fingers between his. She assured him that the chlamydia was long since out of her system. He stared out the window as the man was folding a piece of paper into his pocket, alone for a moment.

Sam blinked. The puppy yelped. A few people stopped to pet the puppy in consolation, others kept along on the sidewalk.

Sam paid with his card and Kay tipped with cash. They exited the restaurant and wandered into the park. Kay asked if she could pet the dog one more time.

"Honestly, you don't need to ask any permission." Sam kissed her forehead. "You want to pet a dog, pet the dog. You want to drink four daiquiris, you can do that too."

She hiccupped and was nearly struck by a car as she sprinted through the one-way leaving Sam on the other side grinning. She sat cross-legged and stroked the pup's head, its ears separated and snapped back upright with each stroke. It was dear.

"Where's uh … Theo, Mac?" she asked the dog with a light babble. "Seriously!" she turned to the arriving Sam. "Where the hell is this dude? You can't leave dogs, let alone baby dogs, by themselves!"

They waited. And waited. For three hours they played parents to the affectionate and loveable tyke. They falsified backstories and entertained others who wished to pet the dog.

"This is my husband Sancho and I'm Sakura, this is our mixed-race son Guillermo. He's half Fijian and half Dutch."

"We are agents that stole him from an evil scientist who wanted take over the world with a cuteness ray that used puppies to fuel its particle beam, we got there in the nick of time."

"This is my dead uncle reincarnated as a dog and only *we* can hear what he says, like that movie with Danny Zuko and the voice of John Maclean."

When evening began to creep in, an actual concern replaced the levity of the webs that they had spun that afternoon.

"Sam, really though … Where is this prick? The dog would've had no water or food? What do we do? Call the SPCA? Call the number on the tag?"

She called the number on the dog-tag, no answer.

"Do we … take it to the pound? Do we … "

"I've got a pretty good idea what we can do." Sam smiled.

And that is how Sam got himself a dog.

Kay's shared accommodation set-up allowed for piles of dirty dishes and take-away boxes, random houseguests sawing logs on the couches, sporadic chore and utility-bill bickering, but no quadrupeds. Since her first date with Sam, however, she spent less and less time at the cluster of private rooms that always seemed to roof double the intended occupancy. Sam and Kay leashed the pup and brought it back to Sam's apartment. She repeatedly tried to contact the owner, but to Sam's clandestine lack of surprise, the dial tone was only abbreviated by voicemail. "You've reached Theo and 'ruff, ruff' Mac, good boy. If you want us, leave us your name and number and bra-size, ha-ha. Just kidding."

The more Kay heard the message, the less she thought about giving the dog back and the more she concocted reasons why the owner was probably using the dog for personal gain. Sam helped by hinting that he left it on purpose. It was easy for them to become attached to the little furry companion, immediately so for Kay who hurt almost physically to have a pet-dog and one that was so reminiscent of her childhood sidekick named Rufus.

Sam appreciated the little fellow more after his first shift back to the office. He was pulled from his desk and interrogated with an inquisition of Catholic proportion. A team of suits investigated the disappearance of Chen and Michelle, levelling Sam and the entire office with a barrage of questions to turn the stones. The senior Chen, Howard, made an ultra-rare appearance in the office to conduct an excavation to turn the earth around those same stones with thinly papered intimidation tactics, swearing to discover the truth.

In Sam's haste and lack of knowledge about Michelle and Chen, his provisional and desperate email contained holes that were considered cryptic and out-of-character.

It was brought to Sam's attention that Harry had never used the name 'Harold'. 'Weighing anchor' is the preferred term to 'raising anchor' and that was something an avid yachtsman like Harry would not mistake. He left out his father completely, who was as close of a confidante as any friend, even his best friend Edwin Chan. As for Michelle, she had withdrawn a considerable sum to lay as deposit on the wedding venue, for which she was going to leave work early.

"I don't know," Sam shrugged during the interviews, "maybe they planned it for a while? I didn't speak to them about personal lives, ever." When asked in surprised tones why Chen favoured Sam for the role, even after being shown the graph and other disparaging but critically honest memos and notes about Sam and his work, he responded with the same remote demeanour: "I guess he saw that I was unmotivated in my current role but that I had a fire in my eye when we spoke about rising up the ladder. Maybe he actually liked me or at least respected me."

The group and Chen, Sr. seemed unimpressed. Sam attributed their skepticism to wine-leg tremors of a bombshell that had exploded only days prior. A smoke like Glaswegian fog and a knelling which bit the inside of the ears and left the cochlea unfurled was still felt like yesterday.

Andy picked Sam up after work on Monday and the friends grabbed some beers as they made their way to the jetty. The boat-launch they used was farther from the main beach area where the trees were not sacrificed for melanoma-seekers and where the cops turned an even blinder eye to shenanigans. Unofficially it was the area where topless bathers and their complimentary perverts dwelled unperturbed.

"Isn't this nice?" Andy smiled, leaned into the stern, his fingers delicately brushed the top of the ocean. "Just a couple of pals, enjoying a few cold enchantés on the open…. Hey! Ladies!"

Andy brought his hand with a splash and waved to a couple of women wading deeper into the waters. The girls snickered and appeared to say something to each other, then paddled towards the lads.

"Andy, I was hoping to use this time to tell you some stuff, I have a lot on my mind and some things I need to … "

"Nice … They look like nice ladies." Andy ignored Sam and stood up on the boat while continuing to signal the mermaids to the gunwale.

"Hey, how are you guys doing?" One of the girls pulled her elbows up on the side of the boat, the other slowed her strokes and idled up beside her friend, curling her fingers around the edge of the boat and panting heavily with just her eyes visible.

"We're good," Andy crouched, "just enjoying this beautiful spring day."

"It's so cold in here," the second girl chattered smilingly, "have room for two more?"

Andy curved his neck back and shrugged his brows up and down, smiling at Sam. "Of course, the more the merrier. Very enchanté." He turned back to offer his hand to the girls. Sam did not move.

Sam screwed his face and shook his head. Andy wrapped both towels on board around the girls and kissed both of their cheeks. "This is called a *bise*! It's very French … Enchanté my belles.…"

"Ooh! French!" one of the girls noted.

"Why is your friend wearing a shirt?" The other moved her attention towards the benched Sam, wearing a button-up faded-denim shirt, sitting with his beer in between his knees, knocked inwards.

"He … He thinks he's fat," Andy said, "I know he's not, he's a babe, right? But he … "

"Aw, he's not fat," the second one said.

Sam nodded and churlishly slurped his beer, purposely making noise. "I'm not fat or skinny, I am perfectly unimportant, average and not at all special or significant."

The second girl laughed and bit her nail. The first was already sitting beside Andy, under his arm, being fed a sip of his beer.

Sam was entirely unamused by the proceedings and that he couldn't excuse himself. He did not listen to the conversations and made it a point to contribute as little as possible to the dialogue around him. Andy tried to sting Sam with contemptuous glares, but Sam ignored his sun-bespectacled friend and stared off into the distance with petulance, wetting his arm and watching it dry. He responded to the second girl only when she made it clear the question was designed for him alone, he never bothered to ask or remember her name.

The sun had dropped from the sky quickly like its string was cut from above. The sub-amateur boys were knee-deep in the water trying to figure out the best way to fix the boat back on to the trailer. The girls collected their bags they had hidden beneath a rock and dusted them off, removing their sundresses and jean-shorts and sliding them over their bathing suits. Andy's light-hearted frolicking mirrored Sam's impertinence. Sam felt the day had been wasted opportunity and now only wanted to solve the Rubik's trailer conundrum and head home.

The rest of the group had been playing with the possibility of heading for a night-cap at a nearby lounge. Andy was sitting in an SUV with his leg dangling out of the open door conversing with the girls while Sam remained in the water waiting to moor the boat.

"Let's go already!" Sam shouted without any jollity to blunt the edges.

Andy appeared to say something and fired up the engine. He slowly backed the trailer into the launch and put the parking brake on, climbing out to help Sam fasten the skiff. The door's sensor-alarm dinged with its metronomic apathy, reciting its obligatory lines like a public-school's compulsory choir.

"I've gotta go home." Sam pulled Andy aside.

"Dude! Why? We've got these chicks lined up and ready for the coup de grace. Just one drink, that's all."

"I don't want to! I've got Kay at my house with the puppy and I don't want to … "

"Wait … the girl? Is she living at your place? You got a dog? Who are you?"

"Yeah, like I said I've got a lot to tell you, but you, you pussy-hound, don't have time for your best friend!" Sam's voice rose enough for the girls to hear the 'pussy-hound' part and appeared to stiffen.

"Ladies," Andy extended his arms, "Sam doesn't mean that, he's just tired from his puppy duties."

"Aww," they both sang. "You have a little puppy? What kind? Is it cute? I bet it's adorable! What's its name? Does it look cute when it sneezes?" the girls shot rapidly.

Sam responded languidly to the girls, "Mac. It's a boy-dog. Golden retriever. Super cute. My girlfriend is going to need some rest, she took the day off to watch it."

Andy looked at Sam sideways.

The boys wrestled with the ropes and pulleys. The jettison was simple. Each go-around to latch the vessel left them with either too much or too little cord to safely snug the boat to the metal frame.

"We understand," the first girl said. "Take our numbers and we'll do it later."

Andy raced splashily to the shore and collected the first girl's number. The second waved and yelled goodbye to Sam. He flicked his wrist and fiddled with the marine rope.

The beach was dark, empty and quiet by the time the men rigged the boat to the trailer. They had not spoken after Andy returned. They had not spoken after they had toweled off. Silence continued as they tested the strength of their lines and piled into the vehicle.

The silence was strange, especially for Sam who was used to Andy's hummingbird incessancy of nonsense and bravura.

"You mad?" he asked Andy.

"I just … " he started, wiping the water and sweat from his face with his t-shirt. "Don't you think you're moving too fast? Your whole life has basically done a 180 in three seconds. Do you think you are, no … You *are* going way to fast, man! You have never been a risk-taker."

"Well, if I had a friend who was willing to listen and talk, just the two of us, then maybe I wouldn't mash the gas pedal so hard. But … To be honest … I feel happy. I told you that. I might even talk my way into the promotion and things are looking up. I can't ever remember a time when things were coming up."

"They might seem to be, but, nothing sounds like it's written in ink yet. You are in the early part of knowing your lady, and I'm sure she is a nice lady, but … You got a dog? Are you nuts? Is it both of yours?"

"We found … well rescued it."

"Who are you—Batman? Spiderman? You know they have places that take runaways and found animals, right? Just because you have taken care of yourself for a big, whole week doesn't mean you can handle a pet."

"I don't know what you're bellying over, you should be happy! Supportive! Are you jealous?"

"Me? Jealous? Of you? Are you out of your fucking mind? I love my life and up until a week ago, you hated yours. I was gearing up to talk you out of suicide, I hate to admit that, but it's true."

"I didn't hate it…. I mean … I wouldn't … "

"Bull fucking shit! Every week it was depression, depression,

depression. You know I have expected to untie you from a noose in your own goddamn apartment? Chloe would've left you to collect flies just to keep them away from her produce. You're delusional. You really might have bi-polar or something, and this is just the upswing. And this new girl … "

"You can't judge Kay until you meet her! She is perfect and makes me feel like a new man."

A thoughtful silence.

"And so this girl has made you become a different person, hmm? It's all her?"

"Well, yes and no … "

"What?"

"I have a new perspective, a new set of eyes.… I'm not going to be a push over anymore. I want to be a better guy and I ain't about to take shit from nobody anymore. I feel tougher, I feel like I can say what I want and do what I want. I feel stronger. I feel like anybody that stands in my way will get erased."

"Jesus, okay … You goddamn psychopath," Andy scoffed. "What happened to you, huh? You kill a man when I left you that night at Mahoney's?"

"I killed the old me, that's all."

The boys were quiet as the SUV rolled from the long gravel road to the smooth pavement. After a period where the only sound was the crunchy squeak of fidgeting on leather upholstery and the low murmur of the air conditioning, Sam spoke. "New car?"

"Nah, mom's ride, needed the hitch."

"Cool. Cool." Sam clicked his teeth.

"Hey, sorry for being a shitty pal."

"Sorry for going a little nuts. I … I wish I could tell you more, but I am learning to recognize and deal with anger."

"Yeah, you've never been good at that.… You used to and then … It was like either nothing or everything got to you. You kind of became a doormat who hated being walked on, but it was like it was your job."

"I'm trying, I'm trying."

"Proud of you, boy … You know I love you."

"Love you too, Andy." Sam tapped the window. "You should meet Kay though … she is awesome.

"I bet, I bet … I will, I will," Andy said while concentrating on something, possibly the wide-angled turn that led off the highway.

Sam arrived home and found Kay sleepily swaddling her arms around Mac with both their knees tucked-up on the couch. He slowly, quietly, took off his jacket and drank the scenery indulgently. So innocent and heartening, he thought, the way they mingled together like a fox and its cub, soft and beautiful, the feeling of longing and attainment at once. An immortal smile heated Sam internally until the warmth traveled outwards and curled the corners of his mouth, creasing his brow. He sniffled. One of Kay's eyes slowly peeled back while her lips stretched with satisfaction. Sam joined them on the couch and felt a purr verve from the dog's youthful, fishbone-thin ribs. It sneezed and buried its head in between the couple. They suppressed their laughing to damp the noise as a god might, when its dimples are communicated through the soft morning dew, glistening with a rainbow hued tincture beneath a drowsy and mellow night-breaking glow.

Sam carried both Kay and Mac to the bedroom, he pulled back the covers and joined them in the dark warmth of the bed and shut his eyes with a sedation of spiritual completeness.

He awoke in a feverish sweat from a feverish dream; the serene plenitude that was his lullaby seemed to be misplaced, in a location that leaked no sound. A grimness was transplanted within him like an accursed kidney, perhaps from a death row donor, which brought a presage with its compatibility. Even when he peered over at the angels beside him, swallowed by sleep and each other, there was no consolation, only an inauspicious stir that forced him to the bathroom.

He splashed water on his face in the unlit room, swamping through the still-vivid segments of his nightmare.

Sam remembered coming to in the centre of the city, perhaps his city, perhaps an amalgam of urban parody, such is the case with dreams. He had a leash in one hand, a cup of coffee in the other. The objects beheld within them neither canine nor cuppa. By some enigmatic nudge, he began whistling for a dog and shouting for coffee. He began booming with purpose and surety. His voice bounced between the buildings in a hollow echo that was unfiltered by the usually shambolic soundtrack of the city. There was no traffic, no cranes or jackhammers, no pigeons or crows or seagulls, no wind rustling the trees, no airplanes overhead, no hawkers, no people. The atmosphere was static and desolate; a city with the vivacity of a tundra or prairie or steppe. Visually, everything appeared normal, there were no signs of war and destruction; no plagues or signs of infection; no bodies, that is, nobody. Only a creeping anxiety that comes from being alone, a fear of why he was. Panic crept, hurrying from corner to corner, still he waited for the little man to permit his passage, shouting for coffee and dog until his voice cracked and his sinuses burned. Finally, he could hear something, his ears discerned a faint clamour, he focused on following the sound, guided by the indistinct. There is little beyond a feeling or predesignated instinct in a dream, like a ride where the cart is bolted to a track, but the mind of the rider is still active.

He jogged. He sprinted. He zig-zagged over the road and sidewalk, through bushes and gardens. He came upon a thick tubular railing that overlooked a large flat concrete terrain. A port with a cargo dock replete with gantry cranes and shipping containers. He braced himself on the railing and stared down at thousands of people and perhaps many more, angry and confused and rattled to a man, being huddled like livestock into the giant rectangular containers. The containers were closed and lifted by crane on to a massive tanker; there were already dozens or so of the containers stacked on the deck of the ship. The vessel seemed to stretch as far as the naked eye could see, appearing to taper and break apart, but not end. The longshoremen were dressed druidic in all black cloaks. They were tall and boney and moved the levers slowly and methodically, not responding to the fulminating herds of citizens they steered and latched into the containers with their faces buried featurelessly within the hoods of their robes. The crane operators were thickset creatures in sheep's blood cloaks, their faces also obscured, their movements smooth and mechanical. Sam stared into the mob. He focused on little pockets and saw people who he had disappeared; he saw Chen, Michelle, Linda, Chloe, Chandra, and the gardener, their faces. He screamed their names, but they did not turn. He saw Andy with pallor that extended from his face to his spirit, shuffling his feet with his hands in his pockets, appearing lost. He cried his name. Andy did not inch. Sam's heart raced as he scrutinized the crowd around Andy, and he saw them. Kay was holding Mac like a newborn, dressed in a white cassock and shawl that was so white that it dimmed all coloration around it, as if it had absorbed the surrounding pigments. He screamed with lunatic lungs that made his face bruise. He searched along the railing for an entry point but found nothing. He looked again to the tanker, filling every minute with another container, and another, and another after those. A man in a trim a nautical themed suit emerged. Not a commodore's sailor-suit, rather a gentlemen's version: a thick reefer jacket, a submariner turtleneck, a wool Breton-cap, rimless aviator sunglasses, and a visibly well-groomed beard. A black and gold ivory pipe was clenched between his teeth and seeped an endless trail of ductile gunmetal smoke that mingled with the dusty horizon. His hands were behind his back, his face was beaming lordly. Sam squeezed his eyes and the man acknowledged his with a wave, swinging one hand widely over his head and yelling 'Ahoy'. He took off his glasses and placed them into his breast pocket, then, tapped the pipe against the handrail, slowly, the clinking sound clangored with ear-piercing rhythm. Sam glanced back down to see Kay treading softly, almost floating towards the same container that Andy was now also shuffling towards with a lost, downcast expression. He grabbed the rail. He sized up the height. He pushed and pulled himself on the railing once, twice, three times....

The alarm had been screeching beneath his pillow. Perhaps adding to the head-aching chime of the captain's pipe clapping against the ships' handrail. The battle cry of recommencing the weekday attrition had not stirred Kay or Mac. Sam was left to contemplate the dream over solitude and cold water cupped against his face. He wanted to forget the dream, and at the same time play it from the beginning. Was it a warning? A promise? A dooming assessment of his debauchery? Was it something that a person with a daringly darker sense of humour would appreciate as satire? Absurdity?

Sam had to leave those questions in the bathroom sink. He toweled his face and sought to replace any significance of the dream with thoughts of the upcoming day, work-over the execs, tasks at hand, breakfast and ...

There was a knock at the door.

Sam grabbed a t-shirt and slowly foot-palmed his way to the door. There was an external buzzer that linked to a landline which should have prompted him to ask who was there and, if deemed important, he could proceed to press '6' and allow the person to then enter the building. *Early for the Witnesses or the Mormons,* Sam thought.

He pressed his face against the eye-hole and perceived two suited figures outside the door. One wearing a grey tweed jacket and khakis, the other in a plain black suit of no estimable elegance.

A second set of three knocks startled Sam, he hopped back a step, then unfastened the locks and slowly opened the door.

"H-Hello?" Sam greeted. "I'm not interested in the Church of Latter-Day Saints...."

"Sam Florin?" the tweed jacket-wearing asked.

"Y-Yes."

"I'm detective Perez and this is detective Diggs." Both men held up their credentials. "We were hoping to ask you some questions ... apologies for the early morning visit." Perez did not seem apologetic.

"N-Not a problem d-detective."

"We are investigating the disappearances of three of your co-workers. Michelle Nguyen and Harry Chen had left a note which you have been questioned via internal inquiry already. There is foul play suspected, and when combined with the disappearance of one Linda Hawerchuk, we are routinely questioning certain people who may have had contact with them. There have been a number of disappearances recently in the city, and we are trying to deduce ... "

Diggs tapped Perez on the shoulder with his pen, he looked down into his black police journal and began. "I'll be blunt. We have come to you Mr. Florin because the disappearances, when taken separately show little signs of continuity, but when we pulled back, they have either happened in your neighbourhood or at your office."

Sam did not respond.

"Do you know an Arturo Carrera, Benjamin Sharpe, Carolina Gomes, Blake Kennedy, Dahlia Moncton, Theodore Kapanen, Laura Henley ... "

Sam again did not respond. When he was certain that the detective was no longer reciting names he said, "No, not a single one. Did... do they live in the area?"

"Lived or worked," Perez said curiously. "Have you noticed anything strange going on?"

"Nothing out of the usual."

"Did your coworkers show any signs of erratic or spontaneous, out-of-character behaviour?"

"No sir … business as usual."

"Do you live alone?" Perez asked.

"Yes, well, no … I live with my girlfriend Kay, well, she stays here most nights…. It's still kind of new, I don't want to jinx it. It's going pretty well … and we just got a dog, so … "

"Not a … Chloe Bellinger?" Diggs dug. Perez put his hands from a folded position to his hips.

"No sir … we broke up, she just left with some guy she was cheating on me with…."

"Interesting … " The detectives eyed each other. "How long ago did she leave? What was the name of the man that she left you for? Did you know him?"

"U-uh, his name was Chandra. I met him once, seemed … fine. I guess a week or so ago. We had not been really with each other for a while, we mostly stayed in separate places…. Different places … Other friends' places … I think they were going, uh, camping, or travelling, to the uh, mountains?"

"The mountains. You wouldn't happen to know which ones or where, would you?" Perez took out his own little black journal.

"I don't." Sam shook his head long before and after his words.

"Okay … " The two detectives glanced sideways at each other.

"Look, fellas, I'd love to be able to help, and if there are any questions, or anything that you think that I can do to assist the investigation, please let me know."

"Thanks Florin," Diggs unimpressively stated.

The two detectives waited as Sam bid his farewell and slowly closed the door. He could hear them speaking at low volume and walking slowly towards the staircase. Stopping twice.

Fuck, Sam thought.

"Who was that?" Kay asked, carrying the pup and rubbing the sleep from her eyes.

"Uh … some detectives." Sam coughed and came back with more surprise in his voice. "They are investigating Chen and Michelle, the two people who ran off together at work…."

"Why would they come here?" she asked.

"Routine investigation, I guess," Sam said, unsure if he was lying or something not dissimilar.

Sam left early, he needed a nice quiet walk to work to clear his head. He achieved two steps on to the sidewalk when a stretch limousine pulled up beside him. A tall and lifeless man in a chauffeur costume emerged and glided around to Sam's side, he opened the door and gestured for Sam to enter. Sam recognized not the face, but a depraved twinkle in his eye.

"Hello Sam," Lucy said, sitting comfortably against the right window in a black tailcoat, black bowtie, black top hat and white leather gloves. "Champagne?"

"N-No," Sam said, his stomach still swirling from the detective visit.

"Suit yourself, it's good for calming the butterflies, relaxing the nerves, distilling the humours…."

"I'll still pass…." Sam said.

Sam could hear the driver's door close and the parking grip release. A chunky shift from park to drive set the car down the street to the boulevard.

Lucy sipped from his flute and stared at Sam. Sam returned with momentarily nervous glances, looking beyond the tinted windows at the slowly passing environs.

"You're reaching a stage of critical mass, young man. You will see your resolve mightily tested, I can inform you, and how you choose to … deal with such examinations, of your will and fortitude, will foretell future success." Lucy wet his lips with the fizzing drink.

"I had a … "

"Yes, but dreams are only dreams, they cannot hurt you. The subconscious will only roar with courage when the body is unarmed. You have always numbed the vexing inner-voices with repression that some might define as ignorance, so why beat down the thicket when the road is unwrinkled."

"What about the cops?"

"Yes? What about them? You were correct in assessing their tampering as merely a function of routine. Have you never consumed any crime fiction media? The description of the post demands an inhospitable and domineering attitude. You have little to fear. You have less to worry about."

"I … I feel like I don't really need the power anymore…."

"I beg of your pardon?" Lucy straightened.

"I feel like, well … One or two of the people I, uh, made gone, were useful, but I can … "

"Do not let your hubris, trepidation or ignorance guide you. You are only beginning to harvest."

"I don't want to hurt anyone that I like or love…."

Lucy laughed. "How pitifully human of you. This is why I am so fond of the very fabric that you and your kind are embroidered. There is always a choice. There is no definitive direction that you must traverse. Human beings are more capable of controlling their emotions than they realise."

Sam chewed his thumb.

"Let me ask you Sam." Lucy offered him a cigarette. "Do you feel bad for doing what you did to those people? Does your heart shed tears and your soul mourn for the unimportant lives that you have eliminated? Did their instant removal bring a fit of disconsolate misery to you?"

Sam accepted and lit the cigarette.

"I argue the opposite. I would contend that after the initial shock of their omission, you were relieved. You were slaked by their vanquishing. You were opportunistic and carnivorous. You were audacious and you enjoyed it. The only thing that disturbs you and disrupts your self-assurance is the fear of capture, hitherto unthinkable. To which I should remind you of a remedy that is as effective as a meteor and commensurately devastating."

Sam smoked silently—exhaling the vapours from his nostrils, chewing the skin beneath his thumb.

"My advice," Lucy broke in. "Keep your head down, work hard and give yourself some respite."

"I guess you're right…." Sam said. "Did you shave your beard?"

Lucy smiled, he ran a hand over his face and his full beard re-appeared. He ran it back down and it disappeared entirely. "Little illusion you learn after many years. I have a ball tonight in Moscow that requires a less fatherly and more striking appearance.”

Sam nodded. He was arrested by Lucy's words. “Moscow? Tonight? I'm pretty sure it's nearly time, you won't make it.”

“Then a perfect time for you to disembark and greet your fate with a wink and a smile.” The chauffeur opened the door and let Sam out. They had already arrived at the foot of his office pavilion.

“Take care, young man…. Keep an eye out for yourself.” Lucy grinned as the door was tightly closed. The driver tipped his cap and seemed to smirk without moving his lips. It chilled Sam.

PART 5

MAC'S SIZE AND Sam's career grew defiantly fast; a Polaroid that too-quickly became a sentimental era following a brief period of staggering change. Fuzz turned to silk. Teeth transformed from little razor-pebbles to sturdier, transfixed cuspids. Infantile yelps dropped and deepened to become distinguished barks. On the career-side, Sam was sent to developmental training classes at the Kool-Aid tasting rooms of his company. He found a new courage and intelligence that he had not unearthed since college, and even then were still largely dormant. He was aflush with new information and skills. Expectations were set low and he was not expected to make an immediate impact, to seize the wheel of a ship that was comfortably set on cruise-control.

It was two weeks later that Sam had a moment to step back and look behind him. A dog whose tail had grown to be a mace when near the coffee table and caused the owners to make a stifling noise when he crawled up on their laps, puppylike with adult weight. A job that was somehow not as difficult as he had always assumed it would have been. A girlfriend who was basically a resident, contributing to groceries, cleaning, cooking and harping about the boxes of Chloe's things that had yet to be displaced. A temperament that was too busy to fall victim to the wrath and anger that threatened a coronary artery bypass grafting. A pair of detectives that appeared at random in Sam's office, eyeballing him with distrust, questioning him, building evidence against him.

His 'power' laid somewhat dormant. His days were long, and he was approached with greater respect at work. He avoided the high-trafficked times of the morning and afternoon-to-evening. He was domesticated. Sure, he occasionally erased someone who took liberties in their tones with his girlfriend, trod upon his Italian loafers or spit on the sidewalk, but that was unavoidable. The truth was that Sam was feeling like his old even-tempered, almost buoyant self. He had signed a new lease on life with a girlfriend and pet that were as happy to see him emerge through the front door, as he was to see them on the other side. Though he dragged around a slightly troubled conscience, he had renewed a prevailing sense of hope and happiness.

All the while, Andy had still yet to meet Kay.

He had found a reason to parachute-away just before she arrived or avoided Sam altogether. The previous Monday was even cancelled due to Andy stating that a throat illness had kept him bedridden and matzo ball soup-fed over the weekend. Sam was more annoyed than hurt, but he was almost too busy to be concerned.

One day the detectives happened upon Sam's residence when he was not present. They knew his schedule and knew he would not be at the apartment, but Kay would. They slickly presented their case, stating that the missing people now included Sam's ex and her new flame. When she asked about Savoy, they intimated that he too was a missing person, previously unsuspected, was now tied into the search.

"Sam," Kay's voice trembled as Sam entered the apartment.

"Yes, my dear," Sam responded, petting the tail-wagging Mac that rushed to his feet.

"There were, um, the detectives, um, came … " Kay had difficulty with he words. "Did … did you know that your ex is a missing person? Just like your coworkers? Just like Sav?"

"What?" Sam clutched his breast with amazement. "All of them? What is going in in this kind, little city."

She was across the room and not moving forward. Sam moved into the living space and he saw her shoulders tense towards her ears.

"What on earth did the policemen say to you?"

"They … They didn't say anything definitive, but they hinted that … " She began to tear up.

"Baby, baby … " He moved closer. "They have nothing that is why they're picking on little old me."

"I told them you wouldn't hurt a fly. I told them…."

"And I wouldn't, I have never raised my fist in anger, I have never been a fighter, I have no impulses to hurt a single hair on anyone's head, ever."

"Then why would they … " She fell into his arms.

"I have no idea…." His face contorted thoughtfully, emptily. "Did they look around here?" He moved a within a pace from Kay.

"Yeah, they petted the dog, they just kind of walked around. I offered them coffee, they said no. They dusted some things…. Asked about your ex's boxes … Are they allowed?"

"It doesn't matter because they are banging their heads, I did about as much as you. I'm totally at a loss why they're picking on me." Sam pulled her for a hug.

"It really freaked me out!" She sobbed slightly then moaned agreeably.

He smirked victoriously, not at Kay's disquietude, but that the police had come and gone, yet again, emptyhanded.

The dog came up on two legs and swindled himself into the action, licking their hands. They both smiled.

"Let's get some dinner," Sam said.

Sam and Kay walked hand-in-hand and watched their growing boy sniff at trees and flowers, jump and tumble with other dogs, and part his ears to allow passers-by to feel his silken coat. "He loves the attention," they joked. "His old owner got him used-to it."

They decided on a little Greek taverna with a blue and white Santorini paint-job that indicated the restaurant was traditional enough for finical, authenticity-seeking non-Grecians. All the lettering on the menu and awing were in sharp Greek inspired Roman letters. The dog precluded a dine-in experience, so Kay went inside to order souvlaki, pilaf, moussaka and extra tzatziki for the pita.

Sam was waiting outside, bending over to loosen the collar around

Mac's neck as a familiar voice entered his ear, the mouth within inches from his orifice. "Hey sexy, can I pet your dog?"

Startled, Sam snapped his head up and saw a smiling Andy, standing beside a pretty little thing in a snug skirt. "Andy! You scared the hell out of me! What's happening?" he yelled with giddiness.

He hugged his friend.

"This is Amelia, she's a nice lady, very enchanté." Andy winked.

"I don't think that's an adjective…." Sam thought aloud.

"It's whatever it wants to be," Andy said, already bent petting Mac alongside a squatting and cooing Amelia. "You just out here pumping out the vibes?"

"Nah getting supper," Sam said. "Waiting for some take out."

"Greek, huh?" Andy looked up at the awning. "Lamb?"

"You know it…." Sam gleamed.

"Eight bucks for two little containers of tzatziki?!" Kay rattled the bells on the door, looking at the bill, "It better … " She stopped.

Andy glimpsed up, his blue eyes were struck with a shred of sunlight that sparkled like ocean derma. He slowly rose and buried his blues downward.

Andy went pale and quiet. Kay was red and silent. Amelia giggled to herself while scratching the dog behind the ear. Mac panted idiotically. Sam squinted and moved his head side-to-side, looking at the drastic difference in Andy and Kay's countenance.

Had he been a more intelligent man, perhaps if he was unencumbered by the weight of his ability and their powers of accelerated status, Sam would have anticipated, like most would have or have by this point, why the silence and radically different and equally apparent expressions were bannered upon their faces.

"Andre … " Kay bit through her clenched teeth.

"Hey, uh … " Andy scratched the back of his head.

"Kayoko … Kay … You know my name you son of a bitch." Her jaw muscles protruded.

"It's been a while…." Andy stumbled in a low voice. "You and Sammy, eh … It's nice to … "

Amelia continued to stroke and babble away to Mac with tunnel vision. An epiphanic realization dispatched the knots that wrinkled Sam's forehead, having been twisted from a regrettable lack of foresight.

"I should probably … " Andy said as he grabbed Amelia's arm to wrestle her from her spell.

"Yeah, yeah you probably should … Asshole … " The words somehow absconded between Kay's tersely locked jaw. "Hey, you, broad … " She flicked her head at Amelia. "This guy is a fucking creep, a piece of shit and a womanizing son of a whore.… You better get out now." The girl's face was stunned, unaware of the previous unpleasantness and she was swiftly escorted away by Andy.

Andy nodded with much difficulty, his motor functions appeared to seize as he walked stiff-legged in the other direction.

"Andy? Your friend Andy is *Andre Lambert?*" Kay said with due recognition to the French pronunciation.

"Andy Lambert, yeah … " Andy said in the English standard. "You guys?"

"I don't … " She shuddered and squinted back anger-born tears. "Let's get home."

They walked without the frivolous, dumb leisure they had departed with. It was non-verbal; horizontal and vertical lines to the second-floor apartment where the brown bags were placed on the table, the dog was unleashed and Kay sat at the table, lit a cigarette and crossed her legs.

"So … you know Andy?" Sam asked after much silence.

Kay licked her top lip with the tip of her tongue, she rolled the tip of the cigarette in a makeshift ashtray of a cereal bowl. She took in a big puff and watched the exit of a heavy cloud of breath. She did not look like she would tear up. She looked as though she could murder someone.

"You could say that, yeah." She took a long pull on the cigarette. "Remember when I said I wouldn't go to Esposito's for pizza? It was your … pal, Andy who took me there."

"He takes a lot of girls there, it's … " Sam stopped when she shot him a vicious eye.

"So … Yeah, I meet this pretty boy, blue eyes, nice everything, and figure 'hey, let's go.' The dinner is nice, he ordered and he made the right choices. Great wine, great atmosphere, real romantic but not cheesy. They had this guy who walked around and played an accordion. He played beautifully. The owner treated him, and me, like a big deal, like it was an honour to have us. Real class." She lit another cigarette while the first lay half-burnt, a wisp of cobalt smoke began to corkscrew until their ringlets broke overhead. "And, of course, he's charming and funny and nice. So, I figure, why not? Let's go back to his place."

"So … you guys had sex." Sam felt a sting in some organ. "I can get over that.…"

"Yeah, we fucked.…" she said coarsely. "But he *fucked* me."

"What do you mean?" Sam felt a stabbing pain behind his navel.

"So this fucking asshole, your best friend in the world, tells me he's allergic to latex. Fine, cool, whatever. He says we can't go to his house because it's under renovations. Of course I don't believe him, but I figure that he has a girlfriend, or a wife, or whatever.… That's on his conscience, not mine. I'm drunk, I'm horny, fuck that other bitch, she should've tried harder. Obviously I'm not thinking the clearest, but like I said … I was drunk. A few bottles of red wine and some Limoncello with the dessert kind of gets you in the mood. The pizza was great, too. It really is the best in the city. Such a loss, I'll never want it again."

Sam went from sitting to standing to sitting to standing, his thumbnail firmly planted in his dry mouth.

"We drove to this little secluded area of the beach, way off the main drag, a little dirt road and bumpy rocks and trees and nothing much else. No streetlights or anything, just dark. Calm and relaxing and also very romantic. We start kind of getting things going and I ask him if he has a condom. He says no, he hates latex. I asked him if he hates it or he's allergic to it. He kissed me, touched me and asked me if it even mattered at this point. I laughed, like a fucking dumb ass and said no, not at this point. Just make sure to pull out, I told him, I told him square in the eyes. We didn't do it very long. I mean, it was in a goddamn car, you don't have the marathon sessions in the backseat. Hot and uncomfortable and really just a place to do your business. But I could tell he was going to cum, and I tapped him. I scratched him. I bite him and tasted blood. I punched him in the face and yelled at him and then I felt it. I knew what had happened, like a squirt of hot water, I knew. I had, at that point, had plenty of sex, but always with a condom. Except for one boyfriend who I used the pill with. But it made me fat and gave me acne. I'm talking pimples on my face, chest, back and everywhere. It also made me a bitch, short-tempered and … "

She put out the second cigarette and lit a new one. She unzipped a lengthy sigh.

"So I jump out of the car and run to the water. I try to wash the shit out of me … handfuls of water up in there, I don't know, I was frantic. He laughed. I swore. He said something that I couldn't hear and I swore some more."

"D-Did he leave you there?" Sam said through his nail.

"No, he's a fucking gent. He's a real stand-up, classy, well-mannered piece of shit. No, he drove me home. He tried to make conversation, but I was so angry. Tried to kiss me, I slapped him, told him to go fuck himself."

Sam was familiar with Andy's tales of conquest and romance. The optics were different when he was the auteur. He chose poorly to add. "He doesn't really … That is to say he isn't the best guy with the ladies, he's … "

"He got me pregnant! And then he iced me out! Completely! Didn't respond, didn't pick up when I called, not a word. No communication. I didn't know what to do." Kay snorted, not sobbed. "I cat-fished him with a girlfriend, I had to do it fast. I got him to meet her and I showed up at that fucking Italian joint and told him off. I let him have it. I screamed and yelled and the manager laughed, that old 'boys will be boys' laugh. You know what he said? 'Might not be mine, and if it is, it probably shouldn't be anyone's.' I was already planning to and did end up getting an abortion. Do you know how much those fuck up your head? To have something, no matter how big, ripped from you? It's like you're pulled into an alien spaceship and all these machines and people with masks just … " Kay now began to weep. "It rattles you from the body to the soul and back."

Sam never heard this story from the collected works of Andy. In earnest, he may have heard the girl running into the ocean to splash her genitals with water, but there were so many stories, so many of them at the beach.

He moved in and wrapped Kay in his arms. He smelled the waft of spices from the bag, grimaced from hunger, but kept a firm hold. "Are you okay? Now, I mean, these days, I mean … "

"Yeah, I just kind of healed up and did some stupid things after. It took me a while to feel like I won back my soul. Even to feel like it settled back in my body. I'm not religious or was raised with anything like that, if I was might be another story. I might be a mother. Who knows? I'm not sad about giving up a thing inside of me that was no bigger than a microorganism, I am still furious about the way he handled it or didn't. My self-esteem was damaged, I didn't know if I would ever feel confident again. I have great friends, Savoy was there for me…. I was surprised he didn't hate me after all the fits and tantrums I had."

"I don't blame you…. I don't … "

"Sam … I don't know if we could coexist in your life. He and I, I mean. I don't know if I can be with you, knowing that he is someone who holds such a high position in your life. I would kill him if I could."

"He's grown up a lot, you know…. He isn't a bad guy at all, he's actually … "

"Are you defending him?"

"N-No, I just … I don't know what I'm doing. This is a lot of information. I think I'm stunned. This has been a crazy day…. For both of us."

"Sam … do you love me?"

"I-I would think so … I mean … I … "

"Do you care about me?"

"Yes!"

"I'm not going to tell you what to do. I'm not going to throw down an ultimatum. I just … Please don't talk about him, to me, ever. Please?"

"I promise."

"I mean … If you really wanted to … Never mind … "

"What?"

"You *wouldn't* talk to him anymore. I know you guys have been friends forever, best friends at that. But … knowing that you value someone so greasy and disrespectful is kind of grating me, right now, and probably in the future."

"So … You *are* giving me an ultimatum?"

"Look, I don't want to be that girl.… I don't want to be the girlfriend who tells her boyfriend what to do but … "

"But?"

Oh, come on Sam, I don't need to go into more detail, do I? Me and him: we can't really exist in the same circle, it's hard for me, I don't think that I'd get over it even if he apologized, which he didn't but still … I don't think that it would matter."

"No, I follow you."

"Good. I am not going to say it's me or him, but there could never be an 'us' with him in the middle."

And so it continued, the conversation at least in partial reciprocity, dwindling to an eventual stalemate with neither person taking monopoly over the moment to proclaim any definitive plans of action or volunteer any rigid stipulations.

For Sam's part, he knew what she wanted, it was obvious. He understood what simple words would instantly bring her back from the withdrawn absence where she ineffectually forked at food without appetite. He did not, it could be argued that he could not, fulfil such a demanding promise, which at the present moment could salvage Kay from the present distress, and in the future leave him isolated. It was complicated. It made him assess what happiness meant to him and its most pleasing shape. A previous lifetime of brethren-like kinship or a potential future where love and companionship were a starry uncertainty.

Supper was slowly gouged and consumed with the speed of an intravenous drip. The dog wagged his tail and panted with dithery, auguring outwardly a keen perception of the disquieting apprehension. Sam tried joking about the price of oil having nothing on the cost tzatziki barrels, but it remained a morose affair, nonetheless. After dinner, Sam benevolently offered to take the dog for a long walk, he had some thinking to do.

Sam had been out of sorts for weeks, since his power became the engine of his existence. Almost a numbness from the volatility of it all. A stunning and surreal mental galvanism that wooded the uncomplicated man's mind more than before. What had normal become? The ability to disperse human beings with the kiss of his eyes and the hate in his heart? A being of netherworld strangeness flickering here and there as though the wick had lost its control of its flame? Work. Relationships. Investigations. Promotions. Dreams. Dogs. Reality. Vengeance. Forgiveness. Understanding. Confusion. The intangible weight of mercury which chose no conclusive cut or die, cast or mold. Impossible, it seemed, was it for Sam to stop and make sense of his previously transparent existence. As lugubrious as things may have seemed, they were clear-cut, only made difficult by Sam's defeatist resignation. He now bore the intangible weight of mercury that showed no cut or die, no cast or mold, a shapeless, shapeshifting heaviness without familiarity. Sam was numb.

He set off with Mac and flashed through the images of the day. Kay's outburst and Andy's solemn retreat. The detectives, who had no physical evidence, could still find ways to continue to impress guilt upon Sam until he was a fractal cube of worry. A man with extrasensory faculties that appeared at random like Calchas interpreting the flight of sparrows. Loss. Gain. Career. Love. Friends. Revenge. Temper. Cops. Weight. Responsibilities. Death. Life. Too. Much.

The evolution of his role, the downloading of tasks, the expectations, the increased output, the mentorships, tutelage, vocational training, the meetings, the suits, the haircuts, the forced laughing, the drudgery of later hours, the paycheques, the entire galaxy of his work universe was an oasis, a vacation still, in comparison to everything else.

Another person may have gone a vastly different route. Crumpling into themselves beneath the tonnage of guilt, responsibility and turmoil. Yet another may have discovered their calling and willed themselves to despotism and tyranny. A third with an equally different position may have chosen a life of seclusion; securing a lifetime supply of paraffin, hunting supplies and granola bars; taken to Walden and become a pontificating hermit with the immediate cure for his disdain of summer cottagers. A billion people, roughly the same number outcomes.

But Sam … But Sam …

The dark-lit sky was a kind, purplish-cum-indigo that lit the road but treated no shadow; that springtime hour when visibility is still clear, but the streetlights impatiently make themselves apparent for fear of being late or missing out. Sam did not realise it, but he was on a mission.

A man walked past him, whose head was cast down in thought, his chin nearly scraping chest. The man lightly collided with Sam and turned to say, "Watch your fuck … "

Another man, possibly afraid of dogs, told Sam, though not by his government name, to restrain his leaping mutt, in no such courteous words, before …

A lady who was emerging from her car, was having a simple conversation on her mobile about nothing seemingly too important; her tone as shrill, nasally, loud as …

The convenience store clerk who said that dogs were not permitted in the …

The drunkard who dizzily nudged into Sam and threatened to knock his …

A snotty young miss who …

Some big galoot with his …

This older guy that …

Some lady …

A …

Sam accidentally, or not, sated his angst with the blinking of over a dozen, eighteen to be specific, people on his block. Some for as little as not reciprocating his nod or smiling when he did not feel like being smiled at. Sam had inadvertently walked far beyond his intended turning point. It was night, black night, the streetlights were now fittingly employed.

An all-black limo glided without noise and stopped beside Sam. He recognized it, numbly nodded to the driver and accepted a lift back to his apartment.

"Sam, my dear, and this must be young Mac, no?" Lucy smiled and patted the fleece of the dog. His face still bare. The lines and face muscles appeared tenser and more indelicate.

"Good guess … How was the ball?" Sam asked.

"Oh you know … balls, galas, vanity to the point of satire, handkerchiefs and hilarity. Costumes and pranks. It was Moscow in limbo, well, in and of, and in spite of itself." Lucy yawned. "It's all so exhausting, really."

"And," Lucy grinned, "how was your day?" He waved his hand down his face and beneath it grew his full beard once again.

"Oh, well, you know … Long day … Lots of … Personal issues, I reckon. I feel like I might have some choices coming up very soon."

"You seem more at ease with regards to our earlier dialogue," Lucy said. "Do you even realize how many people you've just, let's say, removed? On your little promenade?"

"I don't know.…" Sam looked out of the window.

"That's good, that's what we shall call 'improvement'."

"Why?" Sam glanced sidelong at Lucy.

Lucy said nothing but returned a nod and smile.

"Wait … how did you get to Russia and back?"

The car stopped. Sam could hear the chauffeur step out towards the door.

"Samuel," Lucy shook his head, "you have plenty to worry about beyond my means and methods of transoceanic conveyance."

Sam hopped out and waited for Mac, asleep on Lucy's lap for the ride, to stumble out of the limousine door.

"Cute puppy Sam, he's better off with you." Lucy waved with two fingers. "And Sam. You will have to make a choice soon. Good evening, young man."

The chauffeur smirked fiendishly and secured the door slowly.

Days passed. The newspapers ran a plethora of missing person's articles, speculative obituaries, the 'if you have any information please call' ads. It was the talk of the town. Tales circulated about various unsupported and unfounded macabre activities that were taken as possible reasons for the disappearances. Masked men in unmarked vans roving around the city in the shroud of darkness, preying on whomever they pleased, with no distinction for race or gender or age. A real-life succubus that lures victims to her web and pounces on the unsuspecting man or women, foolish enough to think with their lightning rods, snared and feasted upon by demonically possessed meta-human slaves. A group dedicated to the occult, summoning forces from the Necronomicon to extinguish all human life with swirling cauldrons of witches' brew, eye of newt and curses and hexes and the like. An army of the undead that skulks in soundless packs, feasting on flesh and bone, leaving no clothing or hair as evidence due to their vast hunger.

Parents, siblings, lovers and loved ones pleaded with open letters to the editor. A mural of letters and doleful graffiti was haphazardly started by one girl's boyfriend on the side of a building wall. His one-line of spray paint read, 'Must not sleep must warn others I love you Max I will find you'. Around that original piece of simple red paint grew letters, pictures, flowers and stuffed animals. Sam walked by it one day with Kay. He looked at the wall, spotted with indifference pictures of Chen, Michelle, Chloe, the rest. Kay scanned with intent. She found Savoy's area, poems, guitar strings and pictures. She sniffled and placed a little folded up card in a Zip-Loc bag by pin. Sam hugged her. She was rigid and did not lean into him. He kissed her forehead and she sniffed again.

Sam received a visit from a surprise guest. Mr. Edwin Chan tapped upon Sam's office door without any forewarning, asking meekly to step inside and waited to be offered a seat.

"Thank you," Chan spoke. "I won't be long."

"Please, what can I do for you?" Sam tilted back in his chair and crossed his fingers.

"Well … " The Edwin Chan who Sam had previously encountered, the buoyant and confident, square-jawed and wide-shouldered man, was slouching with his shoulders hunched forward. "I know that Harry's dad, and the police, and everyone else has asked you about them, you know, Chenny and Mimi."

Sam winced.

"But, I mean … If they ran off together, then that's … " Chan bit his lip. "It's a shit situation. It really is. But I would still rather they did run off together than get eaten by a werewolf or abducted by aliens."

"Is that what the rags are saying now?" Sam responded staidly. "Well, I highly doubt there are any half-man half-wolf things out there…. Or if there are beings from beyond the stars collecting scalps. That stupid, silly, foolish nonsense."

"Well … What I want to know is … if they said anything to you … Or you heard anything."

"Why would I know anything? I was never really close with them."

"I know, but Mimi talked a lot, she never let anything slip? Chenny never accidentally left any plane tickets or itineraries open on his monitor?

The- They never … " He buried his thick, Rottweiler-like skull into his hand and began sniveling.

Sam rolled his eyes and rolled his chair to his desk, "Hey, hey big guy … Listen … Hey … " He tried to think of what he could say. "I mean, they *probably* just planned it, the two of them, didn't tell anyone, and just decided that, boom, there they go!"

"You think so?" Chen raised his head.

"They were always close, friendly, though maybe when I really analyze it, more-than-friendly, touching. Always eating together. Taking breaks together. Don't believe the papers. They are just really shitty, really fake and really awful people, Edwin."

"Thanks," he snorted wetly, "I needed to hear that. People keep telling me that they'll come back, but, why would I want them to? You know, I wished once or twice it was the cyclone-lady, or the…"

"Cyclone lady?" Sam cracked.

"Yeah, a lady that can make cyclones big enough for one person and catapult them into another area code or the ocean. They die … of course."

"Crazy, crazy stories, my friend. Ed? Call I call you Ed?" Ed assented. "If I hear anything, I will forward the information to you, along with the law enforcement and the big Mr. Chen. But, so far: crickets."

"Thanks Sam, you're a good guy." Chan saw himself out of the door with a painful smile.

"Cyclone-lady? Jesus Christ." Sam smiled as he thought, *What'll they think up next, a man who blinks*? He laughed and knocked his desk, a fine wood under his boney knuckles.

Sam took his leave from the office later than usual, having to wrap up some extra paper work, but left in a fine mood, nonetheless. It was raining but he had an umbrella and the will to make it bloom. He stopped by the 'wall of lost ones' as it was now-officially dubbed by the press and plebs. A single person braved the rain and stood attentively in front of mural. A girl in a yellow rain jacket with a cavernous hood. She and Sam stood shoulder-to-shoulder and had a human moment. The kind of moment when one can enjoy the act alone, but when shared with another, perhaps the romanticized nature of partaking it with complete stranger, produces a sensuous aura, a nonsexual, speechless entanglement of spirits.

Perhaps because the stranger is utterly alien, if it was shared with a lover or a friend, words can muddy and tarnish the intrinsic, indulgent values of the experience. Astride of someone with no name or prior history, the conviviality and sense of true, human companionship remains present, but does not diminish the equanimity; the mind can, soul can, reach out and touch one another, allowing thought and emotion to intertwine. The rain streamed from Sam's umbrella and bounced from the stranger's rubber jacketed shoulder. They turned to face each other and shared a fleetingly wistful acknowledgement of something great, a harmony drifting aimlessly in the ether.

"Can you take a picture of me in front of the wall for my profile page? I think … "

Disrespectful little jerk, Sam thought as he slow-blinked the girl from his side with a malicious snarl. Sure, he was the reason for the memorial wall, but she didn't need to make light of it.

He moved closer to the area where trinkets and notes were stapled and pinned for Kay's friend, Savoy. He picked up her letter, folded neatly inside the baggy. He removed the page and read:

'Dear Sav, I know we've had our differences in the past and probably always will. I will always love you. I am sure you are alive, so this is a stupid and pointless thing, but shut up, it's for helping us, not you. Don't be so selfish. Kidding. You wandering, limitless spirit. You intelligent sphinx of a beastly man. You caring and passionate lover. I miss you. I missed you before they said you were gone. I missed you the day we said our first goodbye and our last goodbye. You are probably playing a banjo on some atoll in the South Pacific or plating poppy seeds beneath the eyes of some military dictator in Myanmar. I don't know, you've lived a life that anyone would trade ten of theirs to have but one day in your creative, beautiful mind. I know you'll come back. I have your jacket, fool, and I'm not giving it back. Okay, maybe if you ask real nice. Say hi to your mom if you see her. Love, Kayoko.'

Sam contemplated crushing the paper into a little ball and throwing it in the trash. He decided better to refold it and put it back how it was. He took a long breath.

"Best mistake ever," he said as he splashed down the street. He began to whistle, opting for the singer's melody. Really nailing the *This is ground control to Major Tom, you've really made the grade* part. He continued through the instrumental section.

He added the claps with his own hands.

It took a few days, but Sam reached out to Andy. Kay had a blood oath against him but Sam was entirely undecided about how he felt. He thought about the episode in front of the Greek joint and the proceeding story of Andy's insensitive and vile treatment was counter-balanced by a long friendship full of love and brotherhood, a kind of blood pact of its own.

Thinking about it was very much like a soup that was too hot to touch. It warmed the metal spoon to a degree that resulted in it being left alone to conduct heat unmolested. All Sam could do was blow and wait, blow and wait, and hope that it would not melt the bowl, the table and the floors below him. He would decide his feelings when he saw him. He settled as much on that.

"Hello?" Andy answered with a question.

"Andy, hey, how are you?" Sam asked, tapping his fingers on his work desk.

"I'm good, good, good … I'm surprised you're calling me."

"Why?"

"You're serious? I'm sure that she …"

"She has a name. And she doesn't control me, I'm a big boy."

"Oh you the man?" Andy jibed and laughed. "Oh well, hello Sam's balls, it's been a while."

"Ha-ha, shut up."

"I joke, I joke."

"So … Beers?"

"Yeah! I still got the boat. Dimitri has been too lazy to grab it. Suns out. We can probably cinch that fucker up a little easier this time, you know, with the experience. And I promise, no chicks! I cross my heart."

"Okay, pick me up from work. No. Pick me up at Mahoney's." He thought for a moment. "Oh! Can you bring me shorts and a t-shirt or something? I don't want to stop at home first."

"*Enchanté*! Hey, you know I still love you, right?"

"I know you do … I love you too, brother."

Sam sat back, rotated his chair to look at the view. He met his fingers in front on his face, appearing in deep thought though thinking of nothing at all.

He dropped in on Kay at the café in the lobby.

"Hey honey, how are you?" he asked.

"I'm okay, busy day, kind of absentminded today. You?" She brushed the hair from her forehead, her face sticky and reflective with hard work. "You want a coffee?"

"Busy, busy, very busy … " He sighed without listening. "Probably have to work late." Sam chewed his thumb. "I'll take a cuppa though."

"Oh? Again? Well, I guess it comes with the territory, Mr. Manager. Do you want me to make something for dinner? Do you want me to pick something up? I have to go to the store to get doggie kibble anyways."

"Sure." He stopped. "Maybe, if I'm early enough, I'll bring home a pie? I'll let you know so you don't go to any extra trouble."

"Aww thanks babe, you know just what to say." She paused.

"Sam, I love you."

"I love you too, Kay."

Sam felt good. That was the couple's first declaration of love. A shame that it had to happen while they were at work, but fitting that it had been at the place where Sam had been hit by the arrow. It felt invigorating; a menthol cigarette on a cold day, a cold chalice on a hot one. He decided to walk around the block, take a few moments for himself. He removed his deck of cigarettes and his lighter nestled from the inner-lining of his breast pocket. He lit with one hand and cupped the smoke from the wind with the coffee in the other. A middle-aged, cheery-looking woman bumped into Sam while she had been trying to swat a wasp and collided with his coffee hand. "Opa!" She laughed. "Lucky thing you had a lid, ha-ha."

Her gladsome response annoyed him. He did not catch any drips of coffee on his suit, but his anger climaxed regardless. "Opa!" Sam crunched his eyes together until he saw a flash of outer-space fabric and then opened them as far as they would go.

He tested the contents of the cup with a shake of the wrist, still a three-quarters full of Joe. He grinned as he resumed to circle the building. He unconsciously and against character flicked his cigarette into a deserted alleyway.

The sound of feet rapidly striking on pavement, an urgent clopping that was somewhere between a run and a walk, approached from behind as he rounded the corner. "Excuse me! Excuse me!" A male voice called to him, frenetic and articulate.

"Yes?" Sam turned. He was confronted a skinny college-aged kid with a long, angular face and a patrol cap, holding the still smoking cigarette stub to his face.

"I think you dropped this," the kid sneered.

"No, I flicked it," Sam responded with a culprit's smile, like a child still holding with felt pen with his fingers the same colour as the still-wet hieroglyphs. "Entirely on purpose, but I … "

"Well, what are you going to do about it? You in your fancy suit and polished shoes made from innocent animal skin. This isn't just your city.…"

Sam squashed the fallen butt under his pivoting heel, picked it up and carried it to a garbage can. "He was absolutely right," he admitted. "But he did didn't need to be such a prick about it."

Andy met Sam in front of Mahoney's. He was sipping a beer while sitting in the boat attached to the trailer secured by the winch of his mother's SUV.

"Pretty sure this is legal." He pointed at the beer. "I'm not *in* the automobile, right?" He wore big dark shades that were halfway down his prominent nose, enough to leave his greatest gift half unwrapped. "I got a cooler and booze already, we can head straight there, make use of this lovely sun!"

The boys spoke of things exceptional in their unimportance with tentative side-glances as if they were playing a hand of poker in a bullring, the brute scraping its hoof and circling the card table, each lad waiting for the other to dive out of harm's way first. Sam guised himself in Andy's 1980s styled neon beachwear. "Did you just hold on to this since we were kids or something? I feel like I'm nine again." Sam squinted at the bright, nonsensical geometric patterns on the shirt and the Haringesque patterns on the busy shorts.

"Nah man." Andy chuckled. "It's just back in style. I don't know why.… I figure that styles repeat every two decades. Remember in high-school when bell-bottoms and flairs were in fashion? After this, the next ones will dabble with baggy-ass clothes and pants below the ass again. I think it comes down to what happened in the decade just before you were born. That's my theory."

The beach was quieter than the previous time. The recent rain had snapped the fantasy of an abnormally hot and sun-filled early spring. The sand was moist and easily impressed by feet and posteriors. Cloud were scattered over the blue sky like fragments of a broken bottle smashed on the ground and being swept lazily in by the bristles of the imperceptible winds high above. Andy kept true to his word, gently waving and only saying '*enchanté*' to the few women on the shore. It might have been admirable if it was not such a simple undertaking, at least for Sam.

They shoved off. Sam held the boat, his legs prickling from the water, evidentially colder than the previous visit, while Andy found a spot for the jeep. Andy leaped in from the shore and rocked the boat, almost putting Sam fully into the drink. Sam caught his balance, though struggled and nearly toppled over again as the boat drifted away while he only had one leg in the aboard. He pulled himself in and landed shoulders first, flailing like a beetle until Andy pulled him up.

Andy controlled the tiller and broke far left, away from the paddle-boards, kayaks and canoes. Away from the people. The shoreline itself became diminishingly hospitable for the leisure-seekers along the northern-side of the coast. The feather-soft grains of sand in the more populated seaboard gradually became coarser, stone-filled and loamy. The loam became dirt and grass, trees with thick pads of moss on their uniforms, rocks that consolidated into shale to compose natural ambits to insulate the public beach area, which were only disputed by teenagers on psilocybin trips or cockcrow fishermen who sell their paltry catch in the Chinatown markets. Quiet as only forests can be, with their steadily off-beat chirruping; the non-repetitive, percussive rustling of groundlings; and the arrhythmic swaying of leaves. The dull chopping of waves against the strake gently swayed the boat with the brushing fingers of a tranquil tide, the kind of peace that causes one to question why war is even a word.

As they drifted farther, the timberland began to resign to steep rockface, sheer and smooth, with chunks of immovable stone that extended beyond the water from their implacable base into the ocean's floor. Meters above stood the detached mega-dwellings of the rich. Views of boundless endlessness with its inexhaustible reflection from mile-wide windows, used in moments of extreme hospitality or extreme forlorn.

The monotonous putter of the engine was cut, the gargling sputter of the propeller churning in the water and the smell of diesel evaporated instantly. Andy sat at the stern with his beer resting on the sleeping power-head. Sam occupied the bow, his arms lurching overboard. The boys' eyes, each thoroughly blocked by tinted glass, stared in opposite directions. The occasional sip, slurp and gulp of beer were the only sounds that disturbed the melodic, even-tempered placidity of the ribboning glassiness that surrounded them.

"So … " Andy traced his finger around the rim of his can. "How's the new job treating you?"

Sam smacked his lips after a swig, sighing cordially. "It's good … I feel like they're kind of holding back, giving me bits at a time, not trying to overwhelm me. I just keep thinking, it can't be this easy.… Chen was a smart guy, smarter than me for damn sure, and he seemed to work way harder. Maybe it's just what I saw or thought I saw."

"Hindsight is twenty-twice, so they say," Andy responded. "He was probably half-working, half-plotting that little escape act he did with that cute Asian chick. What was her name?"

"Michelle," Sam answered.

"Right, right … Did they ever hear from them or find them? Did they try looking?" Andy sat up, grabbing his beer from the outboard. "I mean, with all these disappearances going around, do you think … "

"Yeah, they have this whole big investigation.… Ongoing … Even the big boss conducted interviews. He seemed unconvinced. But … They won't find them. They're probably in Palau or La Reunion or somewhere far off, not wanting to be found." Sam sipped his beer. "They even brought in detectives."

"Woah!" Andy said. "So they figure there's some kind of foul play, no? Or they wouldn't bring in DTs, right? Do you think it's fishy? Do you think they got lured into some cult to farm bananas in Suriname?"

Sam laughed grimly. "Nah, I don't think they're coming back. I think they're gone for good…. But of course … That's just my take on the thing."

"What about all the other crazy disappearances…. Anyone you know?" Andy asked.

"Me?" Sam inflected towards the heavens. "Uh … Nope … I mean I know people who have, but … "

"I know a chick, well knew a chick? I don't know…. Someone who I met, saw her parents' sob story in the papers." Andy looked down and shuffled his right foot a couple of times. "It's sad man…. They have no idea. Demonic forces, extraterrestrials, sects, cults, Nazi surgeons, Government cover-ups, all these crazy ideas, which to me, means they have sweet dick-all. If they're letting the news have their go-around with all these crackpot theories, maybe they're letting the journalists run wild with whatever idea that comes to their minds, you know?"

"I agree with you there." Sam smirked. "They got nothing. Nada amigo, zippy-doo-da." Sam took a refreshing guzzle, squeezing his can to a cored apple shape, and reached for another.

"I will say," Sam added, peeling back the tab of the can, his beer whispering like it had a secret. "I doubt the people had anything in common, any traits or identifiers, other than maybe they were just shitty people…. Maybe they had it coming…. Wrong place at the wrong time. Crossed the wrong guy … or girl."

"I heard that theory," Andy said. "The Cardinal Killer, they called it. Not unlike that 'what's-in-the-box?' flick, but scary. I mean … I'm a whore," Andy quacked, half in jest and half serious "What chance do I have?" He grabbed another beer, squashing his empty can like an accordion. "I just have to stop reading the damn papers, but in my line of work, you're always waiting, and there's always a gazette just lying there to pick up and thumb through. I think the journalists' were just shooting at the clouds for that one though, too many people, they couldn't all be that bad."

"Curiosity killed the kitty, right?" Sam said. "I wouldn't worry about anything. Worrying would give you more grey hair than you already have."

"Hey, the young girls like my hint of grey: it's wise, it's distinguished, it's *enchanté*!"

They both smiled and cast their eyes again in opposite skylines. They engaged in another bout of prolonged silence.

"Andy?" Sam stared down. Andy slowly turned his head towards Sam. "What's your side of the story with Kay?" Andy curled his lips inward and looked down, holding his can with two hands, sloping his wide shoulders down and in, dropping his head and fidgeting with his knees.

"Honestly," Andy returned after a ruminative pause, "it's probably like she told it. I can only imagine what she said, but factually, it's probably pretty damned close to the King James Version."

"Why then … Why would you?" Sam sputtered.

"To be fair," Andy placed his can in between his knees raised his hands in defensive posture, "I am very equal in that I tend to treat most-to-all women with the same level of disrespect." He broke a smile, burying it back into his jaw when he realised Sam was unflinching. "I guess … I guess … I don't know what to say."

"Did you ever apologize to her?"

"I don't think … That is … No, I didn't," Andy respired lowly.

"I mean I've listened to your stories for … our whole friendship, I always found them funny, daring, crazy … *enchanté* as you would say. But, hearing the other side of the coin, the tail to your face, it's … it's sad. It's mean. Are there others?"

"Others what?"

"Others that you've just left with their legs spread towards the interior lights, accidental baby in the oven, needing to get it sucked out? Do you have any kids? That's an actual, honest question."

Woah! Woah!" Andy stiffened. "I don't go around knocking bitches up, driving off with a middle-finger out the window saying 'fuck y'all'. That was an exceptional case." Andy rotated his shoulder and tried to sit more naturally. "I'm sorry it had to happen to a girl you're dating."

"That's not the point," Sam said. "It could be anyone…. It's just not nice."

Sam felt himself getting worked up. He petted the water and breathed slowly.

"Look, I didn't mean to attack you. I just … " Sam exhaled dully. "She was all out of sorts. Still is. Could be a couple things. I don't mean to dump all the blame on you," Sam said as he removed his sunglasses to admire the explosion of colours detonating from the nascent descent of the sun.

"Well, if I'd known you were going to be dating her, I'd never have *enchanté'd* her...."

Sam shook his head with salt. "That's not at all the point.... You shouldn't go around treating any girl the way you treated Kay."

"What, are you my mother? You want me to get on my knees and beg her for an apology?"

"No, that's not what I'm saying, I don't even think that it would do anything at this point."

"So you're picking her over me? Just like that? Some broad you barely know ... Who you've really only started to date, who you are going supersonic fast in making up for lost time ... Just like that?"

"I didn't say that either. Yeah, we haven't been together that long. But I also really dig her, man...."

"You would have dug any pretty little thing that let you stick your dick in her.... Grow up! Man the fuck up and stop doing this to yourself. You *are* a coward, Sam.... But you are also thick and selfish. I mean, seriously, we've been best friends forever, and you would let *one* female come along and reorganize your life? If it wasn't her, you'd be caving in for someone else, or someone else, or someone else still. Don't you see?"

"What? Are you jealous of her? Of me that ... "

"Go fuck yourself!"

"Andy listen ... "

"No, you listen, I almost, just almost had my dog back after being neutered for the past however long. And there he goes again getting stuck under the thumb of another bossy bitch."

"Andy, I'm warning you, please stop, just calm down, just chill out.... Just stop using bad words and talking me and Kay down, I'm begging you."

Sam could feel his agitation level rising against his will. He concentrated with all his might and mental prowess to make himself unassailable and impervious to Andy's slicing criticisms. He began to hyperventilate. He pinched a small parchment of flesh inside his thigh and clamped his fingers until the skin felt it would burst. He bit the inside of his lip and tasted hot iron between his teeth. He grunted from the physical discomfort.

Andy stood up. "What are you doing? Are you having a panic attack?"

Sam's sprouting anger was fighting to break through the soil. He was visualizing a river of boiling blood coursing with a juggernautish, rubicund frenzy through his heat-stressed veins. His heart beat like a war drum, his skin felt tight as the hide stretched over the copper bowl of the same timpani.

"No … " A drip of sweat jiggled and dropped from the tip of Sam's nose. "Say something nice…. Apologize to me, please!"

"Apologize? For fucking what? For you being a pussy? For you not having any balls to fight back? Come on, man … How are we going to hash this out? Call me a bastard, call me a cunt."

"No … " The hodgepodge of negative emotions refused to abate. Sam thought he had them subdued, but they shot back like fever pains. The blackish, reddish animus refused to have its momentum denied. Darkness as when the night orders the day to no longer breathe, the unbreakable association between gravity and the fall.

"Come on!" Andy protested, swinging arms with upturned palms. "Get up!"

"Stop baiting me! I'm not going to hit you! I don't want to hurt you! I don't want to make you gone!"

"First off, you've never swung a fist on purpose in your life, little man. Second, stand up to me! Don't let me talk to you like this! Have some respect for yourself! Coward!"

The boat drifted perpendicular beneath Andy's upright stirring, now sitting adjacent to the longitudinal coastline. The nesting sun soundlessly rhapsodized its peerless brilliance, a merciful exaltation before its merciful repose. The puissant singular beam profited from the still, speculum water and boosted its snarl immensely. The laser-like beam cut into Sam's eyes and sought to force them closed, reflexively and perhaps unalterably.

Sam could not turn from the all-glowing, all-encompassing surface that surrounded the boat and encircled him without retreat, a double-pincer from a famed general. He forced the index fingers and thumbs from both hands to spread his eyes open like a jaws-of-life.

His eyes burned dryly like a chemical blister. The escape of water from his parched tear-ducts only worsened the pain and muddled his vision.

Sam tried to shift his eyeballs to collect any residual liquid in his eyes to spread, quickly being left with the sensation of and unlubricated pestle scraping flakes from a basalt mortar.

"Stop doing that! Just blink you psycho! What the hell are you doing?" Andy stomped, rocking the boat to its fringes.

Salt and mucus ran into Sam's mouth. His eyelids wrestled his fingers with negligent and covetous abandon. Antlike power connected the tips of his lashes together, bending the mince hairs at the middles. The palpitation of his brow felt like a seizure as shockwaves tremored through his body.

"Say you're sorry!" Sam pleaded, unable to see Andy beyond an incomprehensible outline of granulated pixels and bleached-out colourlessness.

"No!" Andy yelled and grabbed Sam by the hands, pulling him to a standing position. "Quit being weird! You're freaking me out! Quit holding your eyes open, you crazy asshole!"

Sam bucked and thrashed his upper-body to rid himself of Andy's hands tugging at his own, which were bolted to his forehead and orbital bone. The men struggled evenly with Sam's corybantic fervency matching Andy's size and strength advantage. The keel endeavoured with hardship to remain even, threatening to capsize with increasing confidence. The calm waters wrinkled around the turtling skiff like the cheek of a man powerless to help.

Sam swiveled his upper body with ferocity. "Let me go! Say you're sorry!"

"Fuck … You!" Andy struggled to contain Sam amidst his violent jerking.

Sam's resolute squirming broke him free of Andy's fetters brought the boat on the brink of overturning. He stumbled over the coil of rope and banged his shin on the centre thwart, he careened into the side of the boat with the backs of his knees, felling him into the yielding embrace of the water.

It was cold at this depth, a hundred meters from the shore and the sun far from its midday acme. Sam did not feel the brisk stinger of the ocean's needling frigidity. His fingers remained fixed as tire-jacks in his sockets. His legs kicked wildly, ineptly; he could feel bubbles escape from his shoes and fill with water and becoming a Chicago Overcoat, more leaden with each tread. Each cycle of his legs became more wearisome, he lifted himself an inch and sank by two. He had not taken with him a well-provisioned reservoir of oxygen. The dizziness already punched him drearily. He looked up and barely made out the bottom of the boat, falling away from him at an impossible mile per agonizing second. The air that he offhandedly rationed exited without his heed, deserting him with gurgling defiance.

The scenery darkened precipitously fast. The closing of his narrowing aperture, a waterlogged vision that liquefied into faint haze of tenebrous and uncertain imagery.

He prayed that Andy and his lifetime of swimming caps and competition medals would plunge through the water like a dolphin and save him. He lost count of the seconds. He heard and felt nothing.

With no other option for escape or rescue he relinquished his eyes and struck his cupped hands upwards. The air-bubbles escaped his convulsing throat with decreasing size until there seemed to be nothing left to exit. His eyes burned beneath their shutters. His head ached sharply and felt like a balloon ready to burst from high heat. A terrific deprivation of sound and sensation encased him with fetus-like void of obscurity. Though he fought, the surrounding eternity of water lanced its way into sinuses and throat, creeping and coating. He was beyond the early stages of tiring, his legs slowed and the reach of his arms truncated with each climbing motion. He could not see the underside of the skiff or the transcendental border between sea and sky.

The spike-less maiden unwaveringly tightened with the single-minded and relentless vendetta of assimilation. Sam began to feel the soulless insentience of the drift. He could not discern any progress through the chaos of struggling for survival, but his tenantless lungs and oxygen-starved brain resigned him to absolute, somatically induced lethargy. A slight pang shot between his ear and eye. Worry decreased. His burning muscles relaxed, floated, weightless. Just a quick nap. A quick shut-eye-rest for old Sammy.

A vision flashed somewhere between his brain and his mind, behind his eyes and all-around him as the water which held him in physical stasis. He was walking on the same pier he had seen the mobs of people, Andy and Kay and Mac, huddled into cargo containers and lifted on to the tanker. He was alone. Only the loose pebbles crunching beneath his feet disturbed the supremacy of silence. Even the chronic descanting of the ocean was denied so much as a chaste whisper, its waves timorous and frozen in place. Sam was only a passenger in a vehicle that he knew well to be himself as if the driver's seat was already modulated and grooved to comfort by a lifetime of piloting. It was still a projection, a movie filmed in the first person with a narrator that did not speak, but seemed certain of the eventually finale. The ghost in the machine watched intently, without surprise and equally without foreknowledge. Sam watched as his legs carried his body swiftly and directly to a large shipping container. It was the only stand-out object in his perspective. The cranes and lifts had all been abandoned. The ship was gone. Sam moved precisely to the clasped door of the container and tried the handle. 'Up and then out, don't just pull it,' thought Sam, 'idiot,' he scoffed. After seeing a hand rise and feel the scratch of nails against head, the body of Sam lifted the bar with no little effort and unfastened the bottom bolt. He pulled with all his might to wrench open the door, roughly double his height. Sam's surrogate peered inside: dark nothing. He stepped in. He turned to face the open door. He pulled the door shut and sat cross-legged. He felt sleepy. Maybe he should lie down.

Sam was not about to die. No, Sam's journey would not be so blissfully curtailed by cryptic euphoria. He was not so lucky. Death is never easy when an acceptable premise, even for a coward.

A vice clamped around Sam's neck and tore him from the water by the scruff like a cub in a lioness' mouth. He shot above the water and landed on the bench, propped up in a seated position. A walloping smack pommeled his back and water cannoned from his mouth and nose, splashing the bottom of the boat. Sam shook his head. The fuzz of nothingness lifted slowly as dizziness slithered out of his ears, replaced by a ringing. He coughed dryly, retching at the saltwater residue that contracted his stomach. He panted, breathed with and without effort, greedily grabbing at the fresh air like a thief's hand in the register.

He spat, a big one then several smaller ones to get the mineral taste from his mouth. He rubbed his eyes and tried to control his breathing. His senses began to return. Cold. Hunger. Pain. The cornerstones of his hierarchy of immediate needs and impulses. His consciousness was slowly breaking through the obscurity, he felt exhausted.

"That was as close of a call as they tend to come, young man," bristled the sultry elegance of an all-too-familiar.

Sam coughed and spat the stubborn water that crept up his esophagus, nodding reflexively. The taste of drowning beginning to subside.

Sam painstakingly lifted one eye to see a grinning Lucy toweling his forearm, pulling down a rolled-up sleeve before buttoning it and patting it down, then covering it with a bunched-up merino-wool sweater cuff that was drawn to the elbow.

A tapping against the side of the boat slowly tilted Sam's head and torso to an upright position, heaving his eyes fully open. It was pitch now, the fog had eased its way around the boat and suffocated the surroundings from his purview. Lucy tapped a pipe on the frame and after filling it with some shredded brown mulch from a golden screw-top cylinder. He then struck a match under his nail and curtly drew several times on the mouthpiece to establish a self-sustaining glowing bowl of sweet-smelling tobacco.

The soft, whistling crackle of the tobacco and the lulling calm of Lucy's exhalations were the only sounds in the pastoral darkness. The moon was affixed in the sky with the humdrum of a night-watchman, the routine surveillance of a cursory flashlight that was more than a millennium beyond old-hat. An unseen hand supported the bleach-white head with its elbow on the table, the other hand tracing a finger over its reflection in a giant coffee cup with a slightness one had to close their eyes to feel.

"The poor moon." Lucy broke the silence. "The sun is spoiled, you know.... He is privy to the rewards of his own tremendous power. Like an adrenaline addict, a slave to his own fear of boredom, he forces with a cat of nine-tails that all activity, all action, the busying of bodies and the concentration of life and official movement fall under his dominion. You have to hold a place of lachrymosity for the moon. Her sibling demands an amplitude of energy from humans. He appeals to their ego, he fetishizes and consolidates his status, silently constructing a chattel industry on many life forms. What does it leave for the moon? Boredom. Slumber. Crime, sure, but to spectate nothing but nocturnal atrocity has scarred the delicate mind of an already wayward soul. Depressed is the moon above, can you not see? Her silent cries and muted agony. Her scapegoating as an accessory to murder and rape. The deception that her children guile from beneath her. Her brother ignorant to it all, and angry when he is left with the pieces of a broken vase beneath his waking eye. When she fails to compose an opus of tranquility and calm she is vilified. She craves for an equal regard as the daylight. She frowns as a mother from the fear that is associated with her. The stars are too distant to converse with. Beneath the glue of her nails creeps predators, apex and insignificant. She is a wandering prophet who recants the most graceful of sonnets, mistaken as a madwoman with a sinister tongue and rueful poetry. You cannot see the blood from her palms for her body disintegrated from the cross long ago. She is so lonely up there all alone."

Sam listened to Lucy's reflection on the moon, he glanced up but found no sympathy. The big lunar rock that clung to the black curtain above looked to him like nothing more than a hole in a giant piece of black canvas with a strong bulb somewhere on the other side. The story did allow him time to recover. He took a deep, plunging breath as Lucy wound down, one that acted on his body and mind as defibrillator. He blinked and shot his head around the boat, he was back.

"Where's Andy?" Sam moved with painful panic, surveying the small interior of the boat and casting his frame over each side, peering into the onyx waters. "Where is he? What did you do with him?"

Lucy eased himself back, folding a leg over the other. "I did nothing. It is what you did to Mr. Lambert that you should be asking."

Sam's ghost surfaced in his face. "I did nothing! We were talking.… We struggled a bit.… I … "

"You boarded the vessel with a plan." Lucy nodded and hemmed. "Whether or not you choose to acknowledge a truth so provocative or try to disparage it, which is a fact."

"No, I don't believe … I would never!"

"Oh! But you did. Your cravenness demanded you whisper your secret into a deep hole in the back of your mind, a reed resolved the depths, emerged from the soil, flowered a mouth and bloomed a voice you followed."

Sam shook his head. He tasted salt.

"You, for what it is worth, knew the outcome. Sure, you may have struggled with the implementation and even fought until near-death to reverse the executive order, but simply by acquiescence to fate, you damned your friend." A burning red of the embers lit the giddiness on Lucy's face. "You knew."

Tears mixed with brine and collected on Sam's upper-lip, he licked them and scowled.

"Be an adult, Sam." Lucy blew smoke rings, thick and circular beneath the lunar beam. "I will not regale you with an explanation of the subconscious processes of the human mind, but even the slightest scoop into the surface of your thoughts would indicate that you have a pyramidal order of elements which you deem as most important. Andre simply slipped to a lower strata and did little to curry himself redemption."

Sam retched dryly over the boat. A spindle of saliva webbed from his lips but little more. Tears fell and blended in the ocean. "Why … Why did you do this?" Sam sobbed convulsively.

"Do not blame the salesman because you purchased a cheap appliance and failed to read the instruction manual."

"But I never asked for this! If I'd known … "

"You did. You are perhaps too weak-minded or defeated in spirit to … "

"Shut the fuck up!" Sam spun towards Lucy. He braced his arms on the sides of the boat, licked a seething glower at the man opposite and blinked. He collided his lashes like the teeth of a beartrap, squeezing out the vinegar from his ducts and slammed them open.

Lucy smirked. His legs and arms crossed, biting his pipe, taking precious little puffs on the mouthpiece. "Really, Sam. That is your great, last-gasp scheme to reverse the travesty of your own ambivalence. Have you ever thought that maybe you are just a bad person?"

Sam tried again. He tried a third time, his eyes nearly bursting beneath the pressure of his squint. Lucy remained, carelessly smoking. "You bastard!"

"Just because I have been affable thus far, conceding and patient, does not mean I have not already pre-heated the stove. Mind your churlish tongue or risk it being fashioned to a slipknot for your own gibbeting." Lucy spoke with controlled fire. An articulate sternness infinitely more threatening than the average lion's roar.

Sam slumped back, exhausted. He looked up again at Lucy in his nautical suit. The hat, the pipe the sweater, an overcoat politely folded on the bench beside him.

"*You* were in my dream…."

"*You* dreamt of me."

"But you were wearing the same thing in my dream, that awful, twisted dream."

"I decided to guise myself appropriately for the seafaring encounter. That is all. A captain and a ghost ship. A damnable cargo with a destination yet to be determined."

"Is this what you wanted, to destroy me completely? To build me up, slightly, and tear me down. To do what? Why did you choose me? Why is this happening?" Sam sobbed but no substance leaked from him. Soaked to the hide but parched to the bones. He slowly drifted his head into his palms, rubbing his eyes, moaning and writhing in place.

Lucy uncrossed himself and leaned in. He placed the pipe on the folded topcoat beside him and rubbed the back of Sam's hand lightly. "How about I tell you a little about myself. A little story, unburdened by my usual affection for prolixity and something that will divulge some confidence in my character."

Sam sat back and observed the man through ravaged, ragged and red eyes. Lucy wiped his hand over his jaw, effacing his beard, leaving the stony characteristics of his sharp, angular face visible. His cheekbones swelled monstrously in the light. His chin tined to a point like an elf with twisted malevolence. A carbonite flame jittered in his opaque irises. There was a heat that whirled around, neither dry nor humid, but an intense burning that burrowed from the heart and clawed outwards.

"One of my earliest memories, at least one of my most memorable recollections from early childhood, was the day that I found a snake. My father, righteous to the marrow of his thick bones, always warned me of snakes. There are many kinds of sidewinding vermin, he would say, and all of them are symbols of pestilence. Snakes, rats, spiders; all things children should not have an innate fear of, such fears are instilled into their unassuming minds through the prejudices and phobias of progenitors, irresponsibly so.

"We had a small, box-shaped house with a big, lush yard; acres of grass, trees and a little pond planted deep in the thicket. I played with frogs, spiders, squirrels, birds, and whatever slick and furry creatures were so brave to sidle against my arm or leg or remain still and not flee without alarm.

"One day I was playing beneath the house. There was a little opening under the foundation, a crack that I could fit inside and no one else could. It was just beside a rhubarb bush that grew wild; once in a while my father would chop away the chubby stems and my grandmother would make a pie, along with raspberries that grew in the thorny bushes beyond the pond. It was dark and damp, even in the hottest days of the summer. Quite nice on those sweltering afternoons. It smelled musty, but natural. The soil and the mildew, the declining concrete walls, I breathed so heavily when I would first step in because I knew the smell would soon disappear and naturalize.

"I would play the way kids do, mumble to myself, watch the wood bugs, beetles and spiders crawl and hide from each other, or act as two ladies who dislike each other in the grocery store, push their carts by while pretending to ignore the other. Innocent and without a care in the world. One day, I saw one of those slick, slippery things slowly wind its way towards me. I was very scared. I shot up and cracked my head against the support beam above. I was dizzy, I had a goose-egg with a little cut, but I escaped. A week later, I recovered the confidence to go back under the house. I was tentative, scared, but wanted to breathe in the sultry dust of raw and damp nature.

"Again, I saw the snake. This time, it had already curled around my wrist by the time I took notice. I shook my wrist and the thing wriggled away, again, its scales shining in the bits of light that penetrated the area. There was something alluring, something sexy and charming about the way it casually danced above the ground, almost hovering, skipping away.

"I thought about it for days. I lay in bed and thought about it. I fished out tadpoles, picked berries, stung my limbs of stinging nettles, all things that failed to distract me from the thing that, the only thing really, that scared my old man. You see, I never cared for my father. He was absent much of the time. When he was around, he made up for his absence with rigid and harsh authoritarianism. Others, most in fact, loved him beyond words. Fought for him. Swore oaths and allegiances to him. Would do any-thing he said. But, I knew a different man. The man who I knew was an implacable grimace with bitter words and a strict belt. The older I grew the more I hated him. Still, I never quite caught up to the hate he has for me.

"I set to find a snake. To catch it and just look at it. I wanted to hear its side of the story. To my luck, I found one, perhaps not the same one, but a snake, nonetheless. Part of me wanted to run; its dead little eyes, the tongue whipping about its straight, emotionless, lipless mouth. It seemed to be wandering pointlessly, noticing me, but unconcerned. It drew closer, and I squared. I forced control over my shaking little body, my head still smacked with the pain from the head injury a week earlier. The snake coolly moved without feet, winding wide, then tight, then wrapping around my wrist. I fought the reflexive tensing of my fist. I wanted it to feel at ease, at liberty. It did not announce itself. There was no fear, no pride, no animosity, and no happiness, nothing remarkable. It was hardly real, more of a thing than an animal. It moved with some kind of intent, but curiosity did not figure on its face or body. Its calmness calmed me. I lifted and spread my hand and let it wrap around my fingers. The little black tongue flickered quickly against my skin, even with the ruddy still-new complexion of a babe I did not feel anything.

"Its body was soft as a ribbon of silk, but it was sheer muscle. Any thickness was not wasted on useless parts, it was a perfect creation. It was taut but pliable, it let me manipulate its curves as it surveyed me. A living piece of yarn, it did not try to bite me. I loved it immediately. I did not want to name it, for I felt it needed to appellation. Snake, serpent, both were immediately the most charmed and prized words in my head. Neither of us were scared, but we each had an empathetic longing that both of us could feel.

"I tried to break its neck. I don't know why. I wanted to test the strength, maybe the fragility of the snake. But I could not. It just curled and bent with my force and straightened itself out. I tried to pull it apart, but its spine was smart. It was elastic. It was durable. It was majestic.

"I took it out of the darkness and with my hands, showed it the light. Its protruding, black eyes seemed unimpressed, of course. I would come to learn a snake never shows emotion, especially through the eyes. Just the stoically blank expressionlessness of a silent, studious creature with infinite patience and a mind full of knowledge. I knew instantly this was the peak of evolution, of creation, of imagination and celebrity.

"I lay the snake, who by this point trusted and loved me in return, on the ground. It obediently wavered like a flag, in place, on the hard-packed soil in front of the porch at the side door. I removed its head with a shovel, one quick and decisive stab, admirably placed. The shovel, lying in a heap of upturned earth, had seemed to call me, beckoning to somewhere deep inside of me. The snake's eyes never changed as its head lay inches away from its body, wiggling in the throes of death. It was beautiful. I picked up both pieces.

"I was smiling so hard my ears were a foot higher. My father swung open the screen door and screamed. To my surprise, he was not proud. He was stunned, then mortified, then angry. I remained with a toothsome smile, a heart full of joy and pride. 'What have you done?' he cried. "'That creature is not good but why kill?'

"To him I replied, 'only a snake may murder its own'. Only the alikeness of two perfect specimens may ratify the downfall of one for the sake of the other. 'I loved this snake, father' I said with two hands holding one snake. 'I loved the snake and took its head off. You must love to kill. You cannot kill what you do not have unlimited love and respect for. I … ' before I could speak more he winged a clubbed hand so hard I thought I would never awake. With one strike he hit me comatose and I dreamt of endless falling. I was convinced I would never land, never again would I not have my heart in my throat.

"But I did. And I was still holding the broken cord. I fell for the length of the universe but held the dead snake as a constant to feel my own presence. Snakes are an amazing species, or maybe just this nameless snake, for when I pressed the two severed halves together like electrical cables, the snake was reanimated. It slithered in my hands. It flicked its tongue and curled around my finger. It buried itself into my veins. I crawled in the gap between its fangs. We fell together. We emerged together.

"I have not seen my father since, but I feel I inspired him eternally, for he has made it his mission to kill all snakes. But … my father has never succeeded in killing them off, or me. Only his countless other children.

I drew to the conclusion that my father never loved me, for I was born a snake. And since he never loved me, his attempts have been lacklustre.

"I have little to no love for humanity. The rivalry of step-siblings perhaps. My lack of affection leaves me in an unnerving position, you see…. For one reason or another, I am unable, if I so desired, to wrap my hands around your throat and submerge your head beneath the water until the bubbles ceased. Just as I could not set a sleeping tenement aflame or issue plague. I've come to feel remorse for the rabble, if only because I know the morbid caprices of their most benevolent and trusted godheads. Parenthetically, given the rash brutishness of his progeny, I can surmise that Father has become more negligent and less compassionate, even with his favourites."

Lucy tapped the bowl of the pipe against the side of the boat, filled it, lit it, forged and ember and puffed thickly. Sam's head remained stooped towards his crotch. He glanced up as Lucy suckled on the pipe, his face grew younger, twisted and foreign in the bracing stroke of pure whiteness gleamed by the moon.

"You want me to feel bad for you, is that it?"

"Do not be ridiculous, Sam."

"What do you want?"

"Diversion mainly. I have read every book, even those yet to be written. I tire with theatre and no longer celebrate the arts as purveyors of eliciting a sense of fantasy, which for me, was sealed long ago in a charnel house."

"Then … "

"To avoid the mush of atrophy, a mind disintegrating into boredom turns easily to mischief. For some reason mischief allows for much more creativity than altruism."

"So, I'm a pawn?"

"In a sense, sure. In another sense, pawns can become kings. The choice of squares is up to you."

The boat jarred abruptly. Sam fell backwards with his shoulders bashing against the narrowing bow. Lucy smirked. He tapped the pipe against the outside of the boat, glowing embers fell and blackened silently against the shallow waters. Sam picked himself up and looked around hurriedly. The boat had drifted ashore. He glanced at Lucy, who smiled with a wink, glided his hand over his face and recast his beard. Immediately he regained the wise elegance of his countenance that Sam had first encountered.

A pair of soft headlights spoke up causing Sam to squint and shield his eyes with a visor made from his curled hand.

"Up we go," Lucy said, already standing ashore, his hand outstretched to Sam. Sam refused the hand and clumsily stepped into the water, lunging his other foot to the softly matted sand. Lucy led Sam to the car with its perfectly round running lights. The engine hummed with such a low grumble it faded into background noise of the lightly tossing ocean. The bonnet ornament had an intrepid angel with her wings fanned out. The grill had a complaisant, long-toothed Parthenon smile of a put-out Brit: still polite in spite of a rubbish situation. Passing by the stately car's aggressively crocheted fenders and spotless whitewalls stood another tall, morose man with a driver's uniform. He followed Sam with marble-eyes, smirking with insolence, until he followed Lucy into the coffee-with-cream coloured interior.

The car moved slowly until the highway, not one rock or pothole was ignored by the shocks and springs, the carriage did not shift an inch the entire ride. "They really don't make them like this anymore, agreed?" Lucy smiled. Sam was unable to contribute for many reasons. The driver nodded without looking.

The car slowly prowled to a liquid stop in front of Sam's building. The park setting was as silent as most cars only after the engine is extinguished.

"This, if I am correct, will be goodbye, Samuel."

Sam looked up at Lucy with strain and sadness, a scintilla of relief and the rest a confusing anger. "What do you mean?" Sam asked with surfeit exasperation, broken and uneasy.

"Come now, my boy. You have been a good sport, and should you choose to defy all expectation, you will no longer have to entertain these insufferable encounters. I, for one, will miss them. You are an interesting character Samuel Florin. A true coward."

Lucy held out his hand. Sam begrudgingly accepted it, numbly and allowed it to be shaken for him. Limp and unreceived, he slid it back against the seat and lifted himself out of the car. "Bye," Sam groaned, look-ing at the ground, mechanically walking through the lobby and up to his apartment. His eyes were pointed down, but he saw nothing. He arrived at his door. It took him several moments to realize something was amiss. He was wearing Andy's neon-vomit beach clothes. He had no phone, and no keys. He scratched lightly then knocked against the door.

Muffled barks and socked heels-steps grew closer before the sound of unlatching deadbolt.

"Oh my god!" Kay said beneath a look that shifted from worry, to anger, then perplexity all in one sentence. "A meeting? Are you … Where are your keys? Why are you wearing those loud colours?"

Sam walked past her and stood motionless in the main room. A lifeless deadpan knurled his face.

"Babe, what's wrong?" She patted his arm. The dog looked up with a hopeful idiocy, wagging its tail.

"I … Andy is gone. He … we … I won't be seeing him anymore." Sam bite his lip. "It was a … tough goodbye."

"Oh babe." Kay hugged him, exhaled profoundly into his chest. The dog licked and nipped at his hands, dropped to his side. "I tried calling. Are you all right? Was it hard? What did he say?"

Sam was stiff and upright. He could not focus. "Yeah, he, uh, fought it a bit, but in the end … what's done is done."

"Let me take off your bag, you look like you've been to hell and back."

"My bag?" Sam asked.

Unbeknownst to Sam, his bag was slung over his shoulder. Beyond its zipper he found his phone, keys and work clothes. "Oh, yeah, my bag, sure."

She slid off his bag and kissed his shoulder, chin and ear. She moved to kiss his mouth. He did not move. His shock made him nothing more than a statue, frozen in disbelief. She pulled back.

"It's okay." She hugged him again, warmly. "You made a choice, and I'm not to say it was the right one. And I won't say it will be easy to get over. But the fact is you made it, it's important. I care so much about you. We can move forward together. I didn't think I would be able to open myself up again. I'm so glad I met you, Sam Florin. I lo … "

"Not now," Sam interrupted. "Another time. I want sleep. I … I need to forget today as soon as possible. I'm not myself. I care about you too. I just need … I just need to forget. To forget about it all."

Sam went to sleep without brushing his teeth or taking off his clothes. In asking for space he declined the bed. He huddled himself on the couch and quietly cried until his head throbbed. He sobbed in the dark, tasting the salt in his tears that transported him back to the anguish of nearly drowning, until sleep mercifully came for him, momentarily freeing him from the pain of his woken mind.

Dissipating him, assimilating him, and becoming indistinguishable as tears in the ocean.

PART 6

SLEEP WAS NO saviour for Sam. He sensed a dark, scratching haunt him. There were no images projected against the back of his resting eyelids, only the soulless, lonely blackness of charred stillness. A haunting and cold shiver terrorized him from the couch to the bed. He accidentally roused the gentle slumber of Mac and Kay, twisted like vines in a cyclone of bedsheets. Even when resting beside the person he cared for the most, dread persisted in gutting him whenever he closed his eyes. He tried to keep his eyes focused on Kay; her eyes lightly met, her mouth slightly ajar to allow the pass of tender breathing. When he closed his eyes and began to fade, a nightmare swirled about him like a cloud heavy with evil darkness.

There were no images and no sounds. No definitive projections or tangible articles. It was a sensation, unlike touch or taste or any other of his human feelers. Condemnation and the pre-eminence of inexorability; a complete and confident doom that patted simple emotions like anxiety on the head with a condescending smile. An eternity of torment in one blink, being ripped apart at a crawl and reconstituted in a flash just so the procedure could be hastened to linger again. He felt the hysterical panic of emptiness when he looked away from her. When he managed to evade the demons and settle into the waters of sleep, a bolt of imagined terror lurked from beneath the bed and wrapped its accursed tentacles, with teeth in place of suction cups, around his neck, pulling him to a place that was without even the light of deepest space.

He must have slept somewhere between these grisly tidings. He blearily took in Kay patting a damp cloth against his head, concerned with grim accountability, sighing with relief as he opened his eyes. The sun of the morning hid behind her like a shy child, a serene halation wreathed around her black hair as a golden nimbus, only her black eyes and reddish lips unveiled themselves.

"Oh thank god," she said meekly. "Any longer and I would've called an ambulance."

Sam groaned questioningly, squinting up.

"You've been sweating and speaking in tongues all night. I couldn't wake you for the life of me. The dog started barking and was running around the apartment all crazy like. You were running a fever hotter than any cup of coffee I've ever sleeved. You were sweating bullets. Look." She gestured at the sheet and pillow beneath him, a perfect outline of Sam was inked into the bed.

He fingered the dampness, it felt as though someone had spilled a drum of water in a stencil of his profile.

She patted his head again. "You kept talking, mumbling, and even screaming here and there. It was like you were possessed.... I thought your head was going to spin around and projectile vomit was next. Forget a doctor, I should've thought about calling a priest."

"I was asleep?" Sam rubbed his face, it was slick as if in the shower.

"Yeah, I couldn't wake you up." Kay reached for a glass of water on the nightstand. "I got you off the couch, remember? You just kind of plunked yourself down and started snoring instantly. I got you up, we brushed your teeth and took off those ridiculous clothes and, before I could wash my face and brush my own teeth, you were dead to the world." She passed Sam the glass of water. "Did you get wasted?"

"No," Sam reflexed, "I mean, I had a beer or two.... I don't think...."

A punch at the door shook the walls of the bedroom.

Sam went to place the water on the nightstand, but Kay pushed it towards him. "You stay, I'll get it."

"No," Sam wrapped his fingers around her arm, "you're not on the lease. If it's the landlord or something, he'll be suspicious. He'll wonder what happened to Chloe and I'll be playing twenty questions however many times in a row that talkative little guy wants." He swigged the water and passed it to her. "Trust me, stay in here with Mac and try to keep him quiet, I don't want to redraw up my lease right now."

Sam shakily took to his feet and stumbled to the bedroom door. The impatient knocking grew louder and more irritable. He grabbed a t-shirt and instantly melted through it. He toweled himself off with the wet rag and pulled another over his head.

He closed the bedroom door softly behind him and yawned. His entire body; limbs, joints and muscles, needed the same compulsory relief of tedium. He smacked his lips and peered through the peephole.

"The detectives?" he alarmed. "This is … "

"Florin, we know you're in there, open up, now, we need to talk," one of the detectives soured without a drop of honey in his plea.

Fuck, Sam thought. He breathed heavily. He was lost, momentarily stunned by the voltage of a reality check. That instant crushing overpowering of the psyche whereby true, waking lucidity and its sharp outlines displace the dreamlike falsity that people entrust as reality. Sam was experiencing the cable break and his elevator-car freefall headlong towards his fate.

It is the most bizarre of moments when the consciousness snaps itself like a rubber band and pushes all moments from a previous life and thought to the hazy flashes of a once dreamt dream, questioning if either lived or lied. The bewildering feeling of the human animal achieving full conscience, a mortality without definition, the lip-biting prayer to a bleak and empty emperor to make it pass and return the state to normal. A tunneling perspective that reality, the real and the unblemished, too fine and too colourful, is nonmechanical and without the routinely passive adherence to robotic reactions. When the automatic steering is involuntarily disabled, the windshield free of cracks and smears and splatters of insect carcasses, the driver is choked by his own impulses and instincts; those so often used as defence for rashness, but in effect, so rarely used in its purest form that the actual muscles have atrophied like the shrivelled wings of the flightless bird.

"Sam Florin! Open up or we will have no other option but to use force!" the detective growled.

Sam shook his head from the rattling effects of contemplating reality and went for the deadbolt. He removed and wiped the dew from his palms on his shirt and accomplished the task with shaking effort. He slowly opened the door. As soon as the hinges began to squeak one of the policemen tried to propel the door wide-open.

"Hey! Open the door all the way! What's the big idea?"

The clasp was attached without Sam's knowledge. "Sorry," he hurriedly whispered, shutting the door and sliding the chain down the track slowly.

The officers did not wait for Sam to twist the knob again. They stormed in with their hands hovering above their right hips. Sam lunged back several paces. The dog barked behind the closed door of the bedroom.

Detective Perez moved his right hand upwards with a flattened palm facing Sam. "Please, Florin. Do not resist."

"Resist what?" Sam whimpered.

"You're under arrest for the disappearance of Andre Lambert and in the connection of several other disappearances around the city."

"I don't understand." Sam cringed.

"Please, Sam, we can talk about this at the station," Diggs said while brandishing a pair of handcuffs, one of the ratchets was held purposefully open-mouthed.

"No, there has been a misunderstanding!" Sam retorted.

Perez, seemingly the good of the duo, shushed and stared into Sam's eyes. "Listen, pal, we found Mr. Lambert's mother's jeep this morning. We found an unoccupied boat bottomed-up on shore. We have witnesses that say the two of you went into the water together, and you came back alone."

Diggs piped up less calmly. "We have video surveillance of you turning behind the corner of a dive bar with a Savoy DeNoon, with only you re-entering the bar and *him* to be reported a missing person since that night. Listen, you fuck, make this easy. Get yourself a little lawyer and come talk about this with us. You think we have just two? We can link to damn near every missing person's case in the goddamn city!"

Sam held his hands up like a bank teller. "I swear, I don't know … I mean. He did it! He made me! I didn't want this power! This ability! I didn't want anything! Maybe … "

Sam noticed the cops looking at each other and slowly moving their hands in unison for their pistols. Ever so slightly they glided their arms downward. One had to blink to really notice any change in the position of their arms.

"Guys, I didn't do anything! I can't control it! I … I need help." Sam nearly crumbled to the ground beneath him. He swayed and sniffled. His face felt hot and his stomach bubbled uncomfortably. A dull headache and intense sweat leaked like an egg cracked atop his crown.

"It's okay.…" Perez said, looking at his partner and taking the cuffs from Diggs with his left hand. His right hand stayed cautiously over his piece. He took soft, long footsteps, lifting his knees with the same silent gait of a black-masked, striped-shirt thief in the old cartoons. "We are not blaming you, we just want to talk … down at the station … we'll find out who put you up to this … who is to blame … that's it, just stay there… "

A surge of rage, only a single filament, flexed like a solitary tendon within Sam. The patronizing speak of the detective agitated Sam with a low-fire pulse, but enough for Sam to look up from his pity, blink effortlessly, and view only a gobsmacked Diggs. The only remaining detective's hands now wrapped around the hairs on his head.

"What the fuck!" Diggs' eyes were so abundant with dubiety that they swelled from his skull. "Where did … What the fuck!" he screamed. Mac began to bark aggressively in the next room.

"What did you do with Santiago? Where did you … What is happening?!" The detective was frozen. His hand shook violently as he tried to lower it to his belt. His fingers trilled jerkily and danced macabrely as he fought to secure them around the light absorbing pistol grip. The handle was nearing the gun; but his wide, terrified expression, the peeled back eyes and frozen jaw, remained constant.

"Don't," Sam squeezed out of his breathless chest, "I can't help it.…"

"You worthless, weak, fucking coward.… I'm going to kill … " Molecules and atoms of far less weight replaced the area which had held the fiery detective a shutter earlier.

The only sound that remained was the scratchy bays from the bedroom.

Sam slumped, he stood, but barely. He wavered and felt dizziness threaten to collapse him like a rickety shack. He was too dazed to drink the relief that was held to his lips like a mazer.

Again, he had to collect himself. He rubbed his soaking face again, and again, his shirt was permeated by sweat.

Kay, he thought as he scraped his fingers down his cheeks. *What could she be thinking....*

Mac's yelping subsided to a fitful, high-pitched whimper. Between the discontinuous whining, the strike of digital pads and rapidly scraping of claws against the inside of the door, Sam discerned a hurried rustling and heel-heavy steps drub against the wooden floorboards.

Sam marched through the empty room to the bedroom. He opened the door and was set upon by Mac jumping onto his lap with a hopeful gaiety, licking at Sam's protesting hands and swaying his entire hind-quarters from the ecstatic movement of his tail.

Kay was shoving articles of clothing into an oversized purse or an undersized duffle. Her eyes were allergy-red, itchy and bothered. She moved as stiffly as her bottom lip, which was bit into by her teeth with such tension that her chin, her entire face, was shades lighter from the strain. Her legs did not bend as they roved around the room, collecting bras, panties and whatever else she saw fit to cram disheveled into her bag.

"Hey." Sam blanked, with the word delivered in an awkwardly confused, nearly expressionless tone. "What ... what are you doing?" He inflected the question with an innocence usually deployed in the soft-handling of autistic children.

She looked at him with, her black eyes ablaze. The instant glare shuddered Sam, the feeling was similar to the chill he sensed when locking eyes with Lucy's footmen. Her chin quivered and her piano-wire jaw loosened. Her eyebrows lifted like a bascule bridge and her teeth relinquished her lips, dripping with wet. Her faced began to strain towards the centre; her forehead, nose and cheeks wrinkled and sunk. Her eyes became dewy, and when hit with the light they sparkled and dropped little pellets that streaked into the lines in her cheek, into her mouth.

Sam approached and opened his arms. She did not move. Sam closed his arms around her and was promptly pushed with all her force, a slap and a punch and an arched-fingered talon swipe followed.

"Tell me...." she seethed at Sam, backing up to his original position near the door. "Tell me the truth! What did you do to Sav?!" Her scream lilted and splintered beneath the weight of her crying.

"I didn't do anything," Sam insisted.

"Liar!"

"I mean ... I didn't mean for anything to happen...." Very quickly, beneath the murmur of her sobbing he said, "I didn't mean for almost anyone to get ... I don't even know what happens to them.... I just blink and, and ... "

Kay rubbed her palms into her face, the trace amounts of eye-makeup that was not fully rinsed off the night before streaked like charcoal sticks from the corners of her eyes.

"Look ... I have this ability and ... "

"Shut the fuck up! What are you talking about?" She bent and heaved, supporting herself on the bed.

The dog barked playfully, looking at one master and then the other, his tail like a windshield wiper in a monsoon.

"Look ... Just before I met you ... you're not going to believe this ... "

She breathed heavy and tried to compose herself. Kay lifted her shoulders from the bed and breathed deeply, a generous intake through the nose and a quavering exhale through lumpy cheeks. "Go on."

Sam pared a sigh with back-against-the-wall mechanics. "I don't know how or why, but I was ... made to have this power."

"Power?" Kay imprudently folded her arms, ran a pinky under her eyelid.

"Yes, and ... I'll try to make it simple ... When I am angry ... I think ... that when I'm in a position where I'm stressed or mad or jealous or whatever, I look at someone and I blink and they ... well ... disappear."

Kay's face twisted with insult and disbelief. She rolled her eyes and swore. "Bullshit. Whoever heard of some stupid fairy-tale garbage? You are lying, just tell me the truth."

"I am! At least that's what I have figured out. How do you explain the detectives? They just vanished! Go and look for yourself! I blinked and they were just … gone!"

"Where do they go? How can I find Savoy?"

"I don't know…. You can't … I think … "

"What!" she growled and sent Mac under the bed.

"Well," Sam scratched the back of his head, refusing eye contact, "I think that the person, the man who forced these powers on me, might be the … Devil?"

"You're fucked!"

"You think I don't know that? For all I know I just sent my best friend to hell!" Sam's eyes stung. "I don't know if that's where they go! If I'm in a dream or if this is all a hoax."

"This is real! Real life! No one has seen Savoy since we were at that dirty bar…. Sam … What happened?"

"I don't know." His face pained with pusillanimity.

She pinched her eyes, empty of emotion.

"It was an accident…. I guess after seeing you guys at the beach. He was just so much more handsome, talented, cooler and better than me. Knowing just a bit of the history, I guess I was jealous and … When he came out I just turned around and it happened. If I could take that one back, trust me, I would. But I can't reverse this godforsaken curse. It just happens. One or two times, sure, I wanted it…. But almost every other time it has been an accident."

"How many people have you … killed?"

"I didn't kill anybody!" Sam irritably retorted through his clenched teeth.

"Answer me you coward!" she screamed.

"I don't know … maybe a couple dozen, give or take."

"Oh god!" Her bones and muscles bowed with fearful protection.

"No!" Sam protested. "I wouldn't hurt an insect! It just happens when I get bothered or something. I don't really know. I would never hurt you." He felt the oppositional force of his intention appear in her body language. "Or anyone for that matter.

"I just get annoyed and they just disappear, like magic. They are just gone and there is no trace of anything. I don't understand it, it just happens."

Her breathing vacillated between fear and anger. "Did you do it to my boss?"

"Ugh, I did it to both our bosses!" Sam derided. "It's how I got a promotion. How I got Mac. How I got single. How I got new clothes. How I got you!"

Kay squatted, appeared to ready herself to vomit, and grabbed her bag. "Get out of my way, you murderer."

Sam held his position squarely. "You have nothing to be worried about, I would never in a million years ever have a negative thought about you. I love you!"

She gave him a death-penance stare before trying to lure out the dog from under the bed. "That's reassuring! Being told by a mass-murderer that you're safe! Why do all you psychopaths always say that?"

"I'm not! But … I'm serious … if anything, most of the people that got … well removed, were because of how much I care about you and want to be with you."

"Mac, come out baby, come out boy.…" The dog did not move. She looked up with a warring face, black streaks of a Maori soldier. "You fucking psychopath. You sick son of a bitch. You're a Dahmer, a Gacy, a Bundy, a Manson, good-for-nothing serial killer and you *will* let me leave here." Sam just stared with sad confusion. "If you love me, please Sam, just let me leave. You are scaring me," she pleaded with her negotiator's voice softened by fear.

Sam looked down to his soaking t-shirt. A swirl of liquid sloshing around in his skull made him dizzy and lose focus. He felt like the sole survivor in the centre of a meteor crater. He looked back at her, now slapping the planks with her hand, demanding the dog emerge from beneath the bed. He was numb.

"I … I wouldn't hurt you, though."

"You keep saying that but I don't believe you. My guess is … you killed Andre last night." She kneeled. "Sure, you felt bad about it, but you did something that was unthinkable. Shit. I didn't even think you would be able to lessen your friendship, let alone end it.… But you killed him, didn't you?"

Tears like shrapnel fell without feel from Sam's downturned face. "I tried to not do it.… He kept pushing me and starting at me.… I tried with all my power to not shut my eyes. I tried to make him apologize, to … "

"Murderer," Kay whispered with sublime derision.

She rose slowly as Sam stood motionless, head buried in his sternum like a decommissioned robot.

"I'll send for Mac." She picked up her bag and slapped him with all her might, pushing by him and cursing. "Don't kill the dog, for the love of all things holy."

"I don't think it works on non-humans," he stated without thinking. "Kay wait." He grabbed her as she neared the door. She shivered off his weak clutch and raised her fist.

"I … I'm not a bad guy." His eyes were ovate and voice soft as a damp cloth. "I didn't want this. I don't want this. I want you. I need you. I need for you to know that this is not me, this is not who I am. This evil magic is not the man you sleep and eat and laugh and share with. This does not define me. I would throw everything away right now, gouge my eyes out, and learn braille so that I could be with you. Smell you and touch you and taste you. I need you, Kayoko. I love you and want you so bad it hurts every part of my body. Please don't leave me, please. If I could take it back I would, I don't know if there is a way I can but … "

"Psycho." She laughed with hushed revile. "I thought you were just a nice guy. Just what I wanted and needed in my life. A pleasant, agreeable, thoughtful man who cares about me and wants me to be happy." She spat on the floor just missing his bare foot. "You might be all those things, but only because you are a wimp. A total loser and an absolute coward. You aren't genuinely nice and affectionate, but scared and selfish."

Sam shook his head out of dispute and distress.

"You and your *power* orchestrated this whole charade to trick me … to trick me into falling for you. And you know what? I might have. I was. Maybe I did. And I might even stay if people like Sav weren't out there. People who are genuinely good and caring, confident and secure in themselves. No … You are only kind because you are too scared to be anything else. You have no voice and no reason. I liked you, not even out of pity, but because you were shy and seemed to be a real, living, nice man. You are far from that. Maybe it just took some devilry to show your true side. You are a bully, I don't know if you were picked-on as a child or just a natural born pussy. But you are. You have no balls and no hope without your voodoo. You were a cute-enough loser before and just a scumbag serial killer now. You're as gentle as a snake in the grass. I'm angry you killed the man I actually love and actually see as my soul-mate. I'm angry that you fooled me with some fake world you created, you fraud. I'm angry you lied to me and let me believe you were a good guy. I will never forgive you and I never want to see you again. I hope you get what you deserve. I hope they staple your eyelids open and you are fully awake while your cell-mates take turns making your life and rectum more of a hell that the one you've brought on the hundreds of lives you've ruined. I hate you. I hate you with all my heart. You lying, worthless motherfucker. You're not innocent and you're not a good person! You fake-fuck. I hate you. Don't hurt the dog."

All the while Sam could not refute the bullseye-placed accusations, he could not help but become agitated. His mind faded in and out, asking himself whether or not he should blink Kay out. Maybe he was a bully, a former clenched-fist stuck at his side that became a machete raised over his head with little impartiality over what head is to be split. Perhaps it was the build-up of having followed the rules of engagement he had inadvisably set for himself; a hopelessly misguided ritual, bombastic in its attempt to be pure and rustic; an abjectly antediluvian code of conduct that he designed for himself to suffer the pitfalls and punji sticks for a Spartan loyalty.

He came to full cognition when she uttered the final Kalashnikov-prattled taunts and oaths. He put his hand on the door to prevent her from opening it when she lifted her fist, knobbed with little knuckles, shoulder high.

Sam blinked, bracing for impact, and kept his eyes shut.

"Let go of the door you monster!" she seethed.

"Please, stop calling me names. I don't want to get mad at you." Sam did not move.

"Open your eyes and open the door you freak!"

Sam's body trembled. "Oh no." He tightened the lasso of skin around his orbs. Tears slithered down his face. He pulled his arm back and kept his eyes shut.

He heard the door open, it did not slam immediately.

"Go ahead, open them, coward," she fumed.

"I … I don't want to make you go away.…"

"Well, either way, you'll never see me again."

The door slammed.

A flush of air hissed from the forceful swing of the door and cooled the beads of sweat that clung to Sam's body. The whisk of air sent a shiver from his skin to his bones like a T-handled detonator sends currents to a blasting-cap.

There was no explosion. Sam's strength, from his legs to his spine, imploded. He blindly palmed the wall to support himself, struggling to stay on his feet.

Sam held the portrait of Kay as if his eyelids were a canvas. The recent Nightingale Kay, swabbing his forehead with an angelic crown made of broken dawn and gluey eyelids. The debased part of him wanted desperately to watch her leave, to drink in her petite body and caudal curvature one more time, for posterity's sake.

He refrained. He held his leaking eyes closed and stumbled to his seat, back against the door. His sadness triumphed in his most immediate faculties, but the underlying fear and concern of what may happen if he opened his eyes twisted a blade deep in his stomach. He felt nauseated, blind and scared. He sat and concentrated on the greyscale backs of his eyes, in the middling infinity of a rain cloud, where the sun burnt in some faraway place and irradiated just enough light to press the sovereignty of a drab, anemic chromoly foreverness.

Mac grumbled affectionately and crawled on Sam's twisted lap, licking up the tears on his face. Sam allowed it for a few moments, basking in the love of something, until the dog stepped back. Sam could hear his paws scrape in place, followed by the mild plea of a soft whimper. It was a while before Sam acknowledged the dog's demand for attention.

"Hungry, boy?" he finally said desultorily and heard the dog's tail whoosh back and forth. "Thirsty, too?" Sam asked with a smiled that cracked like fault lines though his stiff face. "I bet you'll need a walk after."

Sam stood with more effort than he would have liked, petting the dog's head. "Good boy."

The food and water dishes were easy to find as Sam inadvertently kicked them, cursing the poorly placed bowls. He then stubbed his toe on a wooden chair, cursing the disharmony of his apartment's Feng-Shui.

He recovered the dishes halfway across the living room with laboured hands outstretched like beetle antennae, either grasping a firm shape, shrinking away or dancing his fingers about an object like a virgin boy nervously feeling his first breast.

The water was the easiest. He glided his hand along the wall until the wooden floorboards became laminate tiles under his feet. From there he fingered along the counter until he reached the sink and thumbed the ball-handled faucet upward, rotating it to the right, checking the temperature, and filling the dish. He went to place the dish on the floor, arriving knee-level when Mac introduced his snout, lapping at the water furiously, continuing to splash away with his curling tongue once the dish was settled.

The food was something else entirely.

Kay had, what Sam had thought to be the adorable habit of a young person, the propensity of putting food away in different places every time she touched it. With adoration, and eyesight, he would shake his head affably and guffaw. *Oh Kay, you free-spirit.* With the now-foreclosed eye sockets, Sam opened cupboards at head-level and below his waist, feeling the cans, thumbing the ribs of generic aluminium stores, attempting to deduce if one felt more dogfood-like than a potential can of noodle soup or lentils or cream corn. He wanted to open his eyes, just one, just a whisker, just for a snippet. But he could not, he had no idea what the strength or rules of the 'power' were and if she would survive even she was far away.

He had a squadron of stout cans grouped on the counter in front of him. He tapped the tops, each was as replete as the next. He decided to shake them, which allowed him to separate the broths, soups and either fruits or vegetables.

That left him with four. *Fuck it,* he thought. *I'll just eat whichever ones aren't dogfood.*

He scrounged in the drawers for a can opener. The dog's whimpering grew louder as he fumbled among the cutlery, clattering the cheap metal utensils together which made the scraping sound only cheap metals can. He found it. He picked a can at random and sunk in the cutting wheel and clamped in the pinioned wheel with a squeeze of the hand. The contraption rotated the can with a twisting from the other hand.

A smell that could have either been soup or dogfood seeped from the topless receptacle, he leaned towards the latter. "Fuck it" again left his mouth as he felt for the dry dish and emptied the container in a gelatinous tube shape into the dish. Before he could grab a fork to mash down the slimy pillar, Mac had already dove in, the sound of boots trudging through mud as the dog licked and swallowed the unchewed sludge.

Time passed. Impossible for Sam to say how much, for he did not remark the hour he rose, when the detectives came and went or when Kay had made her exit following her jeremiad. Over half of Sam's energy was dedicated to keeping his eyes closed. It was tiring. The natural process of blinking seemed to crave the reverse of a momentary opening. Sam sat in myriad seats and positions, posing questions to himself that he had never once even touched upon.

"Why is it harder to breathe when I can't see? Do blind people keep their eyes closed beneath their glasses? How do their watches work? Do they have special cell-phones? They must have voice commands of some kind, right? How does one use a computer? Will I really go blind if I keep my eyes closed too long? If I fall asleep, will my eyes know to stay closed?"

While far from philosophical and meaningful beyond his temporary condition, it was at that last question, while draped over the couch, that Sam fell victim to a nap. Once again, temporally concerned, Sam was clueless about the length of time he had slept or spent ruminating on the most trivial of questions concerning his predicament.

His mobile alerted him from the bedroom. Though Mac had been whining for the duration of his shut-eye, the prickling tingle of his ringtone forced a dramatic intake of oxygen through the nose. He maintained his firmly closed lids, just barely, and stumbled to the room. He missed the call. He stood in the room, the dog still whining, trying to determine how to call the number back. It rang anew, the sound plus the vibration in his hands made him jump. He picked the phone up, accidentally accepting the call and pressed the device to his ear.

"H-Hello?"

"Florin, where are you?"

"Who is this?"

"Who is this? This is Gavin Suter, Mr. Howard Chen's administrative assistant. Why are you not at work today? We received no email and no telephone call. There is an important training session where we will … "

"Mr. Suter, hi, umm, I have a slight problem."

"A problem? The problem is that you are not here, and we have not received any communication from you at this point in time. You are on probation for the role and Mr. Chen advised me to remind you of that fact, and the additional fact that there are many people who are qualified and prepared to … "

"I am blind."

There was a silence on the line. Whispering on the admin's line followed.

"I'm sorry, can you repeat that?" Suter's voice seemed more distant, as if on speaker phone.

"I-I said that I am blind. I-I woke up this morning and I cannot see. I have no vision. My eyes don't work. I can't … I can't even find the door to leave my house."

More whispering on the other line.

"Is it serious? Have you been to a doctor?" Suter asked hastily.

"I haven't … I can't even see my phone. I have to try and find a way to the clinic.… But, no … I just woke up and … "

"Florin. Chen. Is it permanent?" He spoke with the same distinguished air as his son, only more austere.

"H-Hello Mr. Chen. I-I don't know, it just happened."

"Report with a doctor's note or have the doctor call my personal mobile," the senior Chen demanded. "Do you have a pen to write it down? Or should I email it to you."

"I don't know if I have a pen, I can't even see a computer, let alone a screen."

"Get a pen, I'll wait."

Sam knocked into a few things in his room. He made it to the kitchen and set the phone on the counter, he searched for something to write with and something to write on. Finally he gave up.

"Yeah, okay … " he lied.

Chen told him the number. "And you have the doctor's office call me as soon as they have your results, young man."

"Okay, good … " The other line clicked-off before Sam finished.

Sam hunched over the counter. He took a few steps and again kicked the dog's bowls and stubbed his toe. This one hurt worse, it felt like his little toe was rend clean off his foot. He was still tired. He picked up the television remote and tried to use the clicker from memory. The whir of the set hummed successfully before the sound activated. He felt around the buttons and aurally scanned the stations to find the news outlet. They always mentioned the time.

He waited. War in the Middle East. War in central Africa. Oil crisis this, environmental catastrophe that.

"The time is 11:47 AM," a monotonous voice announced in the Queen's.

Sam did not know what to make of the time. He could not go to work. He did not need to see a doctor. He had no reason to not live out his miserable days in perpetually squalid conditions, sharing tins of grub with the mutt and singing drunken Day of the Dead hymns with a chiding bottle of Mezcal with the odd recess to masturbate sobbingly.

He began to weep again.

Being blind, so they say, is a courageous act on its own. It takes a certain bravery to muscle the handicap and an air of intrepidity to resist the beck and call to submit. Being born without the ability to see is no different than being born to a certain race or gender; simply a clause in the contract of life that has been proven to be far from insurmountable, with exceptional cases of mastery as anyone with ethic and perseverance can achieve. Becoming blind later in life creates a crossroad that proposes the existence of the afflicted-one with either reliance or independence, weakening or strengthening their resolve.

Courageousness, bravery, valor and heroism.

Sam, it had been drubbed tediously throughout his life, was far from possessing the requisite traits for dealing with blindness. He was as far from brave as he was from genius, and that distance receives no warmth from any deep-seated star.

Sam got up and wandered around, contemplated eating, but opted to disregard the grumbles in his stomach until they reached full growl. He stepped in dog urine, twice. He cursed to himself as he swabbed up the pools, one warmer than the other, and realized at some point, he would have to take the dog for a walk. Mac's supplicating was already transforming from a whinny to a cry, and enough time had passed for the breakfast to travel through the little dog's pipework.

Sam grabbed some easy-to-garb clothing, something that he could tell was plain and worn the right way. He grabbed the leash and, before slipping on his shoes, a pair of sunglasses. His plan was not to stray far, but enough to let the dog fertilize his favourite shrubs and return. It may have been the most adventurous thing that Sam had ever done.

The air felt clean against Sam's face, enlightening him to the greasy pours and gritty, dried ocean stuck to his skin. People passed, let their own dogs sniff and play with Mac, strike up simple-minded conversations and pass. Sam was almost cheerful, unable to cast stereotypes on all people he encountered, eventually smiling without force and gaining traction with his spatial awareness. He let his fingers touch the leaves on the bushes and the coarse bark on the trees. He was led by Mac and kept an ear for traffic. When he lowered the shades down the bridge of his nose, the backs of his eyes became lighter, almost ashen. He heard the elderly speak amongst each other in civil, reticent voices. Box trucks would issue two prompt honks before stopping, raising and lowering their roll-up doors and hydraulic platforms, reverse alarms cutting through all else when they pushed the gear in reverse. Cars in the busier roads that intersected Sam's at each side created a border or sorts, and he even tried to count his paces. From what-to-what, he did not know.

Mac eventually tired and led him back to his building, where he tried to remember the toothed identity of his apartment keys like a forensic dental record.

He fed Mac another can of the remaining three on the counter. A stronger smell of sultry flesh swam from the opened lid. Earthily revolting and synthetic at the same time. He had clearly fed his dog human food earlier that morning.

Sam showered. It was easy enough in practice, but his eyes begged to open, trying to make it seem natural and harmless to him, as if they were saying 'just one lash for the soap, one more for the shampoo, a quick two for the towel, old boy.'

It was a veritable nuisance that Sam had to verbally reinforce to himself. "No! Stay closed! I don't want to know what will happen." Somewhere in a naivete that may have been cute for someone younger, Sam hoped he would reconcile with Kay.

All this led Sam, frustrated after another few hours of concentration, also without consuming any water or food which had given him a headache, to rummage through the drawers and find a roll of duct tape. Truthfully, he found packing tape first but after a solid hour of being unable to find the end-piece and get a clean strip he switched to the sturdy industrial adhesive.

With two stubbornly wrenched strips of whining tape he placed them over his eyes, from his forehead to his cheekbones. Ta-da. No longer did he have to worry about clasping his lenses closed, he only had to worry about the loss of his eyebrows when Kay finally forgave him for his unforgiveable atrocities.

He napped from hunger and boredom. He tried to eat but found the search for nourishment made whatever he held at his mouth, either in a spoon or his fingers, unpalatable.

The news anchor welcomed the evening audience warmly to the six o'clock news. 'Two detectives had disappeared earlier in the after …' Sam clicked off the television.

He tried to rouse the pup for a trot but the dog seemed unamused or ill. He slopped a third can of food, again smelling of human or animal decay, into the bowl, but Mac seemed uninterested.

After another circuit around the house, bumping his knee and hip, Sam had just about enough. He went to the linen closet and removed a broom. He unscrewed the brush-head and held the wooden handle, toggling the metallic cap at the end in front of him. It seemed a plausible device, he could feel-out the chairs, shoes, couches and coffee table. It wasn't perfect, the entire top-end of Sam's body was susceptible to hanging branches, beehives and booby wire traps placed at the neck of the average male.

Once more he tried to cajole his amateur seeing-eye dog. The dog had become repulsively flatulent. Sam opined that now was as good of a time as ever to let him rest and get some supper.

He put on his sunglasses and felt his way cautiously down the stairs, holding the railing and measuring each step with diligence. It had seemed easier with Mac leading the way, letting a puppy with no training take the wheel: a leader to blame. He exited the building and thought over his options. To the left was a busier road with a sandwich shop, a taco stand, some street vendors and a corner store. To the right was a quieter passage with Arab stick-meat and a few other options readily accessible. Sam went right.

He walked at first with his stick skidding on the ground but twice, very early, did the stick hit a bump or median strip. The first such embedment nearly punctured his belly with the stick. The second made him jerk, drop the broom handle and hit himself in the pubic region, which made his face squeeze and feel his hairs pulling beneath the eye-tape.

He tried to mimic the side-winding motion of feeling the radius around him. An improvement. When the tip had dug into a divot, there was less force to stiffen the stick and stab him without time to prepare.

He stood at the crosswalk. The sound of traffic was not endless, but entirely misleading. After waiting for a cessation in the rubbing-cloud sound of cars passing, he went to place a foot down from the curb and felt the gust of hot, gas-soaked air whip past his face. A second time must have been a closer call; a horn alarmed him as if it was placed inside of his ear. He waited. He grew more and more tired. He walked up to the lights a street away. He moved his glasses above his face, it was dark now, the back of his eyes showed the same shade as if he was wearing the shades. He shook his head. "Idiot," he said to himself. "You have thick tape, it will always be pure black and dark from now on, idiot."

The bystander crossing had a noise-cutting signal when the little man was flashing. The problem was that Sam had fallen out of sorts, not knowing which direction he should face, where he was aimed or where the beeping was coming from. He breathed heavily and cursed to himself. Sweat was collecting beneath his arms and in the fold of his elbows and knees. He was certain of retreat, but needed to ask a stranger which way was to head home.

People passed by the broomstick-holding man without any response. He patiently requested the attention of anyone with a submissive voice. The only verbalized answers comprised of "I don't live here", "Get away from me", and "Sorry". That last response often arrived even before he had asked a question. He could hear dampened music of all sorts from what seemed like omnipresent headsets. He could hear people conversing and feel as though he could hear their sneering and scoffing at his sad state. His stomach felt as though it was clinging to his spine like a koala to a eucalyptus tree. He wanted to sit. The slight hunch that was required to use the homemade stick was straining his lumbar and the spots where the stick stabbed his soft body were tender. Panhandlers and homeless people ran upon him like rats to a seagull pecked trash bag, picked over by the pigeons and crows, left drizzling and fetid.

A gentle voice spoke to him as a little hand docilely squeezed his arm. "My poor dear, are you lost?"

"Yes ma'am." Sam humbly dropped his head.

"You're blind? Correct?" the voice, an elderly woman's asked.

"Yes ma'am."

"Where are you going?"

"I-I don't know…. I just want to sup and go home. But I can't cross the street and I got turned around and don't know where home is anymore." Sam sniffled.

"Can I take you to anywhere?"

"Al-Basha? I think it's just a few doors down." Sam wiped his nose with his sleeve.

"Okay little angel," the woman said as she looped her arm beneath Sam's.

Sam allowed the woman to lead him about a block leftwards, she spoke softly to him.

"About one day," when she asked him how long he had been blind.

"My goodness," she giggled, "you are so brave, I can't imagine losing total vision and going out the same day. You are a hero.'

Sam sniffled. "Yeah … I guess that I kind of am!"

He felt that she was walking too slow, her little patter was beginning to outweigh her assistance as the smell of falafel and spits of lamb and chicken piqued Sam's olfactory system. He assured her that he could follow the waft of undeniable middle-eastern spices, but she persisted.

"Don't be foolish, it's on my way," she said kindly.

They arrived at the eatery and Sam thanked the woman. "I am so grateful for your help ma'am…. I would be lost and crying in a gutter if you didn't come along."

"It is my pleasure, young man. I know the feeling." A sharp tap tickled the pavement below. "I can still see up close, but anything under the hips is getting difficult. I use this in public so that I don't hurt anyone. You should get one as well. It is the life-saver for people like us."

Sam shook his head, and reached his hand. It was a smooth, ski-pole like staff with a rubberized handle and a plastic ball on the end.

"You're blind?" he nearly shouted.

She laughed gently. "Almost, just hanging on … I will have to learn braille to read my stories now. Radio, just like it used to be for the other stories. Have you ever heard the old mysteries? The Shadow? The Whisper? A Man Called X? Quiet Please? Oh they are wonderful. The suspense and the drama. You will love them!"

"Uh … well … maybe … "

She was quiet for a moment.

"What's that on your face?" she asked. Sam could feel her hands brace herself on his wrists and her breath against his chest.

"What's what?"

"On your eyes?"

Sam hesitated. "Duct tape?"

"But why? Why my boy?"

"Because I can't open my eyes."

"Because you're blind? Because you have lost your eyes somehow?"

"No … my eyes are in my head. And … they work … But I can't use them."

"What do you mean you can't use them?"

"I mean, I am not allowed to open them."

"Allowed or able."

"I can open them, and if I open them I can see. But I am not allowed to open them and therefore cannot see."

"So you are not blind."

"But I can't see."

"By choice?"

"I suppose that is correct."

"So, open your eyes!"

"I'm unable."

"Why?"

"It's hard to explain, I just can't."

"But, if you did, you could see"

"Yes, quite well."

"But you will not."

"That is correct."

"So you slap the lord God and people like myself in the face."

"No, I can't explain. I am able to see, but unable to see … "

She cursed something in a language Sam could not understand.

"Pardon me?" Sam asked.

"Enjoy Hell you insufferable, foolish, pill of a man." She spat on the ground.

"But, you're not blind either…"

Sam heard her clicking down the street, muttering in the same language. She seemed to move quicker, it irritated Sam. If he could only blink that old dame out….

Sam ordered a plate of kebab and a soda. He did not know how much cash he had taken with him, but felt his wallet had lost more weight than the cost should have entailed. On the bright side, which was the same opaqueness to Sam with tape over his eyes, the owner was never as nice to Sam as he was during this visit.

He ate hastily. Drips of yogurt and garlic sauces splat against his shirt and pants like gobs of eighth round boxer spit. He did not care, he could feel the greasy meat slicken his cheeks. He noisily slurped the can of soda, unaware of any potential looks from other customers, or even if there were any other customers. The only sound was a precise, standout violin and other accompanying strings and horns over a goblet drum and cymbals. The faint wailing of a man's voice seemed lost in the burnishing music. The owner and another man conversed behind the counter, Sam could neither understand them nor the song lyrics, but focused solely on the food.

Upon finishing his plate he felt reinvigorated with strength, lest he saw the elder lady again, and as a new man, he was sure that he could make it home. He exited the restaurant and spun right, that much he was certain. He made it to the same traffic lights and was again confronted by the same problem. He stalled, ground his knuckles together nervously with his stick beneath his arm and listened carefully. He tried to examine where the mob moved and to what signal they moved towards or away from. Jaywalkers and right-turning cars made this more difficult, but he was full of food and felt refreshed.

Each shoulder that collided and spun his unbraced body lowered his confidence. Each admonishment towards his clumsiness with his stick and body movement decreased it further. The street was chaotic without permanence. He cussed aloud, perhaps too loud, a vacuum of gasping quietude blotted his vicinity for a spell. The crowd moved along, and a new batch of pedestrians soon refilled the void, bringing clamour and indifference to poor Sam's self-perpetuated perplexity.

He heard a little child, at the age that the voice of a boy and girl carries the same shrill attenuation, asked its father why the man had tape on his eyes.

"I don't know, baby, don't look," the father audibly shuddered.

Sam was worked up again. Vitality plummeted. He lost his direction and felt like crawling into a ball.

"Hey, buddy … Need some help?" a sly voice treated Sam.

"My god, yes, please … My god thank you, I just want to go home."

"What's you address?" the man asked.

"I just live like a block or two that way," Sam pointed, "or was it that way?"

"Address, man," the voice coaxed.

"Eighty-eight 80th Street, my friend," Sam exhaled.

"Cool, it's on my way," the man said and gripped Sam's shoulder. It was a fastened, man-sized grip, like an orderly might lead a patient to shock treatment therapy.

The two walked. The man's grip never loosened.

"Nice night?" Sam attempted conversation.

The man hemmed.

"No, I mean is it a nice night?"

The man agreed with a nasal inflection.

The trip felt longer than Sam felt it should take. He became nervous, "Are we close?"

"Yup, just a right here," the man said.

"Another right? I don't think that's … " Sam nearly lost his head as he was shoved with brute strength from behind, abandoning his stick and landing on his hands skidding across ungroomed pavement.

"What's the … " Sam wailed.

"All right buddy, I don't want to hurt a blind man, so just give me your wallet, keys and apartment number." The slyness in his tone was still present beneath sharp authority.

"Why?" Sam sniveled.

"Doesn't matter. Saw your open wallet in the A-rabs … A no-seeing cat like you don't need all that loot." The man's tone graveled. "And keep your voice down."

Sam became a table, resting on his hands and knees, picking himself up.

"Stay down and get it out of your pocket," the man roared and kicked Sam in the ribs.

Sam rolled on to his back. It was a well-placed, well-powered boot that took his breath and knocked the glasses from his face.

"Why … Why do you have tape on your eyes?" The man's aggression was perforated by confusion. Sam coughed, and rolled to his side. He turned his face towards the direction of the kick and shook his head.

"Yo, you get the loot?" another voice rang from some direction, not far off, bouncing off the walls of what seemed to be an alleyway.

"Nah, not yet, this freak has tape on his eyes, just keep six," the closer male voice shout-whispered back. "Make with the goddamn shit!" He turned his attention back to Sam with another sweeping boot.

Sam would not have resisted but the kicking slowed his movements. He rolled again. He landed on his backside against a wall. He could feel tears squirm around the tape, loosening it slightly, waterlog in the seal of around his socket.

"Hey, freak," the man said, losing patience. "You can't see shit, but hear this?" A flicking noise, followed by a clicking noise, following each other several times. Sam could hear the man smile. "You know what this is? It's a switchblade with bodies on it. I don't give a fuck, I ain't scared of going back to jail. I will kill you.... Now hurry the fuck up and make with the shit."

Sam breathed heavy. Numb. Numb again. The new angry and the new sad. Sam felt catatonic. He heard the blade and its spring flicker like a flame. The sound of a silhouette. The ejection and recall of a death device that could lead Sam to one of two places. He just sat against the wall, his hands braced his back straight. He felt a dirt and grime that was painted atop the concrete, sticking under his nails as he scratched it nervously, like motor oil and sweat.

A far-off belch in the sky started-off the successive hammering of thunder that beat closer to the men each strike. Sam heard the rain before he felt it, the sound of a bubble bursting and the white-noise of overfed skies poured themselves out like hedonists with the ambition to be lavished again.

"Oh Jesus Christ! Justin! Just fucking take the shit out of his fucking pockets, you pussy! It's pouring!" the voice now yelled.

"Give up your goods or I'll fucking kill you!" Justin's voice quivered.

Sam breathed heavy, staring up at the nonexistent sky where the palpable rain washed his face, bounced off the tape and loosened the muck at his fingers.

"Do you not understand?" Justin got his face close to Sam's. "You're going to make me kill you...."

"Then fucking kill me already!" Sam screamed at the man, who must have stumbled back. "Shut up and kill me! Do it! Kill me already!" Sam growled his breaths and waited for the man to approach. There was no sound. Just the rain soaking him to the bones and a few rats flitting past him.

"Jesus Christ." The other man's voice became louder. "Give me the fucking blade, you pussy." Two sets of footsteps approached Sam. The knife was pressed to Sam's throat. "Okay you blind … "

"Stop talking and kill me already you fucking cowards!" Sam thrust his neck and felt the blade nick his throat as the man pulled back. Warm syrup trickled down the side of Sam's neck.

"Do it, you fucking cowards!" Sam's voice cracked. He ripped off the tape and saw the two men. Neither appeared too intimidating by this point, just loose skin hanging from their skulls and unwashed denim. Sam saw a hollow pallor in the lamp-lit dimness, their eyes retreated deep into their skulls and their mouths ratcheted open with disgust and disbelief. They were shaken beneath their facial sores and grey, scaly lips.

Sam emphatically blinked, biting down until his gums turned white and his entire face was corrupted to a wolfish snarl.

They were gone, knife and all.

Sam fell back and looked into his hands. Filth slicked with two raggedy strips of grey tape in his palms, curling and sticking to itself. No use to put them back on, any damage that could have been done, would be done.

Sam hobbled his way home with a limp and bruised ribs. He caught a view of himself from the lobby mirror and felt like punching it until it cracked and turned to sand. He was filthy, blotches of sauce on his front-side and grimy, tar-like dirt on his arms, legs and back. His face was less skin than it was bone. Not that he had lost weight, he viewed the face that looked back at him with reptilian infamy and unfamiliarity. He pulled himself up the steps and achieved his door.

"I wonder if the dog ate the food," he questioned himself. "I'll have to pick some more up." He stepped in the door and was surprised not to be greeted by the wagging tail and greedy tongue of his pup. From his vantage point he could also see that the tubed dogfood had congealed into the bowl with no outside interference. He felt nervous.

The dog lay on his side with his front and rear legs stretched out, his head off to the side with his tongue hanging like a cook's pocket-rag from his mouth. He rushed over and stopped at the cans. Three opened, one sealed. Two cans of dog food, one can of beans with chunks of real bacon; the real bacon seemed to be the draw, emboldened in a yellow circle that had stolen Sam's attention at the grocery store. The room smelled terrible and a pile of soupy brown feces laid behind Mac and a rivalling puddle of vomit in front. Sam placed his ear to the dog's chest.

A very low murmur and a slight rise of his little ribs. Mac's eyes looked in pain, sad and accusatory towards Sam. He writhed and moaned. Sam picked up his phone and looked up some solutions. He filled a bowl with water and wiped away both the vomit and diarrhea, placed the bowl in licking distance and patted Mac's belly. The dog's bloated breast felt hot, moist and his fur was matted with sweat or what Sam diagnosed as dog sweat. Mac's tail flicked once and it panted lightly, raising its head before dropping it back down and closing his eyes.

"Touch and go," he blankly stated. Unblinking and unfeeling.

He looked through his missed calls and email. Several from work of both varieties. A final email with an emergency meeting at seven in the morning with the board. A number of nasty, passive and fully aggressive emails from the upper tier of management. No messages from Kay. No messages from Andy. No reason to expect either.

He opened a chat with Kay and advised her that he would be away for the entire day. That he would leave Mac at the apartment and she could collect the dog, his leash and toys at her convenience. He told her that he did not expect to see her at the café as he would probably be out of a job after tomorrow, if that even mattered. Similarly, he did love her and did not mean to hurt her, if she got it, if it mattered.

The question of if she was alive escaped through the open window of Sam's mind as quickly as it breezed in. He could find out, but why? To torment her? That's a coward's play.

He did make a call. 9-1-1.

"Hello this is an emergency operator," the dial tone gave way.

"Hi, yes, my name is Sam Florin. I have no doubt that the powers that be have a folder or something on me. I accidentally erased two detectives, a Perez and a Diggs. Don't know what happened to them but they're gone.

"Sir … "

"Shut up," Sam interrupted the interruption. "I'm at home, but you already know where that is. I just wanted to tell someone that I didn't mean to do any of it. Except for Michelle Nguyen and Harry Chen. I never liked them, too spoilt, too … well they were jerks. I guess I meant to get some people, the guy with the dog, anyone who crossed my woman, Chloe Bellinger and that guy, can't remember his name … "

"Is this a prank?"

"Chandra! That's the bastard! Yeah, him, and maybe some others. There have been a lot of them. At any rate, I enjoyed some of it, the power I mean, it was … different. I only wish I could've controlled it better. I wish that I could have been a better man.… Well, maybe better isn't the word, maybe just a man … A human, someone who could pick a lane, choose a path, follow a road, you know?"

"Am I a bad person?"

The other end was silent, either having hung-up or being captivated.

He continued venting, as if seated on the plush leather sofa, a psycho-analyst scratching a ball-point away in a moleskin diary. Swiss, with the German way of agreeing without speaking. A good-listener. That is all he needed and wanted at this point, someone to listen. A person who could bare the immeasurable weight of his guilt and sigh with sympathy. Not empathy. Sam did not need the person to try and understand him, just to listen, to listen with silent care. Nodding and humming benignantly as he emptied the contents of his dirt-ridden soul, about how he had fallen so far and earned no sparks.

"Oh! That Savoy guy … I really didn't mean to do that. I mean, he could've been prime minister or president or at least a tribal leader in some South Pacific flea-hole. I was just jealous, but then again, I was a lot."

"Florin! Come out with your hands up!" A voice from the window. Loud, too loud, megaphone-assisted loud.

Sam shook his head and looked at the phone. "Whoa, forty-three min-ute call!" He laughed hysterically. "Maybe I just needed a shrink."

He went to the window. Police cruisers that came from all directions, parked at all angles like knocked over shoe boxes in a storeroom.

"Sam Florin, come down with your hands up, immediately," the mus-tachioed older, but still fiery, officer shouted through a megaphone.

"Okay!" Sam yelled, beaming and raised a thumb.

He walked to the door. A gang of creeping policemen, wearing all-black and carrying assault rifles and obese pistols skulked down the hallway. They looked so small and adorable through the eye-hole, like little pyjama-wearing kids playing ninjas.

Sam latched the hook and walked to the bathroom.

He saw his face and any geniality washed away, missing entirely. He looked deep into his dirty, jagged face, his unnaturally rounded eyes, and little stress cracks, like fissures, broke from every side. Crow's feet that seemed more ostrich-like. Those eyes, all this bullshit because of those stupid eyes. They did not look like his anymore, but like someone else who had taken the wheel and commandeered the zeppelin, drove it straight into a clock tower. They looked terrorized and fearfully unsettled like those of a schizophrenic, who sees our reality painted over with grotesque colours and themes. Staring in a mirror he saw a different set staring back at him; they had the confidence of all the ugly men with beautiful women and fat wallets in all the world. His own eyes, or the eyes in his head that stared back at him, mocked him, jeered him and laughed at what their counterparts were forced to see. The haunted lenses conjured the demons of schizoid panic and unadulterated distress, joy at his tears, a rebuke of his humanity, a cold blade in a hot heart.

"No." Sam shook his head; his age had climbed centuries in a day. The pudge that gave him a youthful ruddiness had dried and hardened like stalactites, dripping any comeliness and innocence into shrewd points of sinister and damnable wretchedness.

A loud thump times three at the front door. Shouting. A harder object, likely the stock of a Mossberg, acutely announced the arrival of the pyjama-clad child mercenaries.

"No," he said again. Blinking and breathing hard. It felt as though each bull-like breath and steel-trap blink cut the lights for a city block, a surge of immense and intolerable force that broke electrical boxes and set power stations alight with welder's torch sparks and towering mauve flames.

"She's right, he was right, they're all right. You're a coward. You've got a dog lying half dead in the living room and the woman you love may or may not still be alive. You don't know, and you won't dare look because you are a coward, a loser. You were born a coward, struggled through life as a coward and now you can try to die like a coward. You simpleton. You had to be stupid and gutless, hmm? You pathetic, fat, dumb piece of shit.

You emotional, disgusting ruiner of lives and happiness. You black hole of human misery. You non-contributing, unimpressive, d-level, d-grade, why-do-you-even-try loser. I hate you. You're ugly and dumb. Idiot. I hate you more than anyone or anything that has ever been and ever will be. Look at you! You called the cops to do the right thing and face the punishment like a man, and now you're just staring at your ugly, pathetic face in the mirror, debating the coward's retreat. Where are your balls? You aren't a man. What more can you lose? You are a disgrace and don't deserve to steal tax money to rot in a cell. I want you to die. I want you to feel the torment and sadness you've made others feel. I hate you. I hate you. I despise your coward guts you fucking shallow, moronic, fucking cowardly idiot! I hate you! Die already!"

Sam blinked.

ACKNOWLEDGMENTS

I WOULD LIKE to start by thanking the creative minds behind the final product: Winnie Fong for the photo, Abby Competente for the doodle and my baby brother Spencer motherfucking Croft for coming through in the clutch. I would like to extend a huge gratitude to Sue for editing this beast and helping me learn how to be a better beast of my own. Kyle Oser and Bobby Parent for their beautiful love-child. Justus and Alex and Perry for their hearts when it was all crashing down. You. It couldn't have happened without You. Bryan and Kyle, I propose a fight to the death over who said it first, then another one about who says it better. And, a special shout-out to all the awful human interactions that made one of the darkest times in my life that much more difficult, it made me a better writer and man. I owe every penny that I make to you scumbags and raptors.